The door opened and Luc strode in. Cher's breath caught in her throat for a moment. He looked magnificent, and Cher couldn't help the lightning ripple of lust that slipped down her spine. She still wanted him, even after all these years and all the past behind them. Anger replaced the desire. How could she still have such strong feelings for him?

He seated himself in the chair Whitaker had just vacated. "I'm not in the habit of being kept waiting."

"I don't particularly care. I have a department to run, meetings to go to, detectives to supervise and..." she held up a piece of paper. "I'm due to be at the firing range in two hours for firearm certification. I'm locked and loaded, so maybe you shouldn't get on my bad side."

He didn't seem fazed. "It occurs to me that you and I have been on the wrong foot since we met."

"And what was your first clue?" My God, I sound like my daughter. She resisted the impulse to slap the side of her head. "Is this your version of an apology?"

Indigo Sensuous

Love Stories

are published by

Genesis Press, Inc.
315 Third Avenue North
Columbus, MS 39701

A Dangerous Deception

ISBN: 1-58571-056-3
Manufactured in the United States of America

First Edition

A Dangerous Deception

by

J. M. Jeffries

Genesis Press, Inc.

A Dangerous Love

by

J. M. Jeffries

ISBN: 1-58571-026-1

When passion and justice collide, love can be lethal. Phoenix Detective Elena Jackson is hunting a killer. Attorney Reardon North is determined to prove his best friend innocent of murder.

With every passing day, Reardon and Elena find themselves more and more attracted to each other. But Elena denies her feelings, afraid that any involvement with Reardon will not only jeopardize her case, but more importantly risk her heart. Reardon struggles with loyalty to his friend, and his hunger to possess Elena.

Their hearts become entangled when cop and lawyer lock horns over one of the city's most sensational serial murder cases. As the body count escalates, they set a trap to catch the killer, which puts not only their love, but lives in peril.

Chapter One

Stanford University

Cher Dawson pushed Luc Broussard up against the white tiles of the shower wall and kissed him, hard and deep. He returned her passion, his hands roaming over her body to create that familiar, blinding heat that always left her writhing with desire and craving more. For a few sizzling seconds she didn't care that he had a final exam in an hour and his entire future rested on passing the class. She closed her eyes as his fingers slid down her slick skin, massaging and caressing her.

Warm water sluiced off their bodies, and Cher gave herself up to the promise of lovemaking. She loved taking long, hot showers with Luc, exploring his body as he explored her. She never got enough of him. She tore herself away as reality crept into her head. "Okay, I kissed you, now get out and get dressed."

His dark brown eyes sparkled with mischief. "I want more than a kiss."

Her stomach tightened against the exquisite hardness of his erection. She wanted him in a way she'd never wanted any man, but now was not the time. She tried to pull away from him, but he slipped his hands around her waist and held her tight to him as he licked her lips. "Luc." She braced her hands against his chest, prepared to push him out of the tub. "Stop that. You have an exam in an hour."

"I'd rather be inside you than writing the answers to a bunch of dull questions." His full, seductive lips tilted upward into a wicked grin. Water streamed over the muscles of his shoulders.

Cher groaned. She drew in a ragged breath as she pushed hair out of her eyes. This man made her legs tremble and her mind go numb. As tempted as she was to succumb, someone had to keep their head. "No test, no graduation, no degree, no cushy job at the State Department."

He laughed a rich, full-throated laugh. "Are you marrying me because you love me, or because of my earning potential?"

Which reflected his moneyed, upper-class background. She still thrilled that a man like Luc would be interested in a girl like her, one who'd spent half her youth homeless and on the streets, headed for a life of crime if not for the intervention of David Dawson, her foster father and her savior. "You're pretty smart, too."

He nuzzled her neck. "The smartest thing I've ever done was ask you to marry me."

Her knees nearly buckled. Tremors exploded throughout her body. "So you're going to smooth-talk me now."

He nipped her at the base of her neck. "I'm trying to be romantic." His fingers circled her breasts, moving inward in ever smaller movements until she couldn't breathe.

Blood roared in her ears like the driving rain of a thunderstorm. Cher knew it was now or never. She had to get out of the shower, or he'd be late. No final, no degree. He'd delayed long enough.

Summoning all her will, she shoved him away, the lure of his lovemaking almost too strong to control. She wanted him desperately, but first things first. "Be romantic after your final exam."

He grinned at her. "You're a hard woman, Dawson."

She thumped him on the chest. "Because I have to be to keep you in line. Now finish your shower and get to class." She didn't want him to be late, not when so much depended on this one last test.

She pushed open the glass shower door, but he grabbed her arm, tugging her back inside the large shower stall.

Luc braced her back against the wet tile wall. "You

thought you were going to escape?"

A shudder of desire ran through her. "A girl can hope, can't she?" She closed her eyes, maybe just a quickie. God knew that until the end of her life, she would never be able to resist him. You are so weak, Cher Dawson.

Luc bracketed his hands on both sides of her shoulders. "Come on, tell me you don't want me."

She leaned her head against the warm tile, knowing she could not escape ... even if she wanted to. She placed her palms flat on his chest and trailed her fingers downward. His muscles contracted at her touch. Slanting a glance up at his face, she debated the wisdom of letting him tempt her into sin. All her choices should be like this. Luc's eyes closed. Her choice was made, she could play his sexual game. Her hands began to descend, but he grabbed her wrists.

"I thought you weren't interested," he said in a deep, growling tone.

She grinned. "I'm always interested, Luc."

He pushed his body flush against her. "Me, too."

Gently he nibbled her lips. Cher opened her mouth, and his tongue slid inside. He swirled it around slowly, just the way she liked, and he explored the depths of her mouth, his thumbs kneading her nipples. The only thing preventing her from sinking to the shower floor was his body crushed against her.

Heat danced around her body. The steamy water

cascaded over their shoulders, and the warmth of his slick skin was an invitation she could no longer deny. The desire for him flowed through her with such intensity, she gasped for air.

Luc snaked his arms around her waist and lifted her. "Wrap your legs around me."

She hooked her shaking legs around his waist as he commanded. She wrapped her arm around his neck. Hot, passionate excitement escalated inside her. Slowly he lowered her on his hardness, filling her so completely she wanted to scream. Her intimate muscles contracted around him. Resting her head against his shoulder, she gave herself up to the rhythmic movements of his hips. In the back of her head she wondered how she could have been so foolish as to deny him for more than five seconds.

Cher wrapped a plush, navy-blue towel around her body. After stealing one last look at him as he rinsed off, she headed for the small, cozy bedroom they shared. When she'd first arrived at Stanford, she'd stayed in the dorms. But after one semester of sharing showers and putting up with her roommate's idea of sharing clothing and makeup, Cher had taken a second job and then moved out to this small apartment. Privacy was very important to Cher. She had wrestled with the loss of it for several weeks before formally inviting Luc to move in. Now she was glad she had him in her life and in her bed. She couldn't imagine a life without him.

She dried her skin and pulled the burgundy silk robe Luc had given her for Valentine's Day around her body. She loved the robe with its matching silk nightgown. She loved the way the silk felt against her skin. She'd never before had anything so finely made and beautiful.

Luc had also presented her with the diamond engagement ring she now wore. She still smiled at the memory of his proposal and the naked longing in his eyes. At first she had considered refusing him, but realized her future was with Luc.

Cher went to the kitchen to make Luc a cup of coffee. By the time the coffee finished dripping, Luc was out of the shower and dressed. He walked into the cozy kitchen, thumbing through a spiralbound notebook filled with his loopy, sloppy handwriting. "Catherine de Medici was Queen Regent of France, right?"

She eyed the notebook. "And ordered the Saint Bartholomew's Day massacre. Either you know it, or you don't. Now is not the time to start cramming."

He grinned. "Just testing you."

He tossed the notebook to her, she caught it, and set the notebook on the oak dining table. "I did manage an A in the class." She managed A's in all her classes. Cher would tolerate nothing less from herself. Not that she was a perfectionist, but David Dawson had given her a chance and she didn't want squander it, or embarrass him by performing badly in school.

"Show-off." He gulped down coffee, kissed her, handed her the cup, and bolted out the door.

She touched her mouth, still burning from his kiss. They were going to have a perfect life together. She could hardly wait for the wedding. They had decided on a late June ceremony, a scant two weeks away. All their plans would soon be a reality.

Cher finished dressing, cleaned the bathroom and straightened the bedroom. Luc was a slob. All those years of having maids to pick up after him was definitely changing after they were married. She didn't want strangers going through her dirty laundry and touching her underwear. Her freshman roommate had been bad enough, but a total stranger was worse.

She touched the square-cut diamond ring adorning the third finger of her left hand. Cher had never expected marriage to be a part of her future. If anyone had asked her what she thought her future was when she'd been eleven, she would have answered, "why bother wondering. I'll be dead by the time I'm eighteen." But fate had intervened in the form of one tough cop who'd taken her in and given her a life and new hope.

She'd never thought a man like Luc Broussard would be attracted to a girl from the wrong side of the tracks. Prince Charming only came along in fairy tales. Luc was charismatic, intelligent, and sexy. Cher really liked the sexy part. Just thinking about how he brought her body to climax started her tingling.

She began cleaning the tiny living room. Luc had insisted on a new sofa. The one she had found at the thrift shop had been lumpy with the springs pointing through. And they shopped for the dark green leather sectional that took up almost the whole room. She'd been appalled at the price, but Luc had stated that leather, well-cared for, lasted a lifetime and had insisted. Besides when they had friends over, everyone would have a place to sit. As an afterthought, he added a large boxy table, which was now piled with their textbooks.

Cher touched her sociology text. She'd taken her last final two days before and was pleased that school was finally over and she could start her life in earnest now. She plumped up the pillows and dusted the side tables.

They were having dinner with his mother, and Cher didn't want Victoria Broussard arriving at a messy apartment. Luc had said his mother was very meticulous in the way her own home looked. This would be the first time Cher had met Luc's mother, although she had talked with her on the telephone a few times.

The doorbell rang, and Cher jumped, startled. Who could be ringing the doorbell at nine in the morning? She folded up the dustrag as she walked toward the door and answered it.

A tall, slender woman stood in the hallway. She was

elegant in brown silk slacks, a tan cashmere sweater and a Gucci scarf draped about her slender shoulders. Her resemblance to Luc testified to the fact she was his mother. Graying black hair framed an oval face. Her skin was the color of burnished almonds, and her eyes were a dark, intense brown. Full lips, expertly painted in a muted red, gave Cher a cool smile. Victoria Broussard reeked of class. The type of woman Cher aspired to be.

"You must be Cher," the woman said brusquely in her cultured Nob Hill tone. "I'm Victoria Broussard, Luc's mother."

"Mrs. Broussard." Cher offered a welcoming smile, but the woman ignored it as she brushed past Cher to enter the apartment. "What a pleasure it is to meet you." Cher's voice faltered. "How was your drive from San Francisco?"

Victoria Broussard stood in the center of the living room looking around and frowning. "I didn't drive. The chauffeur did." She enunciated every word so clearly, so perfectly, that Cher felt put down.

"I see." Open mouth, take out foot. So much for polite conversation. "We weren't expecting you until this evening."

"Is my son here?" Victoria stared at the dusting rag in Cher's hand, a superior look in her eyes.

"He has a final exam." Cher felt as though she'd been thoroughly examined, found lacking in all areas, and totally dismissed. As though she wasn't even a blip on the older woman's radar.

Victoria took a deep breath, her frown deepening. "Graduation is tomorrow night. How can he have a final?"

Cher couldn't help the smile that touched her lips. "Luc has been known to procrastinate." As if the woman didn't know.

Victoria Broussard slanted a piercing, hostile glance at Cher. "You think you know my son so well."

"I love him." She proudly held out her hand with the engagement ring. The ring stood for all the things Cher had never had as a child.

"Love is nothing." A smirk of utter contempt spread across Victoria's beautiful face.

A wave of panic spread through Cher. This meeting was not going as she'd dreamed. She'd expected Luc's mother to embrace her with open arms, and the woman acted as though Cher was the enemy. "Shall we sit down." Cher gestured to the most comfortable chair in the living room, an ivory barrel chair. Another purchase Luc had insisted on.

"No, thank you." Victoria's voice was distant and icy. "We'd best get this over with. I didn't come here to be friendly." She opened a beige Fendi purse, and removed a large white envelope. Holding it by the corner, she handed it to Cher. She withdrew her slender fingers quickly as if wanting to make certain their hands didn't touch. "This is for you."

Cher accepted the envelope with quivering fingers, a lump of panic forming in her throat. She searched Victoria's face for some hint, but all she saw was a lingering scorn in those dark, frosty eyes.

Cher opened the flap. Her knees quaked as she pulled out a half-dozen photographs. Her vision blurred as she stared at the photographs. Bit by bit the world she'd built for herself collapsed. "What do you intend to do with these?" she queried in a strangled voice she vaguely recognized as her own.

How had Victoria managed to get the photos? Her foster father was always so careful. No one knew he was gay, or even suspected. His sterling reputation with the Phoenix Police Department depended on his discretion.

Victoria offered a thin-lipped smile, reminding Cher of a snake about to strike at some hapless mouse. "How I got the photos is no concern of yours. What does concern me is my son and his future. And his future is not going to be with you. You are not going to marry him. If you proceed with your plans, your father will suffer in ways you have never imagined." Victoria waited, one foot forward as though she were a model on a runway. "Now, you be a good girl and pack. I'll be back later, and I want you gone, out of my son's life." She turned and opened the door and with a triumphant smile she left the apartment.

Alone, Cher fought the beginning of shock. She bit her lips until blood trickled down her chin. Her first impulse was to wait for Luc to return, but showing him the pictures and telling him about his mother's treachery made her reel with fear. He'd never believe his mother had engineered this. She was, after all, his mother. And while Cher would believe her own birth mother capable of such treachery, Victoria Broussard was another matter.

Cher tried to tell herself she should trust Luc, that he would understand, but at the core of her being she was deeply afraid. With one word, Victoria Broussard would ruin Cher's father. She would destroy him with a ruthlessness that frightened Cher.

She had expected Victoria to welcome her with warmth and acceptance. Never once had Cher thought the woman would consider her future daughter-in-law to be so lacking as to demolish a man's life and never lose a wink of sleep. What kind of person could do such a thing? But more importantly why would she?

Tears trickled down Cher's face. She didn't know what to do. She walked from room to room, too agitated to think clearly. She had created a house of cards, and all the cards were now scattered on the floor as fragmented as her emotions. She should have known better. A girl from the streets had no future with a blue-blood like Luc.

Cher spread the photographs over the coffee table and stared at them. The damning evidence left her no choice. She wiped tears from her eyes, the loss of her dreams heavy inside her heart. She could barely walk to the bedroom to begin packing, to dismantle the life she had so carefully started building.

Chapter Two

Fourteen Years Later

San Francisco

Tension rippled through the courtroom as the jury foreman stood and announced in a solemn tone. "We, the jury, find the defendant, Edward William Compton, not guilty."

Luc Broussard sat in the gallery, staring at the back of Edward Compton's head. He felt made of stone. The shock of the verdict reverberating through him like church bells. That bastard, he thought, is going to get away with murder.

The judge nodded and thanked the jury before dismissing them. The crowd of reporters in the back row rustled with eagerness as they wrote swiftly in their notebooks, avid eyes darting back and forth between Luc and Edward Compton.

A Dangerous Deception

This can't be happening. Edward Compton was as guilty of the murder of Victoria Broussard as the day was long. How could the jury not see his guilt? It was so clear to Luc. Handsome younger man marries woman twice his age and then casually murders her for the money.

Except there was no money. Luc's mother had lived off a trust fund set aside by his father that reverted back to Luc when his mother died. Edward Compton received nothing.

Luc snapped his reading glasses in half. Intense anger rose in him. He could barely force himself to stand. This was justice? Justice for whom? Certainly not his mother.

Compton rose gracefully to his feet, his face alight with relief. He was an attractive man in the prime of his life. A few years older than Luc. And now he was a free man. Compton's pretty sister, Helen Ramsey, embraced him. Compton turned to face Luc. A smug, superior smirk flitted across his finely featured face.

Edward leaned over the railing that separated the gallery from the defending attorney's table. "No hard feelings, Luc. I told you I didn't kill Victoria. I loved her. I'll always love her, no matter what you think."

Luc stared bitterly at the man. He wanted to leap across the railing that separated them and throttle the man, but Luc knew this wasn't the time or place. He started to warn Edward that he would be watching him, but a hand on his arm stopped the words. His attorney, Benjamin Ryan, inclined his graying head toward the door and tugged Luc away from Edward, pushing through the crowd of reporters who poured out the door after them. As Ben rushed Luc toward the elevator, reporters and media people jostled each other in hungry impatience to get out of the courtroom and file their stories now that the high-profile case was concluded.

"Remember Luc," Ben cautioned, "not a word to the press."

Luc took a deep breath, attempting to restrain the chaos of his emotions and to control his shaking. "He killed my mother." He relived the memory of finding his mother's body sprawled on the floor of her bedroom, a pool of blood surrounding her soaking into the Persian rug. The image was burned in Luc's memory. Never would he forget, nor would he forgive Edward for his complicity.

Benjamin shook his head. "You know and I know that the evidence was weak and his alibi was rock solid. That bastard is damn lucky."

"Too lucky." Luc vowed he would do something to change Compton's luck. No alibi in the world would convince Luc that Edward wasn't involved.

Luc and Ben walked down the hallway and out onto the front steps of the San Francisco courthouse. A cool autumn sun shone down on them. Reporters crowded around them, shoving microphones in Luc's face.

"No comment," he said over and over, steeling himself for more of the intrusive questions, the assault on his private life made public by the nastiness of the trial. He couldn't let the reporters see how the verdict had shaken him, nor how the injustice of his mother's death would remain unpunished, or how her killer would go free. He had trusted implicitly in the justice system. As he hurried toward his limo, he found himself withdrawing from reality, viewing the crowds from an increasing distance.

He climbed inside with Benjamin right behind him. Reporters tapped against the windows and pounded on the roof. Luc signaled the driver and the limo sped away.

"That bastard!" Luc covered his face with his hands. "He murdered my mother, and he's going to get away with it."

Benjamin ran his fingers through graying blond hair. "The case was shaky to begin with. All the evidence was circumstantial, but you pushed. You treated the District Attorney and the police officers as though they were nothing but your hired flunkies." He took off his glasses and rubbed bloodshot gray eyes. "That didn't sit well with them."

"Are you telling me the 'not guilty' verdict is somehow my fault?" Although he and Ben had been friends since prep school Luc felt a second's betrayal that Ben would side with the enemy.

Ben shook his head. "I'm saying there aren't many people in this world who can stand up to you. The D.A.

was willing to go along with this because you're a good friend, and you've contributed heavily to his campaign. But, even the media has been saying you were buying a conviction. You can't afford bad press, Luc. Not any more."

"Dammit, Benjamin." A migraine started at the back of his neck and traveled forward to lodge with blinding fierceness behind his eyes. "He killed my mother. I will do whatever I can to see Edward Compton behind bars."

"You only had this one shot, Luc, and you blew it. Even if new evidence comes to light, double jeopardy prevents him from being tried again."

Luc looked at his hands, at the broken pieces of his reading glasses. "Then I'll find something else. Compton is going to pay."

Luc stared out the window at the passing streets. Except for the four years he'd spent at Stanford, he'd lived his whole life in San Francisco. Yet the city had subtly changed from a welcoming home into a strange, forbidding place. Maybe he had thought he could buy justice for his mother. But the fact was, she was dead and her murderer was free.

Luc spent the next week grieving for his mother in a

manner he had not allowed for himself before. He spent most of the time on the roof of his Pacific Heights mansion staring at the bay during the day, and reveling in the fog that rolled out to the ocean in the morning and returned in the evening.

Inside the cold damp fingers of the fog, he thought about hiring a hit man to rid himself of Compton. But he knew that solving one murder with a second would be equally wrong. He had to find another way to punish Compton, to reveal the man for the charlatan he was.

Even though Luc and his mother had been at odds most of his life, he still owed her. She'd given him life and in her own way, she'd given him love. Nightly, he dreamed that he could hear her screams as she pleaded with her killer.

The autopsy had confirmed she'd put up a fight. But in the end she had lost that battle with her life. The end brought about by a bullet to her brain. And even though Edward Compton had no scratch marks on him to indicate he'd been the murderer, Luc never stopped believing he had something to do with his mother's death. Reasonable doubt. The two words that freed Compton. The defense attorney had done his job. The prosecution had failed.

At the end of the week, no closer to a solution than he'd been at the beginning, he returned to his office. The demands of running a media empire could no longer be ignored. He'd taken all the time he could afford. His business needed his hand.

His secretary and staff were happy to see him. They brought him up to date on everything that had happened in the week he'd been gone. No one spoke about his mother. No one even alluded to the trial. No one spoke about Edward Compton who had announced he was vacationing in St. Croix, and would return in a couple weeks.

Luc sat at his desk, his hands resting on the dark green blotter, not certain what to do next. A pile of mail, and stacks of phone messages waited his attention. But he couldn't bring himself to start going through them. He kept seeing his mother's lifeless body on the floor of her bedroom and wondered if he'd arrived home a few minutes earlier, if he would have prevented her murder.

The office door opened and Ben entered. He was holding a thick file.

"Is there a problem?" Luc asked. Usually, Ben just used the phone, and Luc frowned wondering what had upset him so much.

"I don't know. I want to run something by you."

Luc frowned. "What?"

Ben dropped the folder on Luc's desk. "Four years ago in Phoenix a man named Edward Compton was murdered."

Bewildered, Luc replied, "Excuse me."

Ben thumped the folder. "You heard me." He opened the folder and pulled out a newspaper article, a photograph of a man in an Army uniform and shoved them at Luc. "A friend of mine in Phoenix found this article and sent it to me detailing the death of one Edward William Compton, from Stillwater, Louisiana. Apparently he was murdered four years ago, by a person or persons unknown, only five weeks before your mother met her Edward Compton in Phoenix. Don't you think it's a little coincidental that both events happened in Phoenix?"

Luc read through the obituary, frowning, trying to make sense of why Edward Compton should be dead in Phoenix and alive and married to his mother in San Francisco. The idea that Edward Compton wasn't who he said he was started to grow in Luc's mind, even though he didn't want to leap to conclusions. His insistence had led to a not guilty verdict once before. His gut instinct warned him to proceed with caution. Although his mother's husband claimed Stillwater as his home this could be nothing more than a coincidence. "There could have been two Edward Comptons from Stillwater, Louisiana."

Ben shook his head. "I checked. Stillwater, Louisiana, has never had a population of more than one hundred and fifty-three residents for the last fifty years." Ben rummaged through the folder and then withdrew another paper. "This is a copy of Compton's death certificate. He was stationed at Fort Huachuca. He had a sister named Sylvia who I'm trying to locate right now."

Luc's mind roiled in confusion as he tried to sort through this new information. Was Ben on to something? If so, what? No matter, this fact couldn't be ignored. "How did you get all this information?"

Ben shrugged. "I have a friend in the Phoenix Police Department. She did some digging for me earlier, but it wasn't until last week that she found this article and faxed it to me."

Luc felt as though he'd been punched in the stomach. He almost doubled over with the stabbing pain that clutched at him and radiated down his arms and legs. If the Edward Compton who'd married his mother wasn't really Edward Compton, then who the hell was he? And how could the private investigator Ben had originally hired come up with such a clean record for someone who'd been dead for four years? He should have found a death certificate. "Didn't we have an investigation done on Edward Compton when he married my mother. Why didn't we find out this information before?"

Ben sat in the black leather camel back chair. "The investigation conducted when you mother first met him was just a superficial one to make certain he wasn't an ax murderer. And the detective who investigated the homicide in Phoenix died in a car accident two weeks into the investigation and the files were turned over to the Cold Case Unit and somehow misplaced."

"How the hell do the police misplace an unsolved homicide file?"

Ben shrugged. "Things happens. When a cop dies, or retires, his cases are automatically sent to the Cold Case Unit, which has the discretion to file or investigate. This was filed."

"It should have been investigated."

"Luc, this was a black man shot behind a sleazy bar on a busy Saturday night ... you do the math."

"Let me guess. He didn't rate?" A cold shudder ran through him. "Why did the case show up now?"

Ben shrugged. "The Cold Case Unit has gone through a major overhaul, and all the files for the last ten years have finally been entered into the unit's brand-new computer system. When Beatrix looked the name up again, she found it and shot it right over to me."

"What about the records from Stillwater?"

Again, Ben shrugged. "The investigator simply wasn't looking for anything other than verifying the identity of Edward Compton. What he found looked good: solid church-going family, no criminal record except for some juvenile mischief. And those records were sealed. He had no reason to investigate more fully. No one in the town had much to say about the Compton family, other than the fact that the sister and brother left when they were out of high school. The parents were dead, and no other relatives could be found."

Luc punched the button on his intercom. "Lisa, call the airport and have my pilot prepare the jet. I'm going to Phoenix on business."

"Luc, what do you think you're going to do?"

"I'm not sure yet. You bring me all this information and then think I'm going to sit around and do nothing. We need to investigate."

"Edward can't be retried for your mother's murder in any jurisdiction in the country."

Luc stood. "I know that. But what about this guy." He pointed at the photo of the dead Edward Compton. "What would happen if the Edward Compton who married my mother had something to do with this man's murder. After all, it appears that he assumed this man's identity. What about identity theft?" A new resolve formed inside him. Maybe his mother would get justice after all. Not the justice Luc would have wanted, but something to ease the ache of guilt and sorrow he still felt.

"Identity theft is a federal offense. I think we should let the police..."

"No," Luc almost shouted. He doubted the police would be interested in anything he had to say after the way he manipulated the mayor and the district attorney into filing the charges against the man he knew as Edward Compton. "This Edward Compton's murder is still open." And was too large a coincidence to be ignored. "Maybe I can help justice along a bit. Bring the matter to the attention of the authorities in Phoenix." And if the police weren't interested, well, he did know the governor and had even contributed to his last campaign.

Ben stood. "I'll pack my bags."

"Ben, you don't have to go."

"Arizona is not your stomping ground, my friend." He gave Luc a bitter smile. "You might need a translator."

"I'll meet you at the airport in two hours." This was his chance for justice. Maybe not for his mother. But if his mother's husband was involved in another homicide, he still could be tried and hopefully convicted. All Luc had to do was prove that his mother's Edward Compton was somehow involved in the death of the Army's Edward Compton. Both claiming to be from Stillwater, Louisiana. He could live with Edward serving time for this crime. Any crime. All he had to do was prove it.

Lieutenant Cher Dawson leaned back in her chair, feet on the desk, reveling in the fact that she had beat them all. After eight months, Phoenix Police Department's Cold Case Unit's clearance rate was a whopping seventy-eight percent. The best in the nation. And all because of Cher and her hand-picked detectives.

When her superiors had given her the job, they'd expected her to fall flat on her face. They'd wanted her to fall flat on her face. She'd shown them. She'd turned the unit around, leaving the big brass boys squirming in their offices wondering what new obstacles they could throw at her now.

If only she could celebrate. A nice Marlboro would work, but Cher's daughter, Miranda, had made the honor roll for the second time in a row, and Cher had promised to quit smoking as part of their agreement.

Maybe she should take her guys out to lunch—even Wyatt Earp Whitaker, who just this morning had come in for the one hundredth time this week and asked to be sent back to the regular Homicide. This little ritual had become a game of sorts between them. He told her he wanted out, and she told him no. He pouted, she ordered him back to work. And then the next day, they would go through the same maneuver all over again.

The phone rang. Cher put her feet down on the floor. She started to reach for the phone. Wait a second! I have a secretary. Let him answer the phone. The phone continued to ring and ring. She tapped her fingers on the desk. I'm not answering. I'm not answering. What good was having a secretary if she still had to answer her own phone?

The ringing stopped and she smiled. Allen had finally remembered he was supposed to answer the phone. Allen was sweet, but this job was his first since he'd graduated with an associate's degree in business from the local community college, and he was still learning just what his duties were.

Wyatt Earp Whitaker flung open her door and stalked inside. "Do I look like your secretary?"

"In your dreams." Whitaker was good enough looking but any nocturnal visions of him would be strictly under the nightmare category.

Whitaker jabbed his thumb over his shoulder. "The guy went to lunch." He glanced pointedly at his watch. "In fact, I'm going to lunch now, too. Maybe I'll stumble across a fresh kill."

"If I get lucky maybe it'll be you."

He grinned. "I'm too good for you to get rid of me."

"And that's your problem. Your ego is bigger than your desire to go back to your old unit."

"If I have to keep acting as your secretary, I want a coffee break every half hour and extra retirement benefits."

Cher glared at him. He reveled in his bad-boy act. "You already take a coffee break every half hour."

"What's your point?"

Cher sighed. Verbal warfare with Whitaker was exhausting. He tried her patience, but no matter how he challenged her, she wasn't going to let him get away from her. He was good, almost too good, but his clearance rate made her department look terrific. "Who called?"

Whitaker shrugged. "I'm not your secretary. I don't take messages. But some guy out there wants to see you. Shall I send him in, ma'am? Do you want coffee? Tea? Rat poison?" He batted his eyelashes at her.

Cher swallowed her laughter. Whitaker was a bastard, but a charming bastard. Fortunately, her taste ran to nice men. The few that she'd run into, anyway. "Send my visitor in, Whitaker. And no coffee. I don't want a sexual harassment suit filed because I abused your generosity."

Whitaker grunted. "Darn. What am I going to do with all that good-tasting arsenic I bought yesterday?"

"Help yourself."

Whitaker laughed and left. A moment a later a tall man entered. He stood in a patch of sunshine that highlighted his lean face and brought back all the memories Cher had thought she'd buried. She swallowed, her heart thumping so rapidly in her chest she thought it would leap out and skip around the floor.

Luc.

Luc Broussard looked good, better now than before. Cher hoped to God she wasn't drooling all over her blotter. His hair was still cut close to his head. His camelhair coat and Armani suit fit like he'd been born to it. Which of course he had. Money and influence had made Luc Broussard what he was. Who he was. Just as a lack of money and a lack of influence had made Cher what she was.

Her heart jump-started to light speed as she rose and stepped toward him. "What do you want, Luc?"

"Cher." Luc Broussard stared at her. "You're Lieutenant Dawson!" Something flickered deep in his brandy-colored eyes, and was gone, replaced by a blank stare that gave nothing of what he was thinking away.

Cher got up and closed the door. Her hands shook. What was Luc Broussard doing in her office? Hell, what was he doing in Phoenix? The only compensation she'd ever had was knowing he was tucked safely in San Francisco, and their paths would never cross. And here he was, big as life, rocking her world as though he'd never left. "Yes, I am. What are you doing here?" Her heart contracted and fear filled her. She bit hard on the inside of her cheek and tasted blood. She knew why he was here.

He'd found out about Miranda! His mother would never tell. Victoria Broussard was a venomous viper, waiting until Cher was beginning to feel safe again, and then she'd spring her little trap.

"May I sit down?" Luc gestured at a chair.

No, she thought. She didn't want him sitting in her office, reminding her of the past and the agony she'd spent fourteen years trying to escape. Wiping her damp palms she mentally searched for some reason to make him leave. She knew it was all in her head, but the wound she thought healed exploded into new rawness as though she'd seen him only yesterday.

Her heart thumped so hard she thought she would faint. How could he not hear. He wasn't getting her daughter. No way. No how.

"What do you want, Luc?" she repeated, her voice

amazingly calm.

He tilted his head and studied her. "Is that any way to greet an old friend?"

After the way she walked out on him, she didn't think friend would be a word he associated with her. "I don't think we're friends anymore."

"You could be right. Betrayal precludes any sort of friendship." He slammed his briefcase on her desk.

She was surprised he showed that emotion. He never used to show his anger.

As she walked back to her desk, he popped the snaps on an expensive, black leather briefcase and drew out a red file folder.

Luc was all about class, all about elegance. He wore his money like regular guys wore sneakers—with comfort and ease. No vestige of the boyish quality she'd fallen in love with fourteen years ago remained. This was a man—a hard man with angry edges. Was her abandonment of him what had changed him? This saddened her. Maybe she had been wrong. Maybe she should have fought for him.

Luc glanced up from his briefcase. "I was told you would be the person to investigate an old homicide."

He wanted her to check out a murder! Her stomach flip-flopped, and she felt queasy. He didn't know about Miranda, after all. Her mind raced. She couldn't focus. "A murder?"

"I need a case solved."

"How are you connected to a homicide in Phoenix?" Relief spread through her, leaving her light-headed. He didn't know. She was safe. Miranda was safe.

He handed her the folder. "To make a long story short. My mother was murdered by a man named Edward Compton. A man she married three years ago."

She reached for the folder, carefully avoiding his hand. The last thing she wanted was to touch him. It was bad enough seeing him, touching him would send her into orbit. She flipped open the folder.

Victoria Broussard was dead.

An old movie song sprang into her head. Ding dong, the wicked witch is dead, and she'd taken Cher's secrets to the grave. Cher almost exulted in the old woman's death, then was ashamed of her response. Not even Luc's mother deserved such a lack of compassion. "What do you want?"

Luc sat across from her. "Compton was acquitted of her murder. Yesterday I was informed that a man named Edward Compton from Stillwater, Louisiana, was murdered here four years ago. His death coincides with the appearance of the Edward Compton that married my mother. I want to know if these two men are related and how it affects my mother."

She forced her cop mind to take over. "It could just be two men with the same name." Coincidences happened, and more often than most people thought.

He shook his head. "No. One of these men is not

who he claims to be. You told me once, a long time ago, that coincidences don't happen that often."

Cher shook her head. "I see." She studied the rest of the folder Luc had thrust at her, reading as quickly as she could about the dead Edward Compton whose body had been found in an alley behind a bar in the downtown area.

As she read she was intensely aware of Luc's presence and anxiously wished he'd leave. His return, after fourteen years, in her office awoke disturbing feelings. Sentiments she didn't want to examine ever again. He was the past, and the past was dead. "Are you sure you want to know?"

"Yes, I do want to know. I want to know why one man is dead and the other is alive. I want to know why my mother is dead." His dark brown eyes narrowed as he studied her, his face closed and blank.

My God he was more handsome then ever. He'd finally grown into that incredible chiseled face. His lips were firm and full, his skin the color of polished teak. His long eyelashes were the only thing that gave sensitivity to his rugged features. He was all man.

She wondered what he was thinking. His face had a closed quality to it, and he acted as though he were the only person in the room. If he wanted to treat her as if she wasn't even in the room, that was okay with her. She didn't want him to ask about her or her life.

She turned to her computer and logged into the

office network. She typed Edward Compton's name in. "What's the bottom line for you?"

He glared at her, his lips thinned to a menacing line. "He killed my mother. I want justice."

A file flashed on her monitor relaying no more information than what was in the file Luc had already given her. A Sergeant Edward Compton of the United States Army stationed at Fort Huachuca had been found shot in the head. "According to this report you gave me, there is nothing but circumstantial evidence gathered on your mom's death." She glanced up at Luc. His face had taken on weary lines that showed an exhaustion that hadn't been there a moment before. She fought the urge to comfort him, knowing that would be the wrong move. "Double jeopardy prevents the state of California from retrying him even if you can find evidence proving his involvement in your mother's murder."

His square jaw hardened. "I know you can't try him for my mother's murder, but you can for the other man's murder. I think the person I know as Edward Compton killed the real Edward Compton in order to assume his identity."

"For what reason?" Identity theft was turning into a global problem, but usually the person stealing the identity didn't murder the original holder of the name. She studied the photo of the very much alive Edward Compton. She saw a man in his late thirties and wondered what Victoria Broussard had seen in him besides his stunning good looks. Victoria had to have been in her sixties. Interesting. Cher would never have thought that Luc's mother would be swayed by a pretty face and a fancy demeanor.

Luc folded his arms across his chest, his chin thrust out belligerently. "That's what you're going to find out for me."

Cher remembered that look on his face. He'd shown it to her often enough when he didn't want to do something, or did and wouldn't be swayed. "Really! Assuming that I will is a pretty big leap for someone who doesn't deal in police work." Part of her brain kept going back to the fact that he could just talk to her like nothing happened between them. Maybe that's why he could marry so early after their break-up. Maybe deep down he was an ice man. Okay, she'd left him, but his mother had engineered that little episode. Cher had no choice. Her loyalty to her foster father, David Dawson, had been more important than her love for Luc. She had owed her foster father her life. Not until later, had she realized Luc had given her something of himself to take away with her, but by then it had been too late to go back.

He pointed at the file. "I think there is a link."

Cher shook her head. "Circumstances and coincidence. Admittedly her curiosity flared, but she wasn't going to let on like she cared. She just wanted to know who had the balls to murder Victoria Broussard.

"Something is going on. I should think you'd want

to know as badly as I do."

Every cop instinct, honed through thirteen years on the force, told her something was not right, but did she really want to go sniffing around? Any kind of investigation would keep Luc in her life. Her stomach fluttered.

Oh my God. Not "the flutter." She hadn't experienced "the flutter" since the first time she laid eyes on him strutting his stuff across the campus at Stanford. Panicked, she had to control this emotion running rampant inside her. She couldn't afford to have her secrets exposed. If he found out about Miranda, then he'd find out what a true bitch his mother really was. No one needed to carry that kind of weight about their mother. She could barely handle the truth about her lowlife mom, and she'd lived it because she'd never had any illusion about who and what her mom was. Luc had delusions and Cher wasn't about to tell him different.

She had enough to do in life without adding the complication of this murder or Luc Broussard back in her life. She had to get rid of him. "So what do you want me to do?" Cher wasn't certain she cared enough about Victoria Broussard to investigate, even with her sudden desire to fit all the pieces of the puzzle into some order. She hated untidy ends.

He drummed his fingers on the armrest. "I want you to find out what happened."

Cher rubbed her forehead. She had to think. His

presence in her office put her emotions into overload and her thoughts into total chaos. Her emotions warred with her logical mind. She had to get out of this. "Listen, my detectives are all busy. As soon as one of them is free, I'll have them do a preliminary investigation to see what they come up with. I'll call you in San Francisco. Leave your phone number with my secretary." If that was her best brush-off job, she'd drink her Liquid Paper.

His face hardened, his eyes turned glacial. "You're giving me the run-around." He sounded surprised as though this was his first experience with such an event.

She raised her chin. "I'm giving you the best I have to offer at the moment."

"What are you investigating? If your people are busy, you work on the case."

Was it her, or did he just give her an order? Her mouth opened to let him have a piece of her mind. She wasn't his servant, yet he just dropped an order like she was on his gravy train. He'd never been so insensitive before. Irritation rose in her. "I have detectives who do that. Detectives who are hip deep in their own cases at the moment. I don't do active investigating anymore. That's why I have an office with a name on the door."

His lips twisted. "Is that best you can do."

She glared at him. "Yes, it is."

He stood and gathered his folder and returned it to the briefcase. "Then we have nothing more to say to each other."

That was easier than she thought. "Works for me." Silently she urged him out the door, back out of her life. She didn't like the way the sight of him sent her pulses racing, and her heart beating like a sledgehammer.

"Thank you for your time." Luc left, closing the door after him with a defiant click.

Oh my God. Cher covered her face with her hands. What had just happened? A man she'd once loved, who'd fathered her daughter, had stood in her office asking for her help, and she'd made him leave, refusing to involve herself in his problem. She didn't give a rat's ass about his mother. His mother had ruined her life. As guilty as she felt, a part of Cher was glad the bitch was pushing up daisies. But then she realized that Luc was in pain. A pain Cher could not help him endure, she had her own crap to contend with.

Cher needed a cigarette. Badly.

Chapter Three

Cher sat, waiting. She forced her eyes to remain trained on the giant cactus plant in the corner of the office. The police commissioner's secretary sat at her desk, phone to one ear. She was a beautiful woman with long, blond hair and dark blue eyes. A serious bit of eye candy. The kind of woman a commissioner, with his public image in mind, would have.

Which brought Cher back to the question of why she was sitting outside the police commissioner's office. Didn't she have enough to worry about with Luc Broussard reappearing in her life after fourteen years? And the feelings he dredge up in her. The big, bad lust monster had returned with a vengeance. It had taken a while for her heart to return to its regular beat. Her palms finally stopped sweating about ten minutes after her stomach had unknotted. The last thing she wanted was for Luc to discover he had a daughter or the effect he still had on her.

She reached into her pocket for her gum. She desperately wanted a cigarette. Anything for a cigarette, even if it meant breaking her promise to Miranda. She unwrapped the gum and popped it into her mouth. She chewed ferociously, knowing, she wouldn't get her smoke.

The secretary smiled at Cher. "The commissioner will see you now, Lieutenant Dawson."

Yippee! Cher spit the gum out into the wrapper and dropped the wad into the trash can. Get in. Get out, and hopefully the man will leave you some butt to sit on. She didn't think she'd been summoned for him to admire her performance rating. The man never offered compliments. He had his own agenda, and she had the feeling she'd just been added to his list.

She opened the door and stepped into Commissioner Victor Sanchez's inner sanctum. The office was opulent. Deep pile green carpeting and a huge rosewood desk flanked by the United States flag and the Arizona state flag. Pictures of the commissioner shaking hands with the President of the United States and greeting rock stars and TV personalities lined the walls. Cher sighed. She wanted to sit in that desk someday.

"Lieutenant Dawson." Commissioner Sanchez said in a deep voice. He was a tall, slender man with dark brown hair graying at the temples. His brown eyes studied her as she walked across the room. "Let's jump right to the point." He glanced at his watch. "I don't have time to waste. Have a seat."

And I do? "Of course, sir." She lowered herself into a brown leather barrel chair that was so comfortable she almost drooled.

He opened a manila folder. "I just reviewed the department evaluation on your unit. Impressive."

Cher nearly fainted. "Thank you, sir." But she didn't think he wanted to talk about her performance report. There was something else.

He sat back and eyed her with a glint in his dark eyes. "But, you can do better."

"Of course, sir." With enough money, manpower and departmental support, she could be the reigning goddess of the Phoenix P.D., hell of every police department in Arizona. But how did he expect her to do better with only three detectives and no budget? She'd been given the assignment with Cold Case because someone in the department had been threatened by her and had set her up to fail. She hadn't failed. Her unit thrived and she could afford a moment's pride.

Commissioner Sanchez smiled. "And I'm going to help you do better."

Cher bit the inside of her lip. A sense of foreboding descended on her. "I'd appreciate the help."

"As you know," he continued with a benign smile,

"crime rates have been steadily dropping over the last year, and the department now has more money and enough manpower to be shifted around to those areas where it is most needed. How do you feel about five more detectives?"

Cher wondered what the cost was going to be, but she was willing to play the game. "I could use five more detectives." Short, sweet. I'm out of here.

He grinned, giving her a glimpse of the famous Sanchez charm that had been the reason he'd gotten his job. "I would like to arrange that for you."

She could hear the but hanging in the air. This man really wanted something bad from her, but what? And did she want to be in a position of owing him one. "Thank you, sir, I look forward to picking my new detectives."

"I need your cooperation in a small matter."

She nodded. Okay. Here it comes. The bribe. "You know you'll always have the cooperation of me and my detectives."

Sanchez smiled gravely. "I thought you'd say that."

Let me have it. Both barrels. Her smile felt forced and stiff, her face began to ache. She bit the inside of her cheek to keep herself from blurting out something she'd regret.

"I received a call from the Mayor. You do know who the Mayor is? His office signs our paychecks. There's a case we want you and your detectives to look into."

"Of course, sir." She'd play the game, but she wasn't liking it. When she'd taken over Cold Case, she'd been assured that she would be able to run it her way, and now the Commissioner was superceding her authority, just so that his political war chest wouldn't suffer.

He handed her a file folder, a bright red folder just like the one Luc had given her earlier. "Take a look at this."

Cher accepted the folder. She glanced at it, and Edward Compton's name leaped out at her. She felt as though her fingers would scorch. A bubble of anger surfaced. Luc had deliberately gone over her head. Did the Mayor's campaign war chest just receive a serious cash infusion? "I spoke with Mr. Broussard this morning, and I expressly told him that as soon as a detective was free, I would ask him if he were interested in working the case."

"Ask one of them?" The Commissioner's eyebrows rose.

"My detectives are allowed free rein in the cases they choose to pursue." As if the Commissioner didn't know. Most Cold Case Units in the country were allowed a certain autonomy. The whole concept of CCU was to allow a single detective to pursue one case until the case was either cleared up or considered completely unsolvable.

The Commissioner swivelled his chair. "I realize your unit is unique, but in this matter you have no choice."

"My agreement in taking over Cold Case Unit was

being allowed a certain autonomy." That meant no one was supposed to blackmail her into taking a case she didn't want to accept.

Sanchez grinned at her. "I know you're a team player, Lieutenant. You know how the system works."

"Yes, sir, I do. But somehow, I feel that my loyalties as a police officer are directed toward the needs of Phoenix citizens and not to an outsider from San Francisco."

"But a very prominent outsider, Lieutenant."

Her emotions were on after-burn. Sanchez had aspirations. How high up in the food chain had Luc gone. Mayor. The governor? No doubt about it. The trickle-down effect had just landed with a very loud and messy splat on her shoulders. "Well, since you're going to give me those five officers, there should be no problem fitting Mister Broussard's case into my agenda."

Sanchez shook his head. "I was thinking that solving this case would earn you the five officers."

Cher leaned back in her chair. "Ah. So, the five detectives is you being grateful."

"I can be very grateful." He steepled his hands and stared at her over the crest of his fingers.

She had the urge to smack that smug expression off his face. He had her by the throat, and he knew it. "As soon as one of my officers finishes their case, this will be their top priority."

"This is going to be your top priority."

"Are you saying that I am going to be the investigating officer?"

He leaned forward, a tendril of hair slipped down his forehead giving him a vulnerable boyish appearance. "I want you to give this case your personal attention."

She stopped herself from yelling at him, she hadn't worked a case since dinosaurs roamed the earth. "I haven't worked a street case in years."

"There's nothing like keeping your skills sharp, is there, lieutenant?"

She was snared. The man had her life in his fist, and he was squeezing. She thought for a moment. Give a little, get a little. She wasn't leaving this office without her officers signed, sealed, and delivered. Cher took a notebook from the inside pocket of her jacket and a pen. She wrote swiftly on the paper and then handed the notebook to the commissioner. Okay Victor, I can play the game by the same rules. "I want your signature saying that you will authorize the detectives' transfer as soon as this case is solved."

He frowned after a quick glance at what Cher had written. "You'll have to take my word for it."

"No." She slapped the notebook down hard on his desk and shoved it toward him.

His eyebrows raised to his hairline. "I heard you were pushy."

She waved the red folder at him. "A glacier-cold homicide with no witnesses, on the wrong side of town at three A.M. I think this could take me a while to solve. By then, the mayor's race will have come and gone and you'll be a man who hasn't realized his political aspirations. You sign this piece of paper, I'll be johnny-on-the-spot with this case. In fact, I'll do my best to have it wrapped up by the end of the week. That way you can start measuring the mayor's office for your furniture."

"With backbone like that, I see you measuring my office for your furniture."

She had ambition, too, but she wasn't about to let him see her goal. She pointed at the paper. "Which is it going to be, sir? A closed case or a lingering, festering drawn-out investigation?"

He picked up the pen and signed the paper, but not without an admiring smile.

She grabbed the notebook, closed it and tucked it back into her jacket pocket. "I'll have my secretary type up the official memo. And I'll see that you get a copy along with the press release for the newspapers."

He glared at her. "You're a hard-ass, Dawson."

She smiled. "I do my best, sir." At least she had some ass left.

Luc Broussard waited in Cher's office. He attempted to control the emotion spiraling through him. She was more beautiful now than she been back then.

Maturity had etched character into her angular face. Her skin was still as smooth as satin, and he yearned to touch her cheek. A shudder of desire pulsed through him as he'd tried to forget the very feel of her. Her almond-shaped eyes burned with a fiery intensity. Her hair was still short but now styled into a sleek professional bob. Everything about her still gnawed at him.

He didn't have time to think of the hole she left in his life. When his mother had told him she'd found Cher in bed with another man, any feeling he'd had for her had died at that moment, yet he couldn't make himself stop thinking of her. He had to.

Luc forced himself to study her office. The room was functional though not particularly comfortable. A row of gun-metal gray file cabinets lined one wall. A window with plastic blinds opened onto the street. A few pictures of Cher hung on the walls. One showed her accepting some sort of award. Another showed her shaking hands with the governor, the same governor whom Luc had visited only that morning and who had listened to Luc's request for help and then gratefully accepted a much-needed campaign contribution.

Nothing personal about her showed anywhere. No family photos, no little mementoes that most of the women he knew would litter their desks with. How like Cher to be so austere. She hadn't changed. A part of her was still kept hidden from the world. She had been the most secretive woman he'd ever known. No chitchat, no revelations, no information. She acted as though she'd just arrived on the scene fully grown and ready for all life had to offer. The only time she'd let him see inside her head was when they were in bed together. Never anywhere else.

Even during college, her apartment had contained nothing but the bare minimum she needed to make it livable. She had jokingly said that she didn't like clutter and knickknacks had to be dusted. Her only vice had been books. She'd been a voracious reader—from romances to philosophy. But even then she'd borrow the books from the library, carefully returning them when they were due. He always suspected her lack of possessions was because of a lack of money. Cher was more about dignity than anything else. A quiet dignity that had attracted him.

He tapped his foot impatiently. What was taking her so long? She should have been back by now. How much time did the commissioner need to order her to cooperate with him?

The door opened, and Cher entered her office. She gave him an annoyed glance. He was shaken to the bottom of his feet at the sight of her.

She was still so beautiful, she took his breath away. Her tall rangy body pulsed with the nervous energy of a thoroughbred at the starting gate. She wore a plain, dark navy pantsuit with a red-and-white scarf tied about her neck. A gold chain circled one wrist and a functional watch the other. Her hands were long and slender, devoid of rings. He wondered if her legs were as shapely as he remembered.

A shiver of excitement coursed through him, surprising him. After fourteen years, he still reacted like a giddy schoolboy around her. The fire was still there, smoldering, ready to be stoked into a roaring blaze.

Luc wanted to look away, but his gaze kept returning to her face. And each time he turned his eyes back to her, he remembered their past together. The lovemaking, the fights, the making up. She was too dangerous to his well-being and to his mission. He glanced at his watch. "I'm not in the habit of being kept waiting." He regretted his arrogant words, but he knew he had to hide the excitement he was feeling.

She scowled at him. "I'm not one of your minions. In fact, I'm surprised you weren't sitting at my desk using my stuff."

He had considered doing just that. "Sitting at your desk would be the height of presumption.

"So what's your point?"

He ran his fingers through his hair. "We're not getting off on the right foot, are we?"

She went around him and sat at her desk. "Maybe that's because you're stepping all over mine."

Behind her desk in the big leather chair, she appeared to be all business. He had to admire her. She wasn't intimidated by him. But then again, she hadn't been impressed by him when they'd been in school. Why should things change? If anything surprised him, it was that she was a cop. He would have thought she had started her own company. She had understood cutthroat business practices better than most and had a keen, logical mind. And here she was cop.

Then he remembered, her father was a cop. Why should he be surprised that she had continued a family tradition, when he had done the same thing?

He had set aside his own dreams of a career in the State Department to take over the family business when his father had unexpectedly died of a heart attack. Luc had turned his father's weekly newspaper into an empire containing magazines, a television station, two radio stations, and if this week's merger turned out as planned, he would own a chunk of a major movie studio. "I assumed you spoke with your commissioner."

She shook her head. "No one speaks with the commissioner. He speaks, I listen."

He couldn't stop the small smile from curving his lips. He could just imagine her on the carpet and trying to be polite. Polite was never her strong suit. She was proud, demanding, and formidable. The kind of woman he'd stayed far away from since she'd broken his heart. His late wife, Vanessa, had been her polar opposite. "I don't picture you taking what the commissioner had to say meekly." He couldn't imagine her accepting any ultimatums, so she probably made a deal of some sort. He wondered what the commissioner had lost in order to get her to play ball and follow the rules.

She opened the red folder. "Tell you what. Let's stop dancing, Luc." She glanced up with a decidedly unfriendly scowl marring her face. "You won this round. I'm stuck investigating your case. So the least you can do is stop gloating."

"I'm not gloating." At least not a lot. "I'm willing to let you get to work. But I do want to be informed of your progress on a daily basis."

She sat back in her chair and eyed him with open hostility. "Who made you my boss? You're not even a citizen of Arizona."

He grinned. "I will be soon. As of two this afternoon, I'm a homeowner, and I even picked up an application for a driver's license and registered to vote."

"My. My." She rocked back and forth, her eyes narrowed. "You finally learned to drive."

"I did. Sort of." Actually, he was proud of his driving skills. He hadn't had a parking ticket or a moving violation of any kind in almost four years.

"I assume you mean whenever the chauffeur allows you to drive."

He gave her a solemn look. "Once a year on my birthday, he lets me drive to the mailbox, other than that I'm not allowed to touch his cars unless I'm in the backseat."

She slammed her palms on the desk. "Stop that."

"Stop what?"

Cher stood up. "Stop trying to make me laugh so I won't be angry with you."

His heart did a full tilt at the way she stood, one hand on her hip and her chin jutting. She looked like an avenging goddess, and the reaction to her was immediate. He felt the stirring of an erection threatening. He couldn't believe her display of temper turned him on. How could she still affect him so strongly after so many years? "By rights, I should be the one who's angry. You threw me out of your life." He prayed for his body to stop reacting or at least that she wouldn't notice the effect she had on him.

She frowned and took a deep breath, her breasts straining against her jacket. "That was then, this is now. I think it's time you leave so I can get to work. I want to get this investigation over with so you can be on a plane to San Francisco."

"I live here now." He fought the urge to squirm beneath her intense scrutiny. "I'll leave, but not until you promise to give me a daily report." He couldn't help but admire her composure. When she had been younger, her emotions rarely played on her face but he could still read her. Now, she was more stoic, more guarded. He wondered what lay hidden behind the wary expression she displayed.

She shrugged. "A case goes as it goes. I can't promise you anything."

He straightened his shoulders and prepared for battle. He didn't like being undermined. He had done the dance to make sure she toed the line. "Would you like to explain your lack of cooperation to the governor?" For a second he thought he'd stepped over the line.

Her face darkened with anger and her eyes glittered at him. "You are high up on the food chain, aren't you?"

He resisted a smile. He wouldn't lord it over her, but he couldn't help his smug reply. "Always have been."

She tilted her head. "Not always. Not with me."

His gut tightened. He remembered that she had never tolerated his sometimes snobbish manner or his arrogance. She had never backed down. She was as sassy now as she'd always been. No way would she allow him to manipulate her. To get what he wanted, he'd have to play hardball, and he knew she wouldn't like it. The very thought excited him. His mouth almost watered. He needed something as a wedge. The same type of wedge he'd used with the commissioner. Besides, he understood the commissioner's desire to move onward and upward, and he'd used that ambition and greed to get him to force Cher to take on the investigation, but what hold could he gain over Cher Dawson? Not their past, she abandoned him.

She tapped the red folder with her long, slender fingers. "You'll get what I give you."

Discreetly he studied her wedding finger. She didn't even have a tan line indicating she'd been married once. "Really?" He found himself enjoying their battle of wits.

She pointed to the door. "If you don't mind, I have a case to investigate."

He'd been dismissed. His mouth nearly fell open. He had never been so casually evicted with such an off-hand indifference. What a novel feeling! As soon as he recovered his equilibrium, he would probably be angry. She had done to him what he had never accomplished with her.

He stood, accepting his defeat as graciously as he could. If she wouldn't come to him, he'd just have to stick with her. "I'll call you tomorrow for an update."

"If I'm not here, do feel free to leave a message with my secretary." She sat, flipped open the folder, and lift-ed it to hide her face, ignoring him as though he no longer existed.

"I'd rather have a more direct line to you than through your secretary."

She glanced up. He could see she was turning around his comment in her mind. "Only if you don't abuse the privilege." She pulled a business card out of drawer and wrote on it. "This is my cell phone. I expect only the most important calls on it. I don't give this out to just anyone." She handed him the card.

After all this time, she still had the ability to make him feel like a little boy caught with his hand in the cookie jar. He wasn't sure what to do next. Technically, he'd won this first battle, but she didn't seem to be taking her defeat with any of the humility he would have liked.

If anything he felt as if she just laid down a challenge to him. One he was going to accept.

Luc could do nothing but leave. He stepped into the squad room, closing the door softly when he wanted to slam it, not once but several times. He gritted his teeth. Four men sat in the office watching him. How appropriate that Cher Dawson should lord it over these men the same way she had controlled him. He felt compassion for her detectives, to be under the thumb of such a hard taskmaster. For a second, he felt a touch of respect for Cher. But that emotion was soon drowned out by the fury of her casual ejection of him from her office like he was no more than the hired help. Though he had to admit, he had treated her the same way. He got the distinct feeling that he was in for a long, hard ride.

Cher slapped the folder closed. She was tempted to toss the entire thing in the trash. It hit the desk with a dull thud. She needed a cigarette. She checked her pockets. How could that man waltz into her office looking better then snow on Christmas. Furiously, Cher rummaged through her desk. Why the hell couldn't he get old and ugly. She dumped the contents of each drawer on the floor and knelt over them pawing through the piles with desperate fingers.

No, he had to be sex walking into her office and saying here I am take me, take me. Where were they? Somewhere, some way, she had to have a pack of cigarettes around somewhere, hidden for an emergency like this. She was so turned on she thought she was going to bust. She ground her teeth in frustration.

How dare he! she fumed. He'd been out of her life for fourteen years and he'd just breezed back in, told her what to do and then gone over her head when she refused. Oh dear God, and he still smelled like a day in the woods. His scent teased her and taunted her. She hated that. She couldn't get enough of how he smelled.

She sat back on her heels and reached for her purse. There had to be cigarettes stashed away in some hidden pocket in her purse. She dumped the contents on the floor and searched with ferocious haste while her mind raced. How dare he just show up out of nowhere and start issuing orders like he signed her paycheck! She didn't even take that kind of shit from the department brass. She was not going to hold his bag of crap.

There had to be one here, she never cleaned out her purse. Just one little cigarette. One puff, and she could deal with this crisis.

The door opened and Jacob Greyhorse poked his face in. "You okay, boss?"

She jumped up, feeling guilty. Jacob Greyhorse, face creased with concern, studied her.

"I'm fine," Cher snapped, dumping her junk back

into her purse.

"What are you looking for?"

Her face squinched up. "Cigarettes. Do you have one on you?"

"I don't smoke. And neither do you. You told us under no circumstances are we to be browbeaten into getting you a pack of cigarettes."

She glared at him. "No one else in this office follows my orders, why all of sudden are you adhering to that one."

Jacob grinned. "Because Whitaker says you won't make it to the new year without a smoke. Marco and I have confidence in you. We have a hundred bucks riding on your steely determination to stay smoke-free."

Cher growled. "Thanks."

"You're welcome." He closed the door.

Wait a second, Cher. Whitaker probably has a stash with her name engraved on the package. She hustled into the squad room. Everyone stared at her door and made no attempt to look busy when she entered. Allan, her secretary, crept toward the door.

"Whitaker," she called. She couldn't do this. She couldn't give in to her urges. Especially with Whitaker involved. She'd be better off driving to the other side of town and hiding in an alley. Besides, she'd promised Miranda.

"Boss lady." Whitaker untangled his long legs and stood. He pulled open a drawer, and held up a pack of

Marlboro Reds. "Do you need a little something to get you through the day? I'm your man. Any time." He waved the pack of cigarettes at her, a smirk on his face.

Cher salivated. Her body shook. "What are you working on?"

He glanced at the pile of files on his desk. "I have one 'hacked-up' nun, and a drive-by."

"Greyhorse, what about you?" Cher glanced hopefully at the one man who kept her together.

"A rape–murder-mutilation."

"Jackson?" Cher asked.

"I'm about half-way finished with the stack my sister was working on." Marco Jackson's sister Elena had been one of Cher's detectives until she'd taken a medical retirement called baby. She and her husband were deep in the throes of happiness and pregnancy.

Cher tapped the door frame. "I need someone to do a quick and easy for me."

"Sorry, boss," Jacob said, shaking his head. "No can do. I'm up to my neck with this one."

Marco shrugged. "Maybe I'll see some daylight in six or eight weeks."

Cher turned a hopeful gaze on Whitaker. He sauntered over to her. "I'll take your case if you let me go back to doing real homicides when I'm done."

"No."

"Is that a firm no, a tentative no, an optional no, or a we'll-see-next-week no?"

She lifted her chin. "That's an only-way-you-get-out-of-my-office is to die no."

He picked up a pair of scissors from her secretary's desk. "Does losing a limb count?"

She pointed to the squad doors. "Get out of my face, Whitaker."

She stormed back into her office, grabbed her purse, then stalked back outside. "I'm taking the rest of the day off. If you want me, I'll be at O'Malley's."

Whitaker looked at his watch. "It's only 1:30."

"Whitaker, I'm the boss around here. If I feel I need a personal time-out, then I get one." She slung her purse over her shoulder. Before she left, she wrote a note and taped it to her secretary's computer monitor, ordering him to find anything and everything on Edward Compton, deceased, and headed out of her office.

Once in her car, she called David Dawson, her foster father, to tell him she would pick up Miranda from school. Instead she said, "Luc Broussard is in town."

There was a momentary silence. "Does he know about Miranda?" David was always to the point.

"I told you I would never tell him." Fourteen years ago, she'd been blackmailed by Luc's mother into keeping Miranda a secret and guarding her foster father's privacy.

"Maybe now's a good time to tell him."

"Do you think Miranda is ready for this? She's doing so well in school. She's behaving herself and actually acts like a human being at times."

David laughed. "You've forgotten what being thirteen is all about."

No, she hadn't forgotten, but time had dulled the uncertainty and the pain. "At thirteen I was happy to have a home."

David laughed again. "That didn't stop you from being thirteen. I remember a time..." His voice trailed away as he broke into loud laughter one more time.

"How did you put up with me?" She slipped the keys into the ignition.

"You had your moments, and you were worth the effort."

"Thanks. I'm picking up Miranda from school today, I'll see you in about an hour."

"Miranda is going to think you're checking up on her again."

"I am." She put on her sunglasses. "Just like you used to do."

"At least you're not making her ride home in a squad car."

Cher could still remember the way she had squirmed over that. She'd never once been late again. When David had said be home at a certain time, she'd been there or suffered the humiliation of another squad-car ride. "Trust me. If I had a spare one, I would."

"Okay, I'll see you in a bit."

Cher hung up, feeling better. David Dawson, or Pops as she and Miranda called him, was her touchstone. She'd been a troublemaker from day one. Even her own mother had given up on her when Cher had been five years old. One day she'd come home from school and her mother had been gone. Not that drug addicts made very good mothers, but Cher's Mom had tried. At least for a while, until her own demons became too much to handle. Then Cher had fallen to the wayside.

Cher's world had been rocked to its foundations. Her father, a man she barely remembered, had been almost as stormy. According to his rap sheet, he'd been in and out of jail, until finally he'd met his fate in a back-alley fight when she was only four years old. At five, Cher had started running numbers for a local bookie. And when she was caught trying to steal a classic caddy several years later, Sergeant David Dawson had stepped into her life and taken her under his wing. She'd been eleven years old and wild as she could be. She could barely read except to get from one place to another, and didn't know addition from subtraction.

Pops had changed her. He brought order and love to her life, and she owed him everything. She owed him for things she could never repay. She turned on the engine and gunned out of the parking lot heading for her daughter's school.

Miranda slammed the car door and buckled herself in. She was a slim child, small for her age. A mass of dark brown braids hung to her shoulders. Her face was small and elfin with a waiflike sweetness. Miranda always looked like she was thinking about getting into trouble. Fortunately for Cher, her troubles were purely hormonal at the moment. She'd grown up the last few months, developing tiny breasts and flaring hips. She was going to be a stunner in a few years. And every once in a while, Cher saw Luc's arrogance and charm in her.

Miranda leaned over and took a big sniff at her mother's shoulder.

"What are you doing?" Cher asked, giving her daughter a kiss on the cheek. At times, she didn't believe this poised, almost self-assured daughter was hers.

"Just checking to see if you've had a cigarette."

"If I had, don't you I think I'm smart enough to cover the smell with perfume?"

"Oh, Mom! That would be a dead giveaway. You don't wear perfume."

Cher had to laugh. Her daughter was evil-genius smart. And she loved that about her. She had to work very hard to keep ahead of her daughter. "Maybe I better start wearing perfume."

"No, don't. I like the way you smell. Just plain soap and water."

Cher simply smiled. Her favorite soap held just a hint of vanilla. Vanilla had always been her favorite scent.

"Is something wrong, Mom?"

"Why do you ask?"

She shook her head and her braids danced. "You picked me up from school and now you're staring at me as though you haven't seen me in years."

Smart girl. "I had a bad day at work." Luc Broussard was more than a bad day, he was a catastrophe, but Cher couldn't tell Miranda about him.

"Did they assign you to a new job?" Miranda was fascinated with Cher's job. She thought it was cool her mom was a cop and carried a gun. In fact, to make certain Miranda understood the dangers of firearms, she'd started taking her to the firing range when she was ten.

"No. I just have to work a case, and I haven't done any field work in a long time."

"I thought you were a desk jockey."

"I like working a desk, but every once in a while I feel the need to resharpen my investigative skills." Cher started the car and pulled out into traffic, easing along while keeping an eye on the dozens of kids strolling across the street with little regard for the cars. Cher had never been that young. She'd gone from kindergarten to adulthood overnight.

Her daughter gave a wise look. "Especially when you have such a cute secretary."

"Are you eyeing my secretary? Do I have to take him out and shoot him?"

Miranda giggled. "He's pretty good-looking for an old guy."

Cher laughed along with her daughter. "If you promise not to date until I'm dead I'll take you shopping."

"Mom, you say that all the time." Miranda's eyes went wide. "Do you really mean that?"

"Just the shopping part." Cher wanted to tell Miranda about Luc, but knew deep down in her heart that she didn't want to share her daughter with him and his family. She remembered the painful interview when she'd returned to San Francisco to tell Luc she was pregnant. Victoria had demanded Cher get an abortion, and when Cher refused had given her money with the proviso she never contact Luc again. After all, Luc had just married his childhood sweetheart, the daughter of a prominent banker, and his mother didn't want anything to tarnish the marriage.

Cher had been crushed. Only two months since she and Luc had broken up and already he was married. He hadn't loved her after all, despite his proposal, and the platinum engagement ring with sapphires surrounding the largest diamond she'd ever seen. How could she still be attracted to him?

Things were better left alone. She would clear this case for him, and he would leave. Then she and Miranda could get on with their lives.

Chapter Four

Luc Broussard stood in the empty living room of the six thousand square foot house he'd just purchased. He hated it. He didn't understand why he'd even agreed to buy the house except that his attorney had suggested that being a citizen of Arizona might grease the wheels of justice a little faster.

Luc didn't think the wheels of justice would move at all. Especially with Cher. He had the feeling she wasn't going to help him despite giving lip service to his request. She hadn't been easy to control when he'd first known her at Stanford and she didn't seem to have changed much.

Neither had his anger. He thought he'd recovered from their break-up, but he'd been wrong. The wound ripped open the second he'd seen her again. Not just the hurt but the desire. She was more sexually alluring, more confident, more at ease with herself.

He took off his coat and tossed it on some of the boxes that had been delivered earlier. His footsteps echoed through the empty house as he made his way to the kitchen.

The house was a sprawling ranch on five acres in an exclusive gated community. All the houses in the community had a generic quality to them. They were built to look prosperous and to show off the surrounding developments. His mother would have scoffed and called this an area for people with new money. Broussard money went back to antebellum New Orleans when an ancestor, one of the largest slave traders in the South, had bought respect with money. It didn't matter he was selling his own people, money was money. And money meant power. And power meant you gained what you wanted. Luc wanted justice.

He'd understood very early in life that every hope, every dream, every aspiration his parents had was placed squarely on his shoulders. His parents, although he knew they loved him with all their heart and soul, expected him to conquer the world and carry the Broussard name into the next mllennium. He was supposed to be Ambassador Broussard, then Senator Broussard, and eventually President Broussard.

He had liked the idea of being a power in the government, with Cher on his arm looking chic and elegant. She would have been the ideal asset. Instead she'd left him without ever saying good-bye or giving him an explanation. And he'd wanted to know why she had so callously jeopardized everything she'd had with him.

His mother had comforted him and re-introduced him to Vanessa Mayfield, a woman he'd known since prep school days. He'd even had a crush on her as a skinny fifteen-year-old boy. Within a year they were married. Cher may not have come from blue-blooded stock, but she had a class and sophistication that went beyond breeding. Yet Luc had come to love Vanessa. She had been gentle and sweet, and she had brought peace to his life even as he created chaos for her. Yet, he'd never quite forgotten about Cher.

And until he'd walked into Cher's office only a few hours before, he'd had no idea how big a hole she'd left in him. With Cher he'd had a destiny, and without her he'd had an existence. His business had become his wife, mistress, and lover. His only passion had been accumulating money and power. He wished he and Vanessa had had children because that would have given him something to nurture, but Vanessa had developed ovarian cancer and died before they'd had a chance to start a family.

He wandered around the kitchen. A house as empty as his life. He stared out the kitchen door to the patio. A road-runner darted across the bricks. A hawk balanced on the fence railing. In one claw, a snake writhed. The hawk bent down and tore at the snake with its hooked beak. Luc was in the middle of a The Discovery

Channel animal special. He shuddered. Luc had never lived anywhere but in the comforting confines of one city or another. His existence had been so sheltered, he had never even picked up his own clothes. There had always been a maid, a butler, a chauffeur, or a cook to take care of him.

He would have to hire a staff and rent furniture. He had to live in this house, though the prospect nagged at him. In San Francisco everything was familiar and close. Phoenix was so spread out, and so brown. He felt exposed.

The doorbell chimed. Luc frowned. Who could be visiting him already? He walked through the house, his footsteps reverberating off the walls.

The front door opened and closed. Luc walked down the hall and found his lawyer, Benjamin Ryan, standing at the arched entry to the living room.

"Ben, what are doing here?"

Ben held up a white linen envelope. "We've been invited to a cocktail party this evening. Guess who is going to be there?"

"Who?"

"Edward's sister."

"Helen is here?" Luc smiled. Edward might be in town, too. "What's she up to?" He wondered who Helen Ramsey really was. He'd wanted to do a full-scale investigation, but Ben had talked him out of it. Let the Phoenix cops do their job, he'd said, and Luc had reluctantly agreed, though he chaffed under Ben's edict. He wanted to do something, but Ben had argued that anything he did this time could taint the case.

"I hear she's trying to unload her art gallery."

Luc took the envelope and opened it, pulling out an ivory card with the invitation engraved on it. "You're a fast worker."

Ben grinned. "That's why you hired me. The only thing I couldn't do was scrape up a date."

Luc chuckled. "I don't think I want you scraping up anything for me. Remember that blind date you arranged for me for our senior prom? You'd said her family were horse-breeders, but I didn't expect her to look like Trigger."

Ben grinned. "Trigger was a blonde, too."

"All right, close enough." Luc read the invitation again. "So you've already arranged for me to go and 'press the flesh' as you like to say."

"Call Daphne," Ben suggested, "she'll fly in from San Francisco."

Luc tapped the envelope against his thigh. "I have someone else in mind." Daphne was a pretty diversion and good for a photo op, but she had a brittle, plastic look to her that didn't set well with Luc. Especially after seeing Cher again. Daphne didn't hold up well to Cher's natural beauty.

Ben nodded sagely. "The lovely Lieutenant Dawson? I never did get a chance to meet her when you were at Stanford together."

"There isn't much to say." Luc studied his friend, not wanting to give anything away. "What did you find about her?" Ben never left anything to chance. The minute Luc had mentioned Cher's name, Ben had taken to the Internet to see if she was mentioned and what was being said about her.

"She's a high-profile lady. Phoenix has her Cold Case Unit to thank for finding a big-time serial killer who'd been operating for years and never been caught."

"And that was all?"

Ben took a deep breath. "If you read between the lines of all the articles she's been profiled in, she appears to be a running favorite for a top-brass job in a few more years. She's the golden child of the department. Ambitious, savvy, and smart."

Luc was intrigued. "Anything else interesting?" He didn't want to show his curiosity too much. He didn't want Ben to know that seeing her again had stirred something inside that he'd tried to keep buried for so many years.

"Nothing beyond the obvious. But I could dig deeper, if you like."

Luc shook his head. "At the moment, no. But I'll keep the option open." If he wanted to find out more about her personal life, that meant he cared, and he didn't want to. She'd hurt him once, and he wasn't going to give her another chance. He'd take Cher to the party to help give her an introduction into the social scene that had spawned Edward Compton and set the stage for his death.

Ben opened a window and cool air invaded the room. "Luc, do you think you're on the right track?"

"You mean with Edward?"

Ben nodded. "The link to here is tenuous, at best."

Luc took a deep breath. "He used to talk about Phoenix society with the type of knowledge that he could only have known first hand. And we already know the real Edward Compton was murdered here. Perhaps my mother's gigolo husband has a history of swindling wealthy women. This is the place to start."

Ben turned to face Luc. "How did you get to be so suspicious? I'm the attorney, I'm supposed to have the suspicious nature."

Luc paused while he ordered his thoughts. "My father could smell a good story from a hundred miles. He knew when something wasn't right. There's something not right about Edward Compton. I've felt that way from the day my mother came home and announced they had eloped to Las Vegas."

"Why didn't you do anything then?"

Luc hadn't wanted to hurt his mother with any sordid information. "My mother seemed happy. I didn't want to hurt her. If she married a gigolo, he was going to find out very quickly that he couldn't swindle her out of her money because I held the purse strings. I can't believe my mother was the first. I think the trail may start here. Or at least go backward from here, because no one can truly cover their tracks."

Ben shrugged. "All right. I'm willing to go along with this, but I have my doubts. And as your attorney, I advise you to be very careful about what you say and how you say it to the press and to the police."

"Not a problem. I understand completely. I will be the soul of discretion."

Ben clapped him on the back. "I know you will. I'll see you this evening at the hotel." Ben left.

Luc heard his car start up, and he watched as Ben backed out of the driveway. Then he reached for his cell phone and dialed Cher's cell phone.

Cher answered her phone on the second ring. "Dawson." She wondered who dared call her on her off-duty time. Miranda sat across from her munching a giant chocolate chip cookie. Cher plugged one ear with a finger to reduce the background noise of the mall.

"Cher, this is Luc."

She stiffened. His voice sent shivers down her spine. "What do you want? I did say emergencies only."

Miranda's head snapped up. She mouthed the word, who? Cher waved her hand.

When had she crossed over into idiot land? The last thing she needed was to hear his whiskey-smooth voice crooning sweet nothings over the air waves.

"I'm having an emergency."

"Try dialing 9-1-1?"

"I'm having a social emergency."

This was worse then being a teenager hot for her first boyfriend. Just the sound of his voice sent her pulse racing and her heart thumping so loud, she was surprised he couldn't hear. "What do you need?"

"A date?"

Did he want her to get him a date? Oh that was cruel. "You have got to be kidding. I'm not an escort service."

He laughed. "I was speaking of you and I."

"I'm not going out with you."

Miranda watched her curiously. Cher fought the urge to turn away, to cover the mouthpiece the same way Miranda did when she didn't Cher to eavesdrop. But then Miranda would want to know more about the conversation, and Cher never lied to her daughter.

"Do you want to know more about Edward Compton?"

Okay the lust spell was broken. "I don't care about Edward Compton. You're forcing me to investigate."

"You make me sound like an autocrat."

"Aren't you? Here you are, invading my personal time as though I don't have anything better to do with my life than wait for your phone call."

There was a long pause on his end of the phone. "Why are you so angry with me?"

"Because I don't like being treated like a flunky. And certainly not by some out-of-state civilian who seems to think that moving to Phoenix gives him authority over me."

Miranda finished her cookie and sipped her milk. Then she cradled her chin in her hands and watched her mother, an excited expression on her face. Cher wanted to throw money at her daughter and tell her to leave, but Miranda was already suspicious. Any other unusual actions on Cher's part would send that suspicion sky-rocketing.

"I don't have to be diplomatic. I forgot that you are not one of my employees."

She changed the phone to the other ear and thought carefully about her next words. "If you treat them the way you're treating the Phoenix P.D., I'm surprised they stay with you."

"I pay extremely well."

"You'd have to." Take that, your highness.

She listened to a long silence at the other end of the phone and then Luc said, "I have an invitation to a party tonight. The hostess knew my mother. Edward Compton met my mother here in Phoenix."

Boy, what she would do for a smoke at this moment. "So this is a working date?"

"You could call it that. You have to start somewhere."

"There is nothing I can't accomplish by interviewing these people on my own."

"To the contrary." He laughed. "I'm providing you with an entree into their world where they would speak to you as an equal."

Whoopty friggin' do. "You've turned into a pretentious snob."

"No, I haven't. I'm a realist. These people are not going to speak to you. They will not betray one of their own."

"What makes you think Edward Compton is one of their own?"

"Because he fooled my mother."

"I'll have to call my boss and see if they'll approve the overtime." If they say no, she could turn Luc down. Thank God for cheapskate bosses.

"Don't worry. I'll call your boss."

"If you do, I won't go. I'm not one of your overpaid employees."

"Where do you live? I'll pick you up at six-thirty."

"I'll drive myself." No way was she letting him anywhere near her house where he might catch a glimpse of Miranda. She looked at the clock on the wall behind the cash register. She had three hours to get her glamorous. "I'll meet you at the party."

He gave her the address, and she wrote it down in a

notebook she always kept handy. Then she disconnected without even saying good-bye.

"What's up with that?" Miranda asked. "You were so rude."

"It's nothing. Just the case I'm working on."

Miranda's eyebrows rose. "Are you sure you didn't get busted back down to beat cop?"

Cher shook her head. "No. I'm doing a favor for someone."

"Remind me never to ask you for a favor." Miranda stood and slung her purse over her arm.

"Miranda," Cher said, grinning. "You never ask anything. You demand."

Miranda rolled her eyes. "So what's your point?"

Cher rubbed her temples. She needed to refocus. She needed to calm the raging heat sizzling through her body. Why was Luc still able to make her go weak in the knees? She hated that. She hated the way he could still twist her into knots. "I don't want to talk about my job anymore. I have to buy a cocktail dress."

"Ooh! I saw one at Dillards that would look hot on you."

Cher tossed her empty soda cup into the trash. "Hot is not what I had in mind."

Her daughter laughed. "Then we'll have to go to the food store for a burlap bag with flour stamped on the side."

Cher tugged one of her daughter's braids. "Don't

smart- mouth me, child. I know where you live."

"Come on, Mom." She handed Cher her purse. "Let's shop for you."

Cher parked her Toyota Camry three houses down from the place where she was to meet Luc. She stepped out of the car, and pulled the skirt down. Miranda had chosen a copper-colored satin skirt with a black long-sleeved cashmere sweater. The whole packet had set her back almost six hundred dollars, but even she had to admit that she looked chic. Her toes may be screaming in the black velvet pumps her daughter had insisted on, but she did look good. Miranda was always excited when Cher went out on a date because she always hoped that something good would come out of the date and Cher's focus would be rerouted away from Miranda. Fat chance!

Cher knew what it was like growing up on the wrong side of town. And as a parent, she watched her daughter like a hawk. She had Miranda's number, and Miranda wasn't getting away with anything.

She took a few tentative steps in her new shoes. After a few seconds, walking in high heels again returned to her. She approached the house and stopped a moment to look at it. The huge, sprawling stucco house was ablaze with light. Two turrets framed a boxy structure.

The turrets looked peculiar. Phoenix's attempt at architecture meant copying English castle style, and the whole thing turned out ridiculous. This was the desert. Spanish architecture dominated here, and the owners of this monstrosity should have remembered that.

"Admiring the house?" Luc emerged from the shadow of a large oleander bush.

"Not exactly admiring." More like overwhelmed. She clamped her mouth shut to keep from sighing at the sight of him. She felt like she was meeting a clandestine lover and not working a murder.

He chuckled. "It's an affront, an atrocity."

He stepped into the light and for a moment, her breath stopped. He looked elegant in his gray suit. His shoulders were broad and powerful in the gray material. His hair was close-cropped and neat. She wondered if he wore cufflinks. He always wore them when they were in college if he had to put on a suit. She loved cufflinks, they always seemed so refined and sophisticated. "Be careful." Her hand tightened on the rope handle of her black evening bag. "We're in agreement on something. That's a precedent."

He tucked his hand around her elbow. "But you, on the other hand, you are exquisite."

His touch inflamed her. For a spilt second she was transported back to their college days when he would touch every inch of her body at will. "I want you to stop trying to butter me up." Luc had changed so much since she'd seen him last. He was more masculine, handsome. The boyish quality, she had loved so much when he'd been twenty-two, had disappeared, replaced by a harder edged man. The change left her feeling sad and excited. She had liked that boy, more than she liked the man. Though she had to admit, she didn't know the man. Nor could she risk getting to know him again.

He escorted her up the stone walkway. She tried not to think about him touching her. Luminaries lined the brick path, the candles inside the designer decorated paper bags flickering in the cool night air.

The front door slid open, and a butler, his face grave and stiff, bowed as they entered. A maid waited to take their coats. From the left of the huge entry hall, music and laughter emanated. The overpowering scent of flowers left Cher breathless. She didn't know whether to sneeze or have an asthma attack.

Luc guided Cher into a vaulted living room. A hundred people stood about in small groups with enough room left over for another hundred people.

A tall blond man approached them. "Luc, you made it."

Luc turned to Cher. "Cher, this is Benjamin Ryan, my attorney."

Cher felt the other man studying her. His blue eyes moved up and down her body and lingered for a few moments on her face. She began to worry that her lipstick was smudged or she looked out of place among all these monied people. He winked at her. Finally, she smiled, she checked out.

"My, my, Luke." Ryan squeezed Cher's hand. "In all the time I've known you, you never once mentioned how beautiful Cher Dawson is."

Cher almost blushed. "Thank you, Mr. Ryan." His courtliness embarrassed her. She was not used to such blatant compliments. The men she worked with treated her as a threat, a boss, or another cop.

"Please call me Benjamin."

Luc pointed across the room. "Someone is trying to get your attention." He pointed at a tall, elegant blond woman standing near the buffet table.

Benjamin smiled. "Excuse me, I know when I'm being dismissed." He walked away with a wave.

Cher glared at Luc. "That was rude."

"I didn't come here to socialize."

"Then why are we here."

He turned away from her. "Someone in this room knows why my mother was murdered."

Chapter Five

Luc glanced at Cher, waiting for a reaction to his statement, but her face remained impassive and closed. He wondered what had happened to the girl whose heart had been so open. Her face had revealed every aspect of her emotions, and he had loved that about her. She had been such a lively contrast to the restrained emotions in his own family. What had happened to change her so much?

Their hostess glided across the room toward him. She was a slim, petite blonde wearing a clinging black dress that left little to the imagination. Her collarbone was a bony protrusion at the base of her neck, and her arms were too thin, yet her skin was flawless and her hair beautifully styled into a sleek cap that looked like she'd just stepped off the pages of a haute couture fashion magazine. If she was too thin, most people would be too polite to say anything.

"The legendary Luc Broussard." The woman held out her hand and gave him a well-practiced, too smooth smile. "Benny told me I had to be extremely nice to you. Welcome to Phoenix." She tucked her hand around Luc's elbow. "I'm Kitty Benson Hodges."

"Nice to meet you, Kitty," Luc said. The woman's perfume was cloying, and she hugged against him a little too tightly for comfort. On his other arm, he noticed Cher tense. He liked that. She wasn't as unaffected as she pretended to be. "This is Cher Dawson, a friend of mine."

"Nice to meet you, Miss Dawson. Haven't I heard your name before. Are you a member of the Country Club, or do I know you from the Junior League?" The woman's eyes didn't look pleased.

Cher opened her mouth as though to answer, but Luc intercepted her. "She works for the city."

Kitty's eyebrows arched. "You work?"

Cher smiled. "Somebody has to keep the city of Phoenix running smoothly."

Kitty sighed. "How absolutely charming."

"Well, thank you."

Luc gave her a warning smile. He didn't want her antagonizing these people. Edward Compton had been a part of this social set, and if Cher didn't treat these people with some respect, she wouldn't get any information out of them. One wrong move and they would all close their mouths tighter than clams.

Kitty introduced them around the room and finally left them in front of the buffet table. Luc couldn't help but notice that Kitty's voice was warm and inviting when she had presented him to the other guests, but cool when she had spoken Cher's name. Kitty did not appear to be a woman who accepted outsiders gracefully. Although Cher was nothing but polite, he worried that her police attitude would show.

He took a glass of wine from a tray and tried to hand it to her.

Cher held up her hand. "I'm working."

"You can relax a little."

"I'm wearing a dress I can't afford, shoes that hurt my feet and meeting people I don't even begin to want to know, and you're telling me to relax. Gee, thanks." She took the glass of wine and set it back down on a table.

"Your hostility and sarcasm are going to make getting information harder. These people aren't going to open up to you if you keep acting like a cop." He felt a spurt of annoyance. She was bull-headed and stubborn.

"I am a cop." She lifted her pointy chin. "Your high-handed methods don't intimidate me."

How he'd missed her defiance. It had always turned him on that he had to work hard to impress her. He reigned himself in. He couldn't afford to get entangled with her again. Not after she'd crushed his dreams once.

He wasn't giving her a second chance to explode his world. "I would think you'd care about justice, about getting a criminal off the street."

"Let tell you something." She turned to face him, tapping him on the chest. "I have one cop working on a string of child murders. I have another detective who spent two months tracking down a nun's killer, something which I have put my own personal time into. Another detective is trying to solve a bank teller's murder. I care about justice. And I care about each and every case that has ever crossed my desk from the moment I pinned on my badge to right now." She stepped closer. "But what burns me is when someone uses their position and wealth to carry out a personal vendetta and then goes over my head to involve me like I'm nothing more than a servant to be used as you see fit."

The scent of spicy vanilla invaded his nose. He remembered she loved the smell of vanilla. How could someone, who smelled so sweet, have such venom in her voice? He stepped back. For a moment, he felt guilty. He'd acted insufferably. He was treating her like she was one of his minions, but his mother was dead and her murder cried out for justice. He would use any means possible to see that her murderer was charged. And no one, not even Cher, was going to stop him.

"My mother is dead. I watched her killer go free. A murderer is free. This isn't just about justice for me. A young man in his prime is dead. I can't live with that.

Can you?"

Cher sighed. "I'm going to tell you something, Broussard. If you undermine my authority one more time and treat me as though I'm nothing more than your errand girl, I will drag this investigation out until I retire. You need me. So either be nice, or be gone." She picked up a plate and started filling it with food. Then she walked away from him and sat down in a corner to eat, her eyes roving about the room as though she were studying each face and trying to determine the secrets behind it.

Cher watched as Luc greeted a strange man. They moved away from the buffet table, talking. She seethed as she munched on the canapes. Luc Broussard was a full-of-himself jerk. He was so changed from the Luke she'd known in school. He was cold and distant, and his obsession with his mother's death really disturbed her. In order for her to work effectively, she needed to keep herself objective. Her emotions were taking over and she couldn't afford to be a slave to their dictates. Luc had done that to her once and look what it got her. A heartache that didn't heal. No, she had to remain cool. If her anger bothered him. So what! That was all she could let herself give him.

And that was why this case was a bad one for her. She wasn't impartial, not about Luc and not about his mother. His presence brought back all the hurt and anger at his mother's cold-blooded treatment of her, and his willingness to marry the proper society wife once she was out of his life. She was still angry over his mother's blackmail.

Victoria Broussard had had every intention of ruining David Dawson's life for no other reason than the fact that Cher wasn't good enough to be a Broussard. Cher couldn't raise much enthusiasm about Victoria's killer. She had studied the files Luc had given her, and from what she could intuit, she couldn't help wondering what Victoria might have done that had made her a victim. Had she antagonized her trophy husband? Or had she found out something about him he didn't want her to know?

She had to stop this line of thinking. She was blaming the victim, and no one deserved to be murdered, though she couldn't help acknowledging the poetic justice that solving Victoria's murder had dropped into Cher's lap. The old bitch had to be turning over in her grave.

One thing she had noticed about this party was that there seemed to be an overabundance of unattached women. She found herself studying them all. They all shared a certain sleekness, a certain sense of breeding that made Cher feel as though she were a Clydesdale amid a herd of thoroughbreds. They were all nipped, tucked, and trimmed to perfection and from the gauntness of their faces, anorexia was their favorite food disorder.

A woman sat down next to Cher. She balanced an almost empty plate on her knees and smiled at Cher. "How do you maintain that gorgeous figure and still eat like that?"

Cher glanced down at her plate. She hadn't eaten much yet. And what was on her plate wasn't even a quarter of the food she wanted to sample. Everything on the buffet table had smelled delicious and Cher wanted a taste of all the dishes. "I take karate and lift weights."

"Maybe I should try that instead of my aerobics class. Last year I was into spin, and the year before that into step aerobics. How long have you been into martial arts?" The woman pulled apart a canape and nibbled on a tiny piece of it.

"Twelve years."

"It must be exciting if it holds your attention for so long." The woman nibbled a little more and then took a long sip of water.

"I enjoy it." She really loved the fact that she could knock someone's block off. And it was something she and Miranda did together.

The woman nodded. "My name is Maris Walker."

"I'm Cher Dawson."

"How do you do, Cher Dawson. You're a new face around here. I saw you come in with Luc Broussard.

Such a handsome man. Such a tragedy about his mother. She was a beautiful woman. Had every man in Phoenix chasing her and that enormous family business she had."

Cher leaned toward the woman. "Really."

"Yes," Maris Walker said. "When the very charming Edward Compton caught her, it was such a surprise to all of us. His sister, Helen, is back in town. In fact, there she is." She subtly nodded at an elegant woman in a dark gray cashmere dress studying the food on the buffet table. "I understand she is trying to dump that art gallery of hers. Asked me if I'd be interested. I may have money to burn, but I don't care two hoots about art. I'd rather invest what I have in jewels." She held out a wrist with a diamond-encrusted bracelet. "You can't wear a Renoir."

"What do you know about Edward Compton?" Cher's antenna rose, and she slipped into police mode.

Kathleen grimaced. "A very interesting man. Very charming and very, oh, I don't know..." She waved her well-manicured hand in a delicate motion.

"Did he come on to you?"

Maris rolled her eyes. "No, I'm happily married."

"What about other women?"

Maris lifted her eyebrow. She waved her hand at the women in the room. "He charmed all the rich widows he could find. Why do you want to know so much about Edward?"

"Just curious? Point out some of the women Edward

hit on."

"You're very curious for someone who's so new." Maris stood up. "I'm sorry, but I feel as though I'm being interrogated." She walked away, taking her plate with her.

Cher took a deep breath. She'd blown it. Finesse was not her strong suit. If any information was here, she wasn't going to be able to find it.

She saw Luc across the room laughing with the hostess, Kitty. She was going to need him after all. These people spoke a language Cher couldn't begin to understand. She wasn't certain she wanted to.

She tried to control her sense of discomfort. She didn't belong in this uppercrust social group. She was a child of the streets. She'd run numbers for the local bookie and stolen everything from candy bars to Cadillacs. She'd been one minute away from either prostitution or selling drugs when David Dawson rescued her. She'd survived the carnivores on the street, but she wasn't sure she had the savvy to survive the well-dressed carnivores in this room. Every woman's smile hid an unsavory secret. Every man's smile hid a predatory beast. These were people who knew they had a right to everything and expected to have it. Not because they could afford it, but because of who they were.

The rich were different. They knew it. And Cher knew it. Luc walked through their world as though he were at the helm. Cher resented his easy manner and charming grin. Give her drug dealers and rapists any day. She knew how to break them down into their smallest parts. She knew how to ferret out their secrets. But the people in this room weren't so vulnerable. They had lawyers, accountants, and public relations managers who shaped their reputations, molded their images, and shielded them from the unsavory elements of everyday life.

Luc sat down next to her. "Enjoying yourself."

"Hell, no. This isn't my kind of party. I don't know why I'm here. And I don't know why you want me here."

A gleam of desire showed in his eyes, and for a second, she was transported back fourteen years to their last morning of happiness. He had stared at her with the same gleam. He blinked, and the gleam was gone. "You're not giving these people a chance. They're no different from you and me."

His eyes seemed to reach into her very soul. A lump formed in her throat. She had to remind herself why she was here. Why she was with him. "They're no different from you." She had no place here and from the way the women spoke and acted toward her, they knew she didn't belong either.

"Edward Compton moved in this circle, effortlessly. If we want to catch him..."

Cher stared at him. "What is this 'we' stuff? You sound like a war-weary old-timer on the job. Gee, when did the Wharton School of Business start teaching crime detection methods."

"I don't like you when you're being sarcastic. You weren't like this when we first met."

Cher was so taken aback, she couldn't reply. No word would form and eject itself from her mouth.

He put a finger under her chin and closed her mouth. "It's very unattractive to have your mouth hanging open like that."

She jerked back and shoved his hand away. "You weren't a pompous ass when I first knew you."

He sat back and stared at her. "Excuse me."

Her palms began to sweat, but she needed to say this. "I don't know what happened to you over the last fourteen years, but you've turned into a jerk." God, she'd said it. She'd told him what she thought of him. He'd probably head right to the Commissioner and report their conversation and she'd be on parking meter patrol. Or back to being Officer Friendly in the Media Department, running out to kindergarten classes to teach street safety. Cher tried not to shudder.

Luc burst into laughter. "Okay, truce." He held out his hand. "Let's circulate."

She held up her hand. He took it and lifted it to his lips. He kissed the back of her hand. His lips felt gentle. Cher couldn't move. She couldn't speak. She couldn't think. The heat of his touch raced up her arm.

He lifted Cher to her feet, then led her through French doors that opened to the back patio. The patio was a wonder to behold. A slatted cover, painted white, shaded most of the yard. Just beyond the edge of the patio was an enormous, Olympic-sized swimming pool, the water so clear, Cher fancied she could reach out and touch the bottom. Tables, shaded by umbrellas and flanked by matching chairs, bordered the pool. Along one side of the pool three cabanas lined up like little yellow-and-white striped soldiers.

Beneath the shade of a pink bougainvillea stood Beatrix Hunter with Luc's friend, Benjamin. One of his hands clasped hers, and she laughed at him. She wore a sexy red sheath dress, with a fur-trimmed matching bolero jacket that skimmed her body. Her blond hair was swept back from her aristocratic face. Her makeup was flawless as always.

Beatrix Hunter was a good cop, but her job in the Media Department reminded Cher of everything she wanted to forget about her time there as Officer Friendly. Beatrix was the current Officer Friendly, and seemed to love the job even though she had once confided to Cher that she hungered for something else.

"Benjamin," Luc said, "introduce us to your lovely friend."

Beatrix flashed a bright smile, her smile fading as her gaze landed on Cher. "Lieutenant Dawson! What a surprise to see you here."

Cher responded with a slight nod. "Hunter."

Luc smiled. "You two know each other?"

Beatrix nodded. "When I'm not being a social maven, I'm a police officer in my spare time."

Luc stepped back in surprise. Then he held out his hand and grasped Beatrix's. "Phoenix certainly knows how to provide the city with such lovely security."

Beatrix smiled. "My mother is one of the cochairs of the charity. My presence here is mandatory."

Cher didn't like the way Luc acted around Hunter. They were way too friendly for a first meeting. "Some cops do have lives outside the station."

Beatrix gave Luc a flirty wink and a sexy chuckle as she withdrew her hand. Cher's spurt of jealousy confused her. Why should she even care who Luc was interested in? Maybe if he found a playmate, he'd get out of her life. That would make her job easier. Right?

Beatrix patted Benjamin's arm. She leaned toward Cher. "Benjamin and my cousin Essex went to Yale together. Benjamin is almost a member of the family." She stroked Benjamin's arm.

Beatrix Hunter had a habit of popping up in the most unexpected places, including an occasional Cold Case investigation. Cher determined she wasn't going to end up working with Officer Friendly again, no matter how connected she was to Luc and his shyster lawyer.

After a few minutes of innocuous chitchat that had Cher on the verge of screaming her outrage, Luc drew her away from Hunter. He approached a group of women standing at the end of the bar and started introducing Cher. Cher tried hard to be polite, but she wasn't born to the position. Her cop's tongue kept running away from her. Still Luc kept forcing her to interact with these people until he made his away around the pool, stopping at the last group that contained Edward Compton's sister.

Helen Ramsey gave Luc a cool, distant gaze, one eyebrow raised. "I heard you were in town, Luc." Her voice was low and cultured, but Cher detected a slight Southern drawl.

Cher sensed the woman was lying, but she hid it very well. One thing she could see, they actively disliked each other. "I'm searching for a fresh start." Luc's voice was just as distant. "Allow me to introduce you to Cher Dawson. She's an old friend."

"Cher Dawson." Helen Ramsey's eyes narrowed. "How interesting."

What did she mean by that? Something flickered in the depths of Helen's eyes and was gone before Cher could identify it. "How do you do, Ms. Ramsey." This case was starting to intrigued Cher and she tried to halt her curiosity. She should be thinking about her personal life, protecting her heart from Luc, keeping her daughter hidden and proving she was more than capable of running her department. Instead of having three balls to juggle, she now had four. Sort of like walking into an spotlessly clean house that still smelled of sewage.

Her cop radar were revving into major overdrive.

This woman was a piece of a huge jigsaw puzzle. All the pieces fit, but the very last one. Something illegal was going on, but what? This was one of those cases where everything on the surface looked right, but underneath it reeked.

On closer inspection, Cher figured Helen Ramsey was in her mid-thirties. She had bronze-colored skin and light brown eyes. Her lips were full and sensual. Her cashmere dress was the latest in trendy fashion. She had a sleek, sophisticated quality to her, yet something in her manner wasn't quite right. Cher couldn't put her finger on it, but she had the feeling that Helen Ramsey was no more to the manner born than Cher herself.

Helen gave s light smile and tilted her head at Luc. "You'll love Phoenix. It's a delightful city."

"If you like it so much, why are you leaving? I understand you're trying to sell your gallery."

Helen turned to Cher. "A wise person sheds what they don't need anymore." She twirled her hand in front of her face. "Don't you agree, Miss Dawson?"

Cher shrugged. "Most people tend to rid themselves of what they have only to replace it with more junk."

Helen stiffened. "My gallery is not junk."

"I wouldn't know." Interesting reaction, Cher thought. "I've never been to your gallery."

Helen's breathing changed. Her chest began to rise and fall with agitation. "Then you must have Luc take you around and educate you. I guarantee you'll be a better person for it."

Cher curled her fist. Had she just been insulted? "Maybe not. I'm a cop. I'm used to wallowing alongside the uneducated, unwashed masses."

Helen's full, sensual lips twitched and a tic tugged at the corner of her eye. "I've heard that about police officers."

"We're good at sniffing out the world's trash." Cher relaxed her hand. She always got a rush when she took over the power situation with someone she didn't like.

Helen backed away from Luc and Cher. "If you'll excuse me, I have to mingle. It was a...pleasure...meeting you." Helen threaded her way through the crowd toward the house and out of sight.

"My, my, I wonder what I said?" Cher commented as Helen disappeared into the house.

Luc grasped Cher by the elbow and led her into the shadow of an acacia tree. "I think you need to turn off your bull dozer."

Cher smiled. "All I did was rattle that woman's cage. Trust me, by the time I get home tonight, she'll have placed a call to her brother and the game will begin."

Luc frowned. "Why does it matter if she calls him?"

"You think he's tied to the murder of Edward Compton. If that proves to be the case, I can't arrest him unless he's someplace I can get to him. In Phoenix is better for me."

Luc gave her a long appraising glance. "But you

haven't proved anything yet."

She still wasn't certain she even wanted to prove anything at all, but being so near Luc again after so many years left her reeling with some untamed emotion she wasn't certain she wanted to experience again. Besides, she and Luc had unfinished business. "If I do prove his involvement, I don't want him in New Jersey."

Luc looked puzzled. "Edward is in St Croix."

"I know that." She rolled her eyes. "But he could just as easily move to New Jersey, or anywhere. I need him here. The only way to get him here is to make him think he still has some unfinished business."

"So you're fishing?"

"Before you catch the fish, you have to go where the fish is. And I'd like my fish in town."

"How will that work?"

"Prove he stole dead Eddie's identity and then we can get him. And he'll do some federal time. I have connections in the Justice Department, if we can present a strong case for a stolen identity with the intent to defraud, he can be charged with violating your mother's civil rights. And that's a life sentence without the possibility of parole. Would you be satisfied with that?"

"What about 'dead' Eddie?"

A servant with a tray walked past, and Cher grabbed a glass of sparkling water with a twist of lemon floating on top. "The problem with solving a four-year-old murder is that it's a four-year-old murder."

"Do you think you can prove it?"

Cher took a breath. His fresh, expensive scent surrounded her. She wished he wouldn't stand so close to her. She could feel him on her skin. In her head. She didn't need the added confusion of his nearness. "Last year one of my detectives solved a case that had been lingering on the books for more than twenty years because of a trash bag. If he can solve that one, I can certainly give this one a go-round."

He smiled at her. "You sound very confident."

Her world dropped to her stomach. "I'm only good at a few things in my life, and being a cop is one of them." Besides, the whole future of her unit depended on her ability to solve this murder, she wasn't going to go down without at least trying.

Luc nodded. "Then you're going to have to do a better job of talking with these people." His gaze swept over the guests. "You're treating them all like criminals."

"They probably are. You know what they say 'behind every great fortune is a great crime.'"

Luc shook his head. "You've become very cynical."

"I was cynical when you met me. I've had a lot more practice since then." Especially after his mother got through with her. Cher acknowledged that Victoria Broussard was trying to protect Luc. Cher would do anything to protect Miranda, but the way Victoria had used her wealth and influence still rankled.

Chapter Six

Cher waited at the red light. Even at 10 P.M. the streets were still packed with cars. Streetlights illuminated the sidewalks and those shops still open. A Santa Claus twisted and bobbed in the spotlight of a window with a model train at his feet. In another window, a gaily decorated Christmas tree twinkled with lights that reflected on the glass ornaments. Christmas was almost around the corner and Cher hadn't even started her shopping.

Cher tapped the steering wheel, wanting a cigarette so badly, she was ready to turn into the first convenience store and buy a pack. She'd had a long, hard day. She wanted the cigarette, she needed the cigarette, and dammit she was going to have it.

The traffic signal turned green, and Cher pulled into

the corner mini-mart and parked by the front doors. The fluorescent lights inside the store brightened the expanse of glass windows, showing a dirty sidewalk and an overflowing trash can. As she approached the double doors, she heard a sound from around the side of the white brick building.

Curious, Cher turned and investigated. A yellow pool of light bounced off the side of the building and in the center stood a tall, lanky white kid about nineteen, his head shaved bald and every visible orifice pierced and filled with gold jewelry. He wore a jacket with the Nazi SS symbol emblazoned on the back. He was spray-painting on the side of the building with bright red paint. Nigers go home to Africa… Oh, good, Cher was going to have some fun today after all.

She turned back to her car and pulled her Glock from the glove compartment and kicked off her high-heeled shoes. She needed to kick some ass and she didn't want to ruin her brand- new shoes. She opened the door to the mini-mart. The store was empty of customers. A young woman dressed in a brown-and-white smock, leaning against the counter and eating a candy bar, eyed Cher indifferently.

Cher nodded at the young woman and said, "Call 9-1-1 and tell them an officer is in need of assistance. Tell them it's Lieutenant Cher Dawson. Give them your address and do not, under any circumstances, come out here."

The woman straightened. Her eyes changed from apathy to fear.

"Do it."

"Yes, ma'am."

Cher backed out of the store, holding her Glock in front of her and pointed to the ground. She slipped around the corner and eyed the kid. He'd finished his message and was standing back, an admiring look on his face.

Cher had herself a redneck who didn't know how to spell. She smiled at the skinhead. "There's two g's in nigger, and you forgot the comma after nigger. Where did you go to school, Redneck Elementary?"

He sneered at her, eyeing her up and down with a disdainful arrogance, and started walking toward her. "What cha gonna do about it, bitch?"

She raised the Glock, centering it on his face. "I'm not going to do anything about it. Mr. Glock does my talking."

At the sight of her gun, he froze, and eyed it warily. "Who the hell are you? The fashion police?"

Cher smiled. "No. I'm your worst nightmare. I'm the grammar police. Lieutenant Cher Dawson, Phoenix P.D. Now get down on your knees and put your hands behind your head and shut your face before I have an accidental discharge. I have a twitchy trigger finger."

The arrogance in his face died as he slowly sank to his knees. He opened his mouth to say something, but

Cher interrupted him. "Hark, are those sirens I hear? Sounds like the entire department. Now see what you did. Your little artwork has diverted everyone from more pressing duties. We'll have to add that onto your list of charges."

The screech of brakes sounded behind her. Doors opened and closed, and she heard footsteps pounding toward her. Two uniformed officers skidded to a halt. She recognized Dennis Coombs, a veteran street officer. He smiled at her as his partner went over to cuff the vandal. Cher lowered her gun.

"Dawson," Coombs said, an admiring tone in his voice. "I don't think I've ever seen you dressed like a girl before." He quickly made his way to the suspect.

Cher relaxed. "I always dress like this to go undercover at convenience stores."

He hauled the suspect up and handcuffed him. "Were you intending to use that gun?"

"I have to guard the dress. You should have seen the price tag of this outfit."

"Put your gun away."

"I'm protecting my investment." Cher took a calming breath. Adrenaline still rushed through her veins. She hadn't made an arrest in a couple years and even one as minor as this gave her a rush. But then again, her small triumph meant an hour of paperwork. What the hell, she'd taken an idiot off the streets.

A Dangerous Deception

Cher opened the front door, entered her home, and tossed her black velvet evening bag on the hall table. She slipped the shoes off her tired feet. The kitchen light was on, and she headed there. She stopped inside the door and watched her father.

David Dawson was a tall, slender man with tightly curled gray hair surrounding a face the color of tawny brown-tan. Little round glasses perched on the bridge of his nose, and his eyes, a velvety dark brown, peered out at her filled with all the love he'd given her since her tumultuous arrival in his home more than twenty years ago. He stood at the kitchen counter, swathed in a black baker's apron. Flour coated the front of his apron. He turned and smiled at her. "How was the party?"

Cher laughed. "Okay. You know, I'm thirty-five years old and you don't need to wait up for me anymore. It's not like I had a date."

He pounded a ball of dough into a loaf shape. David loved to bake bread. "The outfit threw me."

She held up a four-inch satin pump. "I realize these could be confused for date shoes."

He glanced at the shoes. "Those are 'ho' shoes."

"There is a difference, you know."

"Yeah, a lamppost and a mini-skirt."

Cher laughed. She seldom won with him. David

was the best friend she'd ever had, and the best thing that had ever happened to her. He saved her, and he deserved nothing less than undying devotion.

"Speaking of dates," Cher perched herself on a stool. "When are you going to have one? Robert's been dead for four years now. You won't tarnish his memory if you go out with another man." Robert had been David's life partner and lost a battle with Parkinson's. Cher missed Robert, almost as much as David did.

David gave her tight smile. Even at the age of sixty-four, he still had an impish quality. "I could say the same for you. You haven't had a relationship for more than five minutes since Luc."

Cher cupped her chin in her hand. "On the day Miranda leaves for college, I'll get myself a relationship. Right now I'm too busy."

"And maybe even get yourself laid."

Cher chuckled. "Are you saying I'm deprived?"

"Lately, you've only cared about two things, your unit and your daughter. CCU is up and running fine and Miranda is almost mellowed out. Maybe having Luc drop back into your life is a sign."

"Of what? That God doesn't like me."

"No, maybe it's time you tell Luc about Miranda, young lady."

Young lady! He only called her a young lady when he thought she was making a bad decision. "I can't."

"I don't need your protection anymore. I'm out of the

closet. I own my own company, so I can't be fired. Seventy-five percent of the clients are gay. Trust me, my being gay is a good selling point."

Cher traced designs in the flour sprinkled across the counter. "I don't know if I can face Luc's outrage after all these years. What am I supposed to say? I hate his mother more than I hate anything, but I can't tell him about Miranda. He'd want to know why I didn't tell him first thing, and I can't reveal to him what his mother did to me. He doesn't need more pain."

"You know what that kind of loyalty means?"

Her eyebrows rose. "I'm a good person and trying to find the right path to heaven."

"No. You still love him."

She jumped off the stool. "I do not. How can you say that? I've moved on. I have a good life. I have a job I love to hate. I have a daughter who makes me crazy. I do not love him."

David faced her, smiling. "One of the benefits of growing older, besides gray hair and creaky bones, is this incredible capacity to understand the human soul. I'm old and wise, but more importantly, I'm right."

She didn't want him to be right, she wanted him on her side. "I'm going to my office." She stamped across the kitchen. "I have a case I've been blackmailed into working on, and the brass wants personal evaluations on my people three days ago. I have work to do."

"Good night, dear." David kissed her on the forehead. "Sweet dreams."

"There's nothing sweet about my dreams."

"That's too bad. I didn't have good dreams until after I retired."

Cher stalked down the hall, up the stairs and into her part of the house. The light was off beneath Miranda's door. Cher stopped a moment to smile at her daughter's closed door. She was tempted to check on her. A few months ago, Miranda had snuck out the house to hang out with her friends, and Cher had gotten a wake-up call. Her daughter was going to head down the garden path if Cher didn't put her foot down. Cher knew all the tricks—she'd done them herself. She'd even used the same old oak tree to climb down and sneak away at night to smoke cigarettes with her friends at Big Murray's Pool Hall. Miranda tried the same thing, except for the cigarettes. If ever a daughter was on a health kick, Miranda was it. And she wouldn't let up her arguments until Cher agreed to follow the same philosophy. The kid should be studying law. Cher resisted the effort to check.

Cher continued down the hall to her office. She had work to do and now was as good a time as any to get some of it completed.

Cher looked at Detective Wyatt Earp Whitaker who

sat in the chair across from her. He slouched, his eyes narrowed to slits, and his mouth formed into a sneer. He looked rumpled, as though he had slept in his chinos and shirt. Even his grass-green tie looked as though it had been folded up into a tight square and then released just for the day. The only oddness about him were his boots. They were squeaky clean and polished to a high shine.

He rustled the paper he held in front of him. He tapped the corner and glanced up at her. "Maybe I'd have a better attitude if I were doing something I wanted to do."

Performance reviews were not Cher's cup of tea. She hated them, but they had to be done and Whitaker's review was hardly sterling. "You're a good detective, and I gave you high marks for what I think is important."

"Yeah, but because you gave me low marks for attitude, my ranking is just average."

Cher shrugged. "Nothing's wrong with being average. Personally, I'm surprised you care."

Whitaker frowned. "You had a chance to get back at me and you took it."

"First of all, do you know how childish you just sounded." Her patience with Whitaker was wearing thin. If not for his high clearance rate, she'd be tempted to dump him. "And second of all, you have not made any bones about showing that you don't want to be here. Now the one thing I can't figure out is if you have a problem with me because I'm a woman, or because I'm black and your boss."

Whitaker's mouth dropped opened. "Have I ever given you any indication that I'm sexist or racist? Is there any evidence in my record that I have a problem dealing with people of color? And I like most women just fine."

Cher wanted to hit him. "If there were, you wouldn't be working for me. And personally, I don't care how you feel about me, women, minorities, or purple people from Mars, as long as the job is done. I was making an observation. One that has obviously made you uncomfortable."

"Send me back to homicide." For a second, hope seemed to flare in his eyes.

Cher studied him for a long moment. "Okay, Whitaker, I'm taking off the white gloves." She rested her elbows on her desk and gazed at him. "Your old unit doesn't want you back." She could see his fist tighten.

His eyes narrowed. "Why?"

Her secretary buzzed her and she picked up her phone. Allen announced that Luc Broussard wanted to see her. "I'll be with him in a moment."

"He doesn't look like a patient man," Allen whispered into the receiver.

Cher took a deep breath. "Get him a latté."

"I think he's had his caffeine quota."

"Then make it decaf, and tell him I'll be done here shortly." She hung up the phone and glanced back at Whitaker. "Getting back to you, you asked why homicide doesn't want you back. You're not a team player. You get your job done and you do it exceptionally well, but you're too maverick for homicide. Especially for someone like Captain Sanders. He hates anyone who can't play nice. Me, I like mavericks."

"Sanders is a tightwad asshole who wouldn't know how to find a clue if it slapped him in the face."

"Is that what you say behind his back?" She rested the palm of her hand against the side of her face. "What do you say behind my back?"

He gave her a lopsided smile. "I refuse to answer on the grounds that I may incriminate myself."

"Spoken like a true politician. So you're not the one who refers to me as bitch-zilla."

A small blush crept up his face. "Nope." His voice contained a certain bravado, and his gaze slid away from hers.

She opened a drawer and pulled out a framed photograph. Her head had been digitally super-imposed over the body of a bright green-brown Godzilla. "You're saying you didn't send me this?" She held out the picture.

"Did you find my fingerprints?"

"I would have had the photo taken apart, but I kind of like it. I'm thinking of getting it blown up and taped to my door." She tilted the photo and smiled at him.

Whitaker's lips narrowed. "You're a real hard case, Dawson." He slid the performance report across her desk. "What are you going to do about my report?"

"Personally, I don't care if you dance around a burning cross wearing a white sheet, or if you prefer to think of women as bitches, just as long as you never bring it to the job and it never gets you in trouble. But your attitude sucks. Not that your attitude makes any damn difference to me, but I have to report it. That is what performance reports are all about. The big guys upstairs want me to look like I'm doing something for the paycheck the taxpayers give me. If your attitude was such an issue, you'd have been gone a long time ago."

"What do I have to do to get out of here?"

He never gave up. "Rigor mortis has to set in and the coroner has to declare you three days dead."

For a second he looked shocked. "Thanks, boss. At least I know where I stand, or lay, depending on how you find the body."

Cher chuckled. "As long as you're not decomposing in my squad room."

For a second, Whitaker's face relaxed, and he looked almost boyish. Cher thought he would laugh, but he didn't. If he wasn't such a jerk, she could almost like him. She dismissed him, and he sauntered out.

Cher drummed her fingers on the desk. She glanced at her watch, wondering how long she could make Luc wait. After putting away all the paperwork on her desk and straightening her pen and pencil, she waited ticking off the seconds. Her in-box was overflowing and her outbox was almost empty, but she couldn't think what she could busy herself with while she made Luc wait.

The door opened and Luc strode in. Cher's breath caught in her throat for a moment. He looked magnificent, and Cher couldn't help the lightning ripple of lust that slipped down her spine. She still wanted him, even after all these years and all the past behind them. Anger replaced the desire. How could she still have such strong feelings for him?

He seated himself in the chair Whitaker had just vacated. "I'm not in the habit of being kept waiting."

"I don't particularly care. I have a department to run, meetings to go to, detectives to supervise and..." she held up a piece of paper. "I'm due to be at the firing range in two hours for firearm certification. I'm locked and loaded, so maybe you shouldn't get on my bad side."

He didn't seem fazed. "It occurs to me that you and I have been on the wrong foot since we met."

"And what was your first clue?" My God, I sound like my daughter. She resisted the impulse to slap the side of her head. "Is this your version of an apology?"

"Of course not, men don't apologize. It's in our rule book."

Cher took a deep breath. She refused to laugh at his joke. "Let me guess, the Guy Code."

He laughed. "I'd forgotten how much you used to make me laugh."

Surprised, Cher didn't remember making him laugh. She remembered making sure he got to class on time, had his meals, and did his homework. "I was always the heavy: reminding you to go to class, do your homework."

He crossed his legs and leaned back in the chair. "You prodded with the best of them."

She smiled. "It's a gift." She settled back in her chair. "What brings you here?"

"Let's go out to dinner tonight."

She didn't want to get that close to him. "I'm miles behind in my paperwork." Okay it was a lie, but one of self- protection.

"I don't believe that." He shook his head. "You were the most organized, efficient person I ever knew."

"Well, that was then. Now I run a squad, and you would be amazed at how much paperwork that generates." She picked up the red folder he'd given her the other day. "Along with the added duty of working a murder case."

He smiled at her. "One thing the years have taught you is finesse."

Curious, she responded, "What do you mean?"

"How very diplomatically you've just stated that I've caused you nothing but added inconvenience since I arrived in Phoenix."

You got that right, buddy. She rolled her eyes. "Damn, I must be getting old."

"More like ripened."

She shook her head, surprised at him. He was flirting with her. "I'm not an orange."

"Pity, I love oranges. You have to eat. We can do it together."

She was going to let that last remark go by, ignoring the sexual innuendo. "I'm a very busy woman. Thanks for the dinner offer."

"You have to eat sometime."

"I'll eat here. Pretty much every restaurant around the office delivers. I'm not going hungry."

"Let me join you...here."

Not a chance. She picked up her black lacquer ink pen. "I like working late because there are no distractions."

He unbuttoned his navy blue suit jacket. "Do you consider me a distraction?"

Cher didn't like him getting comfortable in her office. "Of the highest order." They had too much history between them for her not to be distracted by all the thoughts of what should have been.

"Am I being presumptuous in thinking you are still attracted to me, even though you left me?"

Dropping her pen, she didn't want to go there. "I had my reasons."

He leaned forward, his eyes intense. "You always had a reason for what you did. You just had a hard time sharing those reasons with anyone."

For a second, she debated whether or not to tell him the truth. The irony of the situation was that his mother had blackmailed her and now she was investigating the woman's murder. She was amused at the whole situation. A little part of her still wondered what would have happened after his wife's death, if she had returned and told him the truth. "Things haven't changed."

"Trust was always the main issue between us, wasn't it?"

He was wrong. She had trusted him with her heart, but it was easier to let him believe she hadn't. Her foster father's secret wasn't hers to divulge then, and she couldn't say anything now because any comment would lead back to Miranda. She couldn't tell him about his mother because she knew how devastating such a revelation would be to him, assuming he believed her. Her own mother had been dead for more than twenty years, and Cher still felt the agony and shame over who and what her mother had been. Everyone needed their illusions. Sometimes it was all a person had to cling to. She had no right to reveal to him the kind of person his mother really had been. Anything she said to him was suspect. Even in her own heart. Was she revealing information to him to get back at his mother, or defend herself? She would never be sure of her own motivations. "I simply don't want to discuss this any further. That part of our lives is ended." She was being cruel, but she felt that brutality was what he needed to get rid of him. Besides if Victoria Broussard had interfered in Cher's relationship with Luc, Victoria had probably interfered in other areas of his life. On some level, Luc probably already knew about his mother, but his allegiance to her would forever keep him silent. "We need to move on."

His eyes narrowed. "You're hiding something from me, aren't you?"

A chill ran through Cher. Your child. My still raging desire for you. She was full of secrets. "I'm not that good a poker player." She could tell he didn't believe her. Nervously she straightened her evaluation folders.

The door to Cher's office flung open and Edward Compton's sister, Helen Ramsey, stalked in. Cher's secretary followed behind her. Cher smiled at him and nodded. He backed away and closed the door. "What can I do for you?"

Helen glared at Cher and Luc. "How dare the two of you cast aspersions on my reputation and the reputation of my brother. I was told you were asking questions about us. My brother was found innocent of all charges. You stay away from me and Edward. Otherwise, I'm going to file a complaint with your superiors claiming police harassment."

Cher stood. "And charge me with what?"

Helen Ramsey put her hands on her slim hips. "I'll have your badge."

Cher smiled. This just made her day. "You are way too used to dealing with California cops. This is Arizona, and we are still a frontier state. You need to calm down, right now, or I'll be forced to have you arrested."

"On what charges?" Helen bristled.

"You come flying in here, in the middle of a police station, threatening me and disturbing my peace."

"I haven't threatened anyone."

"Wrong." Cher crossed her arms. "That's your interpretation, but not what I heard. And since I'm one of the good guys, who do you think the county attorney is going to believe?" She pulled back her jacket. "You see this badge. It gives me permission to kick your ass any time I feel like it."

Helen's lips thinned, and her brown eyes went cold. "Are you threatening me with physical harm?"

Cher glanced at Luc. "Luc, would you please step outside and lock my door on the way out."

Luc stood. "Cher." His voice held a warning.

"You go on now." She took off her suit jacket. "Helen and I are gonna have us a little girl talk."

Luc moved to block her way. "I'm not leaving."

Cher unfastened her watch and tossed it on the desk. "This is going to get ugly, and I don't want you to see me get my bitch on."

"Cher, you must think about this a moment before you do anything rash."

"This woman is giving me a rash." Cher shooed him with her hands. "I'm the law in these parts and can do whatever I want."

Helen backed up, her hand wrapped around the front of her throat. "I don't know what the two of you are cooking up, but it isn't going to work. You can't threaten me, my brother and I know our rights."

"I'm cooking up my dinner plans," Cher said. "I'm not threatening you, or your brother. I was simply investigating my meal possibilities."

Helen paled. "I don't know what you're talking about."

Cher held up a finger. "Well, I don't know what you're talking about, accusing me and Luc of conspiracy when all we were talking about was where to have dinner. Now call me suspicious, but that statement makes me think you have something to hide."

Nervously, Helen glanced back and forth between Cher and Luc. "I'll leave for now." She gave Cher a menacing stare. "I know all about you, Cher Dawson. I know what kind of woman you are. You don't frighten me. I know how to take care of people like you."

Cher felt a shiver of apprehension ripple down her back, but managed to keep her face calm. This woman knew all about Luc's mother and the blackmail. Did she know about Miranda? "You have five seconds to leave my office." She rested her hand on the phone.

"This isn't over." Helen reached behind her to grab the doorknob.

Cher nodded at the woman. "You're right. It isn't. Not by a long shot."

"I'll be speaking to my attorney."

"I'm sure I will be, too."

Helen left.

Cher raised an eyebrow at Luc. "Now, that was interesting."

Luc closed the door. "Cher, did you really mean you'd arrest her. Don't you think that was going a little too far?"

Cher burst out laughing. "I was just having some fun."

"That is a strange idea of fun."

"When you're a female cop, attitude is everything. People think a woman is nothing more than a Barbie with a badge. If I don't jump in and control the situation right away, I might as well be a Barbie. That woman was afraid of me, the same way she'd be afraid of a male cop."

"You didn't answer my question. Would you have hurt her?"

Cher sat down, shaking her head. "Nope. I might have broken a nail. Besides the paperwork is a pain."

"I'm going to pretend that you're making a joke."

"You do that." Civilians just didn't understand. "Now, I have work to do, you have to leave."

He buttoned his jacket. "What about dinner? I insist on it."

"No." She had her karate class with her daughter. No way was she going to miss her major mother-daughter bonding night. "I'm busy." Mending fences with him would reveal too much. As she repositioned her in-box, she thought about all the questions she would have to answer—like why she'd kept Miranda a secret and why she'd left him? She needed to keep Luc at arm's length, and she could see her refusal to go to dinner frustrated him.

He stood and checked his tie. "You know, I never could resist a challenge."

She studied him. He looked ready to take her on. "I don't know what you're talking about, and I don't want to know." She gestured at the door. "I'm not your personal police force."

"I was hoping we could talk about my mother's murder."

She shook her head emphatically. "Let me state something to you and please listen. I am not investigating your mother's murder. I was 'ordered' to work a case involving the death of one Edward Compton. I'm not here to entertain you, or keep you informed. I'm doing my job. And that job does not include dinner or social functions unless they have something to do with the case. I don't want to be your friend. I don't want to be your partner. I don't want to be your employee. I'm not here to soothe your ego."

Luc glared at her. "When did you turn into such a ruthless shrew?"

About five minutes after meeting your mother. "That's none of your business."

Luc left, stalking out of her office with a look on his face that told her he wasn't done with her. But she could handle him. Just not now. Having him so close rekindled too many old feelings. Feelings she'd rather forget.

Allen poked his head into her office. "Boss, are you all right?"

"I'm fine."

Cher pushed back from her desk and walked to the window. She stared down into the street. What was she doing? She had to keep him from finding out her secrets. The only way she could do that was to make him into an enemy. She just wished he'd play along.

When she'd first met him, she'd been dazzled by his class, his culture, his moneyed background. Against her better judgment, she'd allowed herself to be vulnerable in a way she had never been before. She had opened her soul to him, and his feelings had overpowered her. She'd been swept along by the dream that he really loved her and would do anything for her. But in the end, he'd done nothing.

Once she was out of the picture, he'd tamely allowed his mother to arrange a more fitting marriage for him. When Cher had found out he'd gotten married, she had been devastated. She had returned to San Francisco to tell him about her pregnancy, but his mother had stopped her at the door, listened to her tale and given her money for an abortion. On a departing note, Victoria had told Cher that Luc hadn't bothered to come after her because Cher was little more than an amusement for him.

That Victoria would so callously arrange for the

death of her first grandchild and the revelation that Luc had never loved her had sent Cher fleeing back to Phoenix, vowing she would never have any contact with that family again. She had buried her feelings deep inside her and spent the rest of her life being a good mother and a good cop. And here was Luc back in her world again, rocking it to the foundations. She had to stay away from him. Never again would she allow him to see inside her. Never again would she allow him to touch her heart.

She survived once because she'd had a baby to love and cherish. She hadn't had time to feel sorry for herself. She was older and tougher now, but her love for Luc was still simmering beneath the surface of her anger.

Chapter Seven

Luc sat in his car and replayed the scene in his mind. He saw that Cher had been agitated. Not that she had showed a lot of it, but little signs he remembered from before kept appearing. She had fiddled with a pen on her desk and then straightened a pile of reports. She had moved the in-box and then realigned it with the corner of her desk. All the little things that brought back his time with her as though it had been yesterday.

In school, she had been driven to succeed. Even then, she hadn't taken crap from anybody, not even the professors. She stood up for herself and for people who were powerless. He remembered the first time he'd seen her. She was pushing some big linebacker across the quad. At first he'd though they were playing, until she punched the guy in the stomach and yelled at him to pick on people his own size. The linebacker had been a foot taller than Cher and outweighed her by a hundred and fifty pounds.

A young Asian man, his glasses dangling from one ear, had been picking books up off the ground. When the linebacker had taken off, Cher had helped the young man recover his possessions.

Cher was dangerous as well as seductive, and until Luc met her, he hadn't realized how much he disliked the women he dated. Looking back, he had always dated women of whom his mother approved.

Cher was a whole new world for him. She was mysterious and secretive and hadn't come from a moneyed background. She hadn't attended gala parties, the opera, or even the theater. She was jazz, football tickets, and hamburgers. Everything that had been forbidden him during his childhood. Broussards did not associate with riffraff and even as he plunged whole-heartedly into a relationship with her, in the back of his mind he knew his mother wouldn't approve. And somehow that had made Cher even more attractive, until the day his mother's words came back to haunt him.

He remembered that last day so clearly. It was etched in his mind. He'd returned from his history final to find his mother sitting primly in the living room, a drink in one hand and a cigarette in the other. He had asked where Cher was, and his mother had dropped a bomb that ripped his world apart. His mother had arrived early and found Cher with another man.

At first, Luc hadn't believed her. Cher wasn't like that. She loved him. And for her, love also meant complete loyalty. But his mother had insisted, even asking him if he thought she was lying. How could Luc answer a statement like that? His mother was his mother. He'd trusted her, even though he knew she was as much a predator as Cher.

He always wanted to know what the other man possessed that he didn't. His pride kept him from going to her once she'd left. And his need for her expertise kept him from demanding an explanation now. But the longing to know gnawed at him the second he laid eyes on her again. If nothing else, he should be allowed some sort of explanation.

Luc started his car and pulled out of the parking garage. As he turned on to the street, he picked up the phone and called his attorney.

Benjamin answered on the first ring. "Hello, Luc. What's up?"

Next to his mother's death, Cher's desertion has been the most devastating event in his life. He'd understood death, there was an inevitability about it. But Cher's desertion made no sense. "Benjamin, I want you to do something for me."

"Something interesting, I hope. I'm bored."

"I want everything you can find on Cher Dawson. Not just stuff on the Internet, but her address, home phone, everything, anything. No stone left unturned, Ben."

"Even the last man she slept with?"

"Right down to any hidden tattoos." Luc would find out what she was hiding from him.

"Right-o," Benjamin replied.

Luc could almost see Benjamin rubbing his hands together. Normally, Luc reserved such a comprehensive investigation for his competition, but in some ways, Cher had become his competition. As well as a woman he wanted to possess. Normally he never let the personal invade the professional, but with Cher he always found himself making the exception.

"Thanks, Ben. When can you have it for me?"

"I should have a preliminary report by end of business tomorrow," Benjamin replied.

He needed to convince Cher that this was an investigation to be taken seriously, not the whim of an angry man trying to prove something. If finding a skeleton in Cher's closet helped the investigation along, then so be it. He could live with being a jerk.

Miranda leveled a kick at Cher and knocked her down. Cher fell to the mat, her head snapping against the vinyl, her breath knocked out of her. She glanced up at her daughter, amazed Miranda could kick so hard.

"Mom." Anxiously Miranda leaned over Cher. "Are you okay? I didn't mean to hit you so hard. I'm sorry."

Cher found her breath. "Remind me to never get on your bad side."

Miranda grinned as Cher struggled to her feet. She took a deep breath and smelled sweat.

"I'm sorry, Mom, but you don't seem to have your mind on what you're doing. Can I get you a cup of water?"

Cher limped to the side of the room and sat in an orange plastic chair. Her whole body ached. She was getting too old for this crap. She carried a gun, why did she need self-defense? "Yes, that would be fine."

Miranda bounced to the water cooler. As she bent over the spigot to fill the paper cups, Cher could see small elements in her daughter's face that were part of the genetic heritage from her father. Her lips were shaped like Luc's and her eyes were the same dramatic brown. Her cheekbones sloped the same way as Luc's. Miranda still had some growing to do. The rangy quality to her arms and legs told Cher she would probably be tall, topping out around five-eight, maybe even five-nine. God, she and Luc had made a beautiful child. She didn't think in a million years she would ever get this lucky again.

Cher leaned her head back against the wall and closed her eyes. How much longer was she going to be able to keep the secret? And was she being fair to Miranda? Miranda had the right to know who her father was. Her queries in the past had elicited only vague explanations from Cher. Miranda assumed that Cher had simply indulged in a youthful indiscretion and didn't want to talk about it.

Cher had society to thank for her daughter's lack of curiosity. Miranda's own friends were mostly from single-parent families with a mother in charge of the children, the fathers long gone and so out of the picture no one ever talked about them. One girlfriend had had enough stepfathers over the last seven years to form her own basketball team. Miranda's only comment had been she was pleased Cher didn't fool around. Cher hadn't known how to take that.

Her daughter returned with the cup of water. She sat next to Cher. "Mom, what's up with your chi? You've been unfocused all evening."

"I left my chi in the locker. I can't seem to focus right now. This case I'm working isn't going too well."

"Can you talk about it?"

It warmed her heart that Miranda wanted to know about her work. "No. I wish I could, but you know I can't discuss an active case."

"Why? Are the details gruesome? Or because you don't think I'll understand?"

She stared over the rim of the paper cup. "Because I don't break the rules."

"Not according to Grandpa." Miranda grinned, looking very pleased with herself.

Cher shook her head. "Grandpa's telling tales again, is he?" She took another sip of the cool water. "Go back out there and kick some behind."

Miranda giggled. She jumped up and ran back to the class while Cher sipped the water her daughter had so thoughtfully brought her. She couldn't complain. Miranda was a terrific girl. Her only problem at the moment was being thirteen. Cher always thought Miranda was her reward for making the right decision between Luc and David. This way she always had a piece of Luc with her. The best part.

Cher had worked and struggled for everything she ever had. Once she realized there was a life beyond the streets, she had worked hard to keep what she had found, what David Dawson had given her. And she wanted to make him proud. That man had opened his home to her and given her his heart. She owed it to him to make something out of her life, no matter what the cost. Giving up Luc had been the payment. she had accepted that sacrifice.

Why, when everything was going good, did life have to throw her a big, nasty spitball? Compton's case was a spitball of the highest order. She had a dead Eddie Compton and a live, out-of-town Eddie Compton, and one very angry sister who probably wasn't a sister. She hadn't seen anger like that since she'd been on patrol during her rookie year on the force. Helen Ramsey was hiding something. Why else would she get so worked up? Note to self: check out sister.

They were both concealing something. That didn't necessarily mean murder, but Cher hated when people kept secrets from her. She had a fanatical need to find out what was going on. She understood secrets because she had so many of her own and understood the motivators.

Looking back, besides Miranda and David Dawson, there were maybe three other people who knew what her childhood had been like. Cher had always been honest with her daughter about the past. Honest about everything except Luc. She hadn't even told Luc about her background. Another secret. He'd come from a privileged background. Cher had come from nothing. And in a deep way, she was ashamed.

Cher decided she'd goofed off long enough. Nothing was settled, only more convoluted than before. She hated that. She stood, tossed the paper cup in a trash can, and went back to join the class.

After class, Cher called her best friend of eleven years, Lily Alexander. She offered to hand-deliver Lily's favorite food—pizza—in exchange for a favor.

Cher had met Lily, who was writing a nonfiction book on a crime that had happened in Phoenix, and needed to interview Cher. They had struck up a friendship. Lily had the best contacts on either side of the justice system. If information could be divulged, Lily was the one person who could track it down. She had once intended to be an investigative reporter, but an incident in college had derailed her plans, and she turned to true-crime writing.

Cher wasn't ready to start an official investigation on Helen Ramsey. She needed to proceed with caution, no matter how strongly Luc pushed her. She didn't want to look incompetent in front of him or stupid in front of her boss.

As Cher drove through the wrought-iron gate, she saw Lily waiting just inside the double doors of her sprawling adobe ranch-style house.

Cher rolled down her window and stuck her hand out to wave. Lily had a smile on her medium brown, waif-like face. Short, dark hair curled tightly about her face and huge brown eyes. She waved and went back into the house. Cher knew Lily seldom left her home. She was agoraphobic, so people came to her and brought the world with them.

After Cher parked the car. She and Miranda got out.

Lily waited for them in the hallway. After helping themselves to the plates and sodas, Cher sent Miranda to the living room to eat so she could have some private time with her friend.

"So what do I own to the gods of buddies to get this unexpected visit."

"Can't I just want to see you?" Cher stared at the wall of Lily's office. A huge saltwater aquarium containing a variety of brightly colored fish swam back and forth, and provided the room with an exotic underwater theme.

"What's on your mind?" Lily picked up a slice of pepperoni pizza and bit into it.

"Luc is back in my life," Cher said with a heavy sigh.

"Great." Lily bounced in her chair. "You can have the wedding here."

Cher grimaced. "You know, Lily, behind that tough Rottweiler exterior you show to your fish, you are an incurable romantic."

"Oh, I get it." Lily frowned. "So this isn't a good thing? Is he back because he found out about Miranda?"

"He fixed it so I have to personally investigate a murder that may be related to his mother's murder." Cher bit into her pizza. Cheese caught in the corner of her mouth, and she swiped it with her tongue.

"That old witch is finally dead?" Lily put her plate on her desk, jumped to her feet and went to the liquor cabinet. "Let's open a bottle of wine and celebrate. She's gone, out of your way, out of your life, no longer standing between you and Luc."

"I'm driving."

"You and Miranda can stay over. We'll have a slumber party, and I'll figure out how to get you and Luc back together."

Cher rubbed her throbbing temples. She didn't want Luc back. Not now. Not ever. They had too much ugly history to overcome. "I don't want Luc back in my life. Besides, Miranda has school tomorrow."

Lily shook her head. "You and Miranda have a closet full of clothes here. She won't go naked, or wear dirty undies. Stop arguing. Call Pops and tell him you're spending the night. Tell him you need a girl night, and then get the wineglasses. And we'll pull out our war chests and see what we can do for you and Luc." Lily opened a drawer and pulled out a corkscrew.

"Lily, there's never going to be a me and Luc."

"His mother's dead. You're free. I can't see how you can deny your feelings for him."

"My feelings mean nothing." She'd gotten over him once, she could do it again. "Do you know how he's going to feel if he finds out what kind of person his mother really was?"

"Don't kid yourself. He knows. He's a smart man. She didn't fool him."

"She was murdered. That changes the way he thinks about her. She's probably a saint in his mind."

Lily deliberated over the many bottles in the wine cabinet. "I don't think so. I think he feels guilty over her death because he didn't love her as much as he thought he should."

Cher tapped the arms of her chair. She suddenly lost her desire to eat. "How did you get to be so smart about family dynamics? You had a Beaver Cleaver life. Your parents stayed married to each other. Your mother wasn't a crack junkie hooker. Your father came home every night at five to dinner on the table. I know what it's like to be disappointed by your parents. Some people don't want to know the reality about their mother and father. I didn't want to know what my mother did for a living. Do I really need to make sure that Luc knows his mother was a maniacal, manipulative bitch? Luc doesn't want to hear that from me. That woman ruined my life for some sort of ideal."

Lily shrugged. "Your childhood sucked. So what. Get over it. You're a woman now. Welcome to the real world. You did okay. You made something out of yourself and obviously you knew what your mother was and that didn't stop you from accomplishing something with your life. Give Luc a break. He's a grown man."

Cher didn't allow many people to talk to her so bluntly. But Lily was special. "I know all of these things already, but thank you for reminding me."

Lily found a corkscrew. "Go call Pops and tell him you're staying over. And don't forget the wineglasses."

Cher didn't want to go home. She called David from the kitchen phone while she hunted for the wineglasses. Pops didn't question her decision, but did remind her that he had meeting the next evening and wouldn't be home for dinner. Cher reminded him Miranda had soccer practice and they'd be home late.

Lily's cabinets overflowed with the best crystal and china. She should be the poster child for internet shopping and mail-order catalogs. Cher chose two Waterford goblets and headed back to the office, stopping in the living room to tell Miranda they were staying.

Miranda sat in front of the huge TV screen playing on the Nintendo, a plate of pizza on the floor next to her and Cher's two very expensive, designer Bengal cats curled up in her lap.

Cher waved her hand in front of Miranda's face to get her attention. "Go out to the car and get your homework. We're staying."

Miranda whooped. "Great, now I can finish playing Mutant Killer Babes."

Cher hid a grimace. "That sounds like so much fun. Whatever happened to Pong?"

"What?" Miranda glanced up from the TV screen.

"Never mind. That was a game I used to play back when the dinosaurs roamed the earth."

Miranda giggled. "The seventies, right?"

Cher tugged on one of the thin curly braids. "Brat."

Miranda laughed turned back to her game.

"Don't forget your homework," Cher warned as she headed back to the office.

"I won't," Miranda promised.

While Cher had been gone, Lily had opened two bottles of wine and set them on her desk. She had also started a fire in the fireplace, which added a cheerful glow to the room.

Cher handed her the glasses and Lily filled them. She handed one to Cher and then sat down in a plush leather chair and sipped the amber liquid.

"What are we going to do?" Lily asked.

"I understand Tibet is very pretty this time of year, but then again you know how you feel about nature and wide-open spaces."

Lily shuddered. "I'm not a nature girl." She glanced around her office. "I like four walls and roof."

"Obviously," Cher had developed a deep fondness for Lily over the years.

Lily took a sip of red wine. "You know this could be a big cosmic hint that you need to tell Miranda the truth. And maybe you need to tell Luc about Miranda."

Cher closed her eyes. "I've been keeping this secret for fourteen years. My daughter is going to hate me. Luc is going to hate me. I'll have to move in with you and your cats to escape all the anger."

"So you move in with me. They'll get over it. Give them a chance. How do you know they are going to hate you?" Lily jabbed at the air with a finger. "You want to examine every angle before you do anything. Why can't you be the same woman in your personal life that you are in the office. You're dynamic, confident, and you don't worry about the consequences, you just do what's right."

Cher's mouth fell open. "I didn't know you thought I was such a wimp."

Lily gave an exasperated sigh. "I didn't say that. You want to carry the weight of the world on your back. You want to make everything nice for your family and the people you care about. Forget about upsetting people. Pretend you're on the job and stop worrying so much. It will work out."

"I don't think I can." Cher didn't want to rock her world with all the secrets she'd kept hidden for so long. She'd finally managed to straighten out her relationship with Miranda. She was happy with her job. David was doing well with his firm. Until Luc reappeared in her life, everything was great. She didn't want turbulence in her life. She'd had her drama quota as a child. She didn't want any more. Luc's presence was upsetting the status quo. She wanted her life to stay on an even keel.

"Okay, Cher, I've listened to your little whine session. Now tell me why you're really here."

"No keeping secrets from you. I need you to do a little of your voodoo for me."

"On Luc. I can have it done by tomorrow."

Cher shook her head. "Not Luc. I'm looking for background on a Helen Ramsey. She's a local socialite here in Phoenix. Does all the charity stuff. Owns a gallery."

"Why am I rummaging around into her business and

you're not?"

The hairs on the back of Cher's neck stood on end. A sure sign that something was amiss. "Because I'm not ready to do something official yet. I just have a hunch." Besides Lily didn't have to play by the rules. Cher did. She didn't even know where this attitude was going to take her, she just knew she had to follow the thread of it. And maybe Helen Ramsey was the place to start.

Lily frowned. "Am I smelling the possibility of a new book coming out of this?"

"Maybe."

She rubbed her hands together. "Give me the juicy particulars."

"We're talking money, murder, sex."

Lily laughed. "Three of my very favorite things." She rubbed her hands together. She refilled her wineglass, took a long sip, and sat back in her chair with a thoughtful expression on her face. Cher could tell the little wheels in her head were spinning.

Luc didn't know if he was doing the right thing, but that didn't stop him from inviting Detective Beatrix Hunter out to dinner. Cher was not connecting with the people in his social group and Beatrix Hunter's family was a charter member.

He waited for her in the lobby of the jazz bar and four star restaurant called UpNorth. Beatrix had highly recommended it. Through the open door to the restaurant he could see the building had originally been a church. The stage was currently empty, but a trio had been playing while Luc waited.

Luc hadn't listened to much jazz since Cher. The memory was too painful. He was an opera buff and preferred classical music, but the sounds emanating from the stage while he waited for Beatrix had him reconsidering his taste in music.

Beatrix Hunter entered. She wore a blue satin evening suit with a diamond pin on the lapel. Her fair hair was coiled about her head like a crown. Her blue eyes danced. She was beautiful with a Princess Grace elegance. Her pale beauty was everything Cher wasn't. Cher was fire, and Beatrix Hunter was ice. For the last few years he'd preferred the ice queens. With Cher back in his life he sensed he wanted to get next to the heat again.

"Mr. Broussard." Beatrix held out her hand. "Imagine my surprise when you called me."

"Thank you for coming, but most of all, thank you for your assistance to Ben."

She waved her hand in an airy gesture. "The curiosity factor was enough all by itself. I thought my job ended with my legwork for Ben."

The hostess seated them and a waiter approached for

their drink order. Beatrix ordered a cosmopolitan and Luc ordered a martini with two olives.

"Detective Hunter, you are much more than leg-work."

She patted the back of his hand. "Beatrix, please. What can I do for you?"

He smiled. "Maybe I just called you for the pleasure of your company."

"You just keep deluding yourself."

He lifted his menu. "Interesting remark."

"I saw the way you looked at Cher Dawson. You two have history." She lifted her menu and fanned her face. "I sense a certain heat between you. I wanted to find out the truth."

He raised his eyebrows. "And that's your reason for coming."

"Maybe."

The waiter set the drinks in front of them. Luc thanked him. He opened his menu and read each offered item and found he was going to have a hard time making a choice. Luc loved good food and from what he read everything sounded terrific.

Beatrix barely glanced at it before she closed the menu and set it down on the table in front of her. "Why don't you tell me how I can help you."

"You're very direct."

"I've been a cop for almost six years now. Directness becomes a part of you."

"From what I understand, you play some sort of role called Officer Friendly."

She smiled. "Right. I visit schools and act as the spokesperson for the department. Children ask very pointed questions and so do reporters. The best training I ever had for going one on one with Ted Koppel was done standing in front of a room full of six-year-olds. Hold their attention and everyone else is a piece of cake." She snapped her fingers.

"Ted Koppel. I'm impressed."

"He was a nice man, but he could be a barracuda. He thought I was going to be a minnow."

The waiter returned and took their order. When he left, Luc sat back and studied Beatrix while she seemed to be studying him. Should he confide in her? Cher wasn't being very helpful for what he needed. He hoped he could make Beatrix into an ally.

"Are you going to tell me what you want from me?" Beatrix asked.

"Right now, I want to ply you with food and get on your good side."

She chuckled. "That's easy enough. If you really want to get on my good side, a pair of hand-made Prada shoes is my greatest weakness."

"I can have Senora Prada come and fit you herself."

"I like your style."

"I wish Cher Dawson did."

Beatrix leaned her arms on the table. "You have to

understand something about Lieutenant Dawson. She took on a unit that was frankly the wart on the backside of the Phoenix P.D., and for last several years, our department has gone through several large scandals. As far as public opinion was concerned, Phoenix P.D. was public enemy number one. Dawson has been very pro-active in wanting to clean up the department. And rocking the boat is not a popular position. Plus the fact she is a woman of color, and had to fight ten times harder for everything she's achieved. Police departments were notoriously clannish. She's in a position no woman of color has ever reached in the department. She has a lot to prove. And you're complicating things for her."

"I just want justice."

"That is perfectly understandable. You're not going about it the right way."

"If I did what Cher wanted, I'd be on the bottom of the pile."

Beatrix smiled. "Let me explain something. To you, your mother's homicide is the most important event of your life but every murder victim's family feels the same way. Cops want justice. We want to bring closure to the family, to get criminals off the street, but you're looking at a department that, for the most part, is already overwhelmed and overworked. We have too many cases and not enough people or money to solve them all. People want law and order until we say 'show me the money.'"

Luc was amazed by her candor. How could anyone

think this woman was just a debutante playing at being a cop? She really cared. She gave him insight into what it meant to be a police officer, especially Cher. "Have you ever considered political office?"

"I am from one of the most politically conservative families in the country. But my personal views would shock the most liberal of souls."

"Can you help me?"

Beatrix tilted her head and studied him. "Whatever I can do, I will do. But I won't step on Dawson's toes."

"I understand that and I appreciate your loyalty to your fellow officer. Cher doesn't fit in with the people she most needs to talk to. She treats them like suspects. People with money expect to be treated with kid gloves. And if not, they hide behind their lawyers or their money or they take prolonged vacations in Tahiti and whatever information they have goes with them."

"Isn't it a shame that the wealthy, who commit the same crimes as anybody else, expect to get away with it."

"I'm not here for a moral lesson, I want my mother's killer punished."

The waiter refilled their water glasses.

Beatrix clasped her hands together and rested them on the table. "Lieutenant Dawson won't take it kindly if I interfere in her case."

"You're an ambitious woman. Do you want to be Officer Friendly for the rest of your career?"

She grinned. "You've discovered my greatest fear. I

know what I do is important, but I didn't join the department because I wanted to be a spokesperson. I could be on a Paris runway making a lot more money. But I'm not sure angering one of the top officers in this department is going to further my career."

"I can help with that."

"I'm sure you could, but look at it this way. I can help myself." She leaned forward, her face intense. "In case you forgot, I have the same connections you do. I want to earn my place in the department on my merits, not my connections, or yours."

"I didn't mean to insult you."

She gave him a brilliant smile. "No insult taken. Most people think I'm dabbling at being a police officer."

"I had no such misconception."

She inclined her head. "Thank you. Mr. Broussard, I would be more than happy to help you in any way I can. However, as I said before, I will not undermine Lieutenant Dawson's investigation."

Luc felt a spurt of anger. "She's not investigating. She's dabbling."

Beatrix shook her head. "Dawson never lets anyone know what's going on inside her head. What you consider to be dabbling is just her style. Trust me, she's working your case, but she's doing it her way. She'll get results."

"I'll have to accept your authority on that." Maybe he'd underestimated Cher. She'd been a very cautious person in school. He'd forgotten how careful she'd been. In some ways, she'd been secretive. She was being secretive now. He'd have to get close to her, see what she was doing. Maybe even keep her company somehow. He wasn't certain how to accomplish that, but maybe the background report Ben was doing would give him a hint on how to approach her.

"So tell me about you and Cher."

"We do have a past." Even now, so many years later, he still felt anger at how poorly she'd treated him. One moment, she was madly in love with him and planning their wedding, and the next she was gone with no explanation, no hint of why she'd done what she'd done, despite his mother's explanation. What had made Cher give up her dream? Had the other man been so much better than Luc?

He'd been hurt at her betrayal, but his mother had made sure he'd had little free time to grieve. The business needed him. And his mother found Vanessa for him. For a while Vanessa had eased the pain, but his final answer had been to devote himself to expanding the family business.

Beatrix leaned forward. "Why am I not surprised?" She squinted at him for a moment. Then her vision cleared, though there seemed to be a knowing glint in her eyes.

"You just looked at me as though you know my most secret of secrets."

"Maybe." She smiled. "I'm going to speak to her first thing in the morning about your case and see what we can work out together. But do be aware, I'm not promising anything. Dawson can pretty stubborn. I've faced it before."

"Why do I have the feeling I just made a deal with the devil?"

Beatrix laughed. "Not a devil, just a baby demon in training."

Luc studied her. Something he'd said had given her an opening with Cher He ran the conversation over in his head, but couldn't figure out what had meant so much to her. He used to understand women so well, and now he didn't have a clue. Maybe he was getting old.

Chapter Eight

Cher's favorite diner was a haven for off-duty cops. Two uniformed officers sat at the long counter, steaming cups of coffee in front of them. Two plain-clothes detectives had commandeered a booth at the back of the diner, one of them staring at the screen of a laptop computer, tapping the keyboard feverishly. The other detective consulted a spiral-bound notebook and spoke to his partner.

Cher sat on the red vinyl bench in her own favorite spot in a corner facing the door where she could see who was coming in and who was leaving. The file containing the dead Eddie Compton's paperwork, which Allen had finally found for her, was spread across the cracked Formica table. Smoke curled around her. She liked sitting in the smoking section and made a point of coming to the diner on Oatmeal day at the Dawson household. Pops had stuffed enough oatmeal down her as a child to feed a third world country, and she wasn't going to eat anymore of it, no matter how it benefitted her heart. Of course, Miranda was a different story. She loved the stuff and experimented with different additives to enhance the flavor. Today was Tabasco sauce. Cher was glad to have an excuse to leave for the station extra early.

The diner served the best breakfast food in Phoenix and the secondhand smoke almost made her feel like she could indulge herself. She took a deep breath as she read through the coroner's report. Death by a single gunshot from a .38 to the left cheek. Real up close and personal.

Included was the ballistics report, fingerprint report, and the coroner's final report. The victim had been killed around midnight, judging from the contents of his stomach. Aside from assorted alley debris, the only other intriguing find was two black hairs belonging to an African-American woman clinging to the jacket lapel. Did dead Eddie have himself a little date before someone shot him into the afterlife?

A shadow fell across the open case file. Cher glanced up to find Luc Broussard standing next to her. A knot twisted in her stomach. Her mouth went dry. What the hell was he doing here? "You're back again." And looking as devastatingly delicious as always.

He sat across from her on the opposite bench. "Good morning. Mind if I join you?"

She glared at him. Somehow she didn't think he'd take no for an answer. "I'm eating my breakfast." She gestured at her fruit plate and cottage cheese. Maybe if she tried hard enough she could wish him away. Whenever he was around he did strange things to her equilibrium. And her sense of self-preservation.

"Your Detective Whitaker told me you'd be here. I thought I'd join you for breakfast." He signaled the waitress who nodded.

Cher felt a rise of irritation. "I'll be sure to give him a proper thank-you when I get into the office."

"You have quite a shiner. Who hit you?"

Cher fingered the bruise on her cheek. "Karate. Three times a week. I wasn't too focused last night."

"Why is that?"

Why couldn't she get this man out her life? He invaded her thoughts. Wasn't that enough? "My tech stocks are in the toilet."

"Keep the tech stocks, but diversify with some biomedical ones. It's a good time to buy."

She shook her head. "I don't have enough ready cash; besides, I'm thinking of going more conservative with money markets."

"You'll take a bath come tax time."

"Why are you here? I don't think it's to talk about the stock market."

"You're right. You and I have unfinished business."

Cher sipped her coffee, delaying an answer. Unless

she could start controlling her reactions to him, she'd end up in trouble again. The change in Luc made her nervous. He possessed a steely determination that hadn't been there when they'd been at Stanford. He didn't need her to remind him about class and homework anymore. Someplace between then and now, he'd become a man. A very desirable man. The kind of man she knew he'd always be, and she felt oddly vulnerable, and a little sad because she hadn't witnessed the journey.

She wondered what kind of father he would be. Miranda would like him. They were a lot alike. In fact, Miranda was more like Luc than she was like Cher. She had the same tall, rangy look, the same high cheekbones and sensual lips. Yeah, Luc's mug was stamped all over Miranda's face. One look at Miranda, and Luc would know where she'd come from. He would see the Broussard family lines stamped so clearly on her face.

"So speak your piece. What do you want?" Cher asked as he pulled the sports section toward him.

"Frankly, I don't know. I woke up this morning, got into the car, and somehow my driver ended up at your office and your detective sent me here."

She put down her pen. "It occurs to me that you've become a world-class smart-ass."

He grinned. "I had a fabulous teacher. How about dinner tonight?"

She was so very tempted to give in to her craving to be in his company. No matter the consequences, but she couldn't. "You never give up. What makes you think I'm not hot on the trail of dead Eddie's killer?"

"Because you're eating your breakfast."

"It's the most important meal of the day. If I don't have a good breakfast, I'm cranky. If I'm cranky, I can't investigate. And I've been told when my blood sugar is low, I get a little trigger happy."

He held up a hand, laughing. "Okay."

She loved the sound of his laughter. Back in the old days, they had laughed a lot. At silly things sometimes, like now. Delicious shivers of anticipation crawled over her skin. She could feel herself becoming more deeply entangled in his web. If she weren't careful she'd be trapped in her desire for him, and that would lead to things she needed to keep hidden. Not only for her sake, but in a way his, too.

A huge, burly man wearing a patrol officer's uniform approached their table. He had bright red hair and a thick neck. "Hey, Dawson," he growled.

For a second Cher couldn't remember his name. Then it popped out at her. "Morning, Sorenson."

The man sat next to Luc, shoving him to the side. Cher enjoyed the startled look on Luc's face.

Sorenson growled. "I hear you've been doing a great job with Cold Case." He didn't look happy. He'd asked Cher to take him into Cold Case, but she'd refused. Sorenson was a man who kept his grudges alive.

Cher shrugged. "Every once in a while I get lucky.

Let me introduce you to Mr. Luc Broussard, an old acquaintance of mine. Luc, this is Sergeant Sorenson."

The two men sized each other up. Cher could see that Luc was wondering who Sorenson was, and Sorenson was wondering who Luc was. Not that Sorenson cared. He was just needling her because that's what he did. He'd never gotten over the fact that even though they'd gotten out of the gate at the same time, she'd left him far behind. The fact that she was not only a woman, but black, rankled him, too.

Sorenson glanced at her. "Too lucky, if you get my drift."

"Always, Sorenson. Don't you have a doughnut shop to visit? I hear you like the ones with the holes in the middle."

Sorenson frowned. "You never get over being a smart-mouth."

"And I hear you never get over being lazy," Cher retorted.

Sorenson glared and shoved himself out of the booth. "I'll be seeing you, Dawson. I'm always watching your back."

"Unless you're the lead dog, the view never changes."

Sorenson stalked out, his footsteps heavy on the tile.

Luc leaned toward her. "You must have a more interesting history with him," he jerked his thumb over his shoulder at the retreating cop, "than you do with me."

"Sorenson, in a nutshell. I passed him in the academy and he's never caught up. He wanted into Cold Case because he thought the job would be soft. He thinks I'm the problem. The problem is that he's his own worst enemy. He has no idea how to win friends and influence people."

Luc lifted an eyebrow. "And you do?"

"When I need to, you'd be surprised."

"This I want to see."

"Don't hold your breath." Cher tossed money on the table and slipped out of the booth. She stood and stretched her shoulders. "I'm going to share my theory with you. You think because you don't see me with my nose to the grindstone that I'm not doing my job."

He shifted slightly, eyes averted. He gave a short nod.

"Okay, tell ya what I'm going to do. The evidence room is now open, how about you and me taking a tour and see what we can see."

He leaned toward her. "Isn't that against the rules?" he whispered.

"Oh, no." She was amazed at how smooth the skin on his dark face looked. She wanted to reach out and touch his cheek, to see for herself. "You're Luc Broussard. Rules are made to be broken at your convenience."

Again, he looked uncomfortable.

"We need to stop by the doughnut shop for some bribes. So let's go." She was almost to the door by the time he caught up with her.

She stepped out onto the street, pulling on a jacket. A cool desert wind ruffled her lapels. The sky was a bright blue, but filled with puffy clouds. She headed toward her car.

"Wait," Luc said, "I'll drive."

She laughed. "You mean your driver will drive."

"Same difference. I've seen you drive. I would like to live to my fortieth birthday. The older I get, the closer I get to a heart condition."

She waved her hand. "Stop worrying. Phoenix is flat. And I have an automatic." She opened the door to her Camry and gestured for him to get into the passenger side.

"Let me tell my driver to follow us."

Cher slipped into the car. "Hurry up. My case is getting colder." He gave her a dirty look. Now that she was ready to go, she was in a hurry.

Luc opened the passenger side and slipped in, buckling his seat belt. Cher glanced at him and froze. At his feet were Miranda's pom-poms. She'd been practicing for the cheerleading team at school.

Luc picked up the pom-poms and glanced at Cher. "I never pictured you as the cheerleader type."

Come up with a good lie, Cher. "My...uh...neighbor's daughter. Took her to school. I've been trying to remember to give them back to her." She stumbled over the words. Cher found it difficult to be dishonest.

Luc tossed the pom-poms into the backseat. Cher sighed with relief as she put the Camry in gear and turned onto the street.

For a few minutes, Luc clung to the arm rests, but eventually relaxed and leaned back to enjoy the drive. Phoenix was at its best with all the Christmas decorations lining the light standards and in store windows. They stopped at a traffic signal, and Christmas music blasted from a loudspeaker mounted over a door to a store.

Christmas was Cher's favorite time of year. She had missed a lot of Christmases as a kid and now she enjoyed every moment of the shopping, the secrets, and the anticipation.

Luc studied Cher. She bounced slightly on the seat in time with the music. Christmas had special meaning for Luc. The first time he'd seen Cher had been the day before the campus closed for Christmas vacation. Christmas decorations had dotted the lawns, and lights had hung in the windows of the dorms. Someone had opened a window and "Rudolph the Red-Nosed Reindeer" had been playing.

That one moment had changed his life. It was engraved in his memory as though it had just happened yesterday. Being in the car with Cher now opened the floodgate to emotions he'd kept at bay for so long. He'd admired her courage and had wanted to know her better.

The first thing he had done when he'd returned to campus after the holiday, he'd searched her out to give her an antique Christmas ornament he'd seen in a shop. He'd told her it was to commemorate their first meeting. He wondered if she still had it.

"Shades of deja vu. You're thinking about it, too."

She glanced at him. "About what?"

"About the first time we met."

"That was long ago. We were different people."

"Do you still have the ornament?"

Her hands clenched on the steering wheel. "I still have it."

"Thank you."

"For what?" she asked.

"For not throwing away everything that we had."

Her face tightened with tension. Luc knew she had something else she wanted to say, but she didn't. He wondered again why she was holding back. What secret was she hiding from him? Suddenly, he wanted to know more than anything else in the world.

"Oh, look, we're here." She turned into a small strip mall with a doughnut shop at the end.

He waited in the car while she went in. Through the windows he watched her as she pointed out what she wanted. Her body was fuller than he remembered. The nervous energy that had ruled her while they'd been in school seemed more in control. She had always been a fidgeter, but no longer. On the whole, she seemed calmer, more serene. And he liked the way she was now.

She had grown into that woman he had sensed she would be. He liked what he saw in her. She had changed the bright, flashy clothes she'd worn in school for more somber colors. He remembered a bright plaid red skirt she had worn a lot with a black cotton sweater. She had draped a matching scarf about her neck and had looked very sexy. She still looked sexy, but in a tougher way.

She pushed her jacket back, and he saw her sidearm at her waist. The day he entered her office to find her, he realized he hadn't been surprised that she was cop. Somehow, he always knew she would end up on the force. She had talked about how much she admired law enforcement, and her career choice seemed natural to her. He knew her father had been a cop, and he had admired her own determination to follow in her father's footsteps.

Luc's own father had been a crusader, too. He had used his paper and media connections to inform the public about the injustices in society. Luc had always wanted to be just like his father, a man who worked for good. So he understood why Cher wanted to be like hers.

Though he had wondered about her mother. Cher had never once spoken about the woman, and every effort on his part to learn something had been met with stony silence. Another of her secrets. Cher was full of secrets, and he wondered if he had every really known her. Watching as she paid for the doughnuts, he realized that he'd known her passion and sensuality, but she'd always kept a part of herself hidden. Now that he was older and maybe a little wiser, he wanted to find out what she didn't want him to know.

When he said that trust had always been a problem for her, in the back of his mind, he'd thought if he worked on her feelings, she'd open up to him. But she never had, and now fourteen years later, she was just as closed and private as always.

How could he get her to trust him? When he'd first proposed to her, he'd thought then she would open up. But she hadn't. He decided if he just learned to be patient she would eventually learn to trust him, but then she was gone. Maybe she had left him because he'd pushed too hard. But then again, she was tough. Tougher than he was. She would have let him know when he'd strayed into forbidden territory. So what had sent her running away from him?

She opened the door and got into the car. She handed him the box of doughnuts. A fresh, yeasty smell filled the car, making his mouth water. "I'm not much of a doughnut eater, but these smell great." He closed his eyes and took a deep sniff. He wanted to hold on to this moment with Cher.

She smiled as she started the motor and put the car

in gear. "Best doughnuts in Phoenix, maybe even Arizona."

A few minutes later, she turned into a parking structure attached to a multi-story building.

Inside, they took the elevator to the basement and when they exited, Cher handed the box of doughnuts to a pencil-thin cop sitting at a desk.

"Hey, Dawson," the cop said. "Thanks." He opened the lid and the doughnut smell permeated the small room.

"Hey, Bainbridge."

A wide smile spread across Bainbridge's face. "Glazed, jelly-filled, and maple twists." He looked up at Cher. "You know what I like." He gestured at a door. "Go right on in. Everything you wanted is on the table. Just sign in."

Cher picked up a pen and wrote her name on a sheet of paper attached to a clipboard. She handed the clipboard to Luc, and he signed just below hers. Her handwriting was still loopy and bold and for a second Luc studied it. Her signature hadn't changed much. He smiled, remembering all the notes she used to leave him reminding of his schedule for the day, or to go to the library to study for a test. Even back then, he'd been amazed at her ability to be so organized, to remember details that always escaped him.

A cardboard storage box waited on a rectangular wood table that was scarred from years of use.

Cher opened her purse, removed latex gloves and pulled them on. Then she opened the box.

Luc leaned closer. A musty smell emerged from the box to mingle with the doughnut aroma from the entry room.

Cher lifted several evidence bags out of the box. She opened each one and drew out a black suit, which she set on the table and followed it with a shirt that rippled as though it were silk. Luc studied the silk shirt. The shirt was stained a dark brown over one pocket, and Luc realized he was looking at old blood. According to the report he'd received on Compton, he'd been a staff sergeant stationed at Fort Huachuca. What Army staff sergeant could afford to wear silk shirts?

He glanced at the collar and saw a tag that announced the shirt was handmade in England. Luc was startled. He wore the same brand and he knew that no Army staff sergeant could afford five-hundred-dollar silk dress shirts.

He pointed at the tag. "Do you see this?"

Cher tilted her head. "Nice clothes."

"No. This is beyond nice. This is English tailoring at its apex."

She took a second look. "Speaking of English, try talking American to me."

He reached for the suit jacket.

Cher slapped his hand. "Don't you touch anything."

Luc felt the heat from her skin through the latex.

And he drew back quickly, scorched by the raw passion that radiated through him. "Why not?"

"You're not a cop. I can't have you contaminating possible evidence."

"Didn't the cops go through this all once before?"

"Yes, with gloves on." She spread the collar of the suit jacket. "Now explain to me about these fancy duds."

Luc removed his own jacket and held the collar open to show her the label. She compared the label of his jacket to the labels on Eddie Compton's clothes. "Mr. Compton and I seem to share the same tailor."

She eyed him up and down. "I see. Which makes a girl wonder how Mr. Compton could afford to share the same tailor as you. You didn't, by chance, happen to misplace the family fortune."

He laughed. "I've tripled it."

"Hm." She removed more evidence bags from the box.

One of the bags contained keys. Cher opened the bag and drew the keys out. "What do you think?" She extracted one and held it up. "A 911, a 912 Carerra, a Spyder?"

Luc frowned. "Are you telling me that Mr. Compton owned a Porsche?"

She waved the key. "According to this key he did. The case reports said the Porsche never turned up." She stared at the clothes. "Tell me, how do rich people hide money?"

Luc hadn't been expecting that question. "Why are you asking?"

"I checked over dead Eddie's records, and there was no trail of money. He had two thousand dollars in a savings account and two hundred odd dollars in a checking count. He had an old Chevy pickup, a credit card, and a video card. But nothing to indicate a Porsche, or the kind of loot that buys clothes like this." The reports also stated he had a sister. Cher started to wonder what the real sister might know and where was she. It occurred to Cher that Sylvia Compton was dead, too, but she didn't want to go down that path.

Luc pulled out a chair and sat down. He held up a hand and counted off on his fingers. "Swiss accounts. Accounts in the Cayman Islands. Antiques, art, jewelry, mistresses."

She gave him a sharp glance. "Do you really stuff your mistress with your cash?"

He had to think about that one. "I don't have a mistress, and my mattress is a mattress. I keep my money in the bank. I don't hide my assets. I believe it's a federal crime."

"Which would you choose?"

"Art."

"Why art?" She had refolded the silk shirt and returned it to the evidence bag.

"Because dead guys don't paint again and the body of their work, if they're good enough, only appreciates.

How would you hide your money?"

"Coffee cans buried in the backyard."

"Then it doesn't get interest."

She smiled. "Or leave a paper trail. Rule number one, don't advertise. Eddie didn't." She picked up another bag and opened it. "Let's say dead Eddie put his cash into clothes and cars... "—she held up a Rolex watch and a diamond pinkie ring— "...jewelry. There's only one question, I need to know..."

Luc finished her sentence. "Where did he get the money in the first place?"

She pointed a finger at him. "Makes a girl wonder. Maybe dead Eddie wasn't a very good Eddie."

"He could have been killed by someone who wanted to rob him."

"Then why leave all this behind?" Cher swept a hand over the Rolex watch and diamond ring.

"Do you think he was taking bribes?"

"Good cops never assume anything. But then again, I don't see evidence of a lottery win, or a family fortune."

"But you are suspicious."

Cher smiled at the box. "In my line of work, being suspicious is good. Suspicions lead to interrogations. Interrogations lead to arrests and arrests lead to convictions that make me look good."

"Is looking good what's most important to you?"

"No." Cher returned everything to the box and closed the lid. "One more criminal off the street is what's important to me." She stripped the latex gloves from her hands and put them in her purse. "I think I just found my first clue. Write that down in your diary, Broussard."

Luc was impressed. An exhilarated thrill ran through him. He'd helped her and felt proud of his part. "So where do we go from here?"

"I have to head back to the office." She glanced at her watch. "I need to think about this for awhile. I need to move some puzzle pieces around."

Luc frowned, feeling as though he were being dismissed. She'd found something important, and she had to think about it. "What do you have to think about?"

"Contrary to popular belief and television. Investigating is not a contact sport."

"I thought only men used sports analogies."

"I like soccer."

"Only kids play soccer."

For a second her face showed a touch of panic, then the panic was gone, hidden behind a cool facade. "Haven't you ever heard of the World Cup?"

Luc wasn't much of a sports addict. He shook his head. "Sorry, I'm too busy to watch sports."

"I feel sorry for you. You need some fun in your life."

"Like a soccer game."

Her whole body went still, and he saw a flash of something in her eyes. She grabbed her purse. "Let's get out of here. I have work to do."

Chapter Nine

Cher couldn't wait to get away from him, and his prying questions. Why she brought him here was beyond her. Just what was she trying to prove? She practically shoved him out the door. She signed out, and Bainbridge noted the time. She waited impatiently for the elevator to arrive. Every nerve in her body screamed with tension. She had to get rid of Luc.

When the elevator came, she punched the floor for her office and the main floor. When the door opened on the lobby, she waited for Luc to leave.

"Luc, I have some phone calls to make."

He remained in the elevator. "Does it involve the case?"

"Maybe, but I can't have you breathing down my neck. Now, go away."

He lifted his chin defiantly. "Make me."

"Stop acting like a child. I can throw you in a choke hold."

His eyes narrowed. "You just want me out of your hair."

"I want you out of my life." The words slipped out before she could stop them.

"Then solve my case, and I'll be more than happy to get out of your life."

"You can start by getting out of the elevator." The desk sergeant was watching them curiously. "Don't make me do my best police brutality routine on you. I need time to think things through. I can't do that with you breathing down my back."

"Then let me take you to dinner tonight."

"I don't know where this little piece of information is going to take me. I don't want to make plans. I never know where inspiration is going to come from. I'll call you if I have some breakthrough thought that you need to know."

She could see the reluctance on his face, but she wasn't going to back down. "Running down information is pretty boring."

"I can stand boring."

"No, you can't. You'll be bugging me every five minutes and I won't be able to string two thoughts together. Go home, I'll call you if I have any inspiration. I promise."

He started to step out of the elevator, then he stopped and reached into his pocket. He handed her a card. "In case you need it, this is my new phone number and address."

She frowned at the card. "You managed to have all your utilities up and running already?"

"I even have cable."

"I'm impressed."

"You could come see." His face took on a hopeful look. "I believe I even have ESPN."

"Cable is not a luxury item. I have it myself. Go home."

He stepped back, and the elevator doors closed. Cher stared at the card. Nice neighborhood. There was nothing second class about Luc Broussard.

Cher pocketed the card. The elevator doors opened, she stepped out, and entered her office to find it completely empty. Not even her secretary was at his post. He'd left a note tacked to her door saying he was out and would return in an hour.

Whitaker's desk was a mess with folders piled high in such a haphazard manner Cher was certain one good breeze from an open window would topple it. Jacob Grayhorse's desk was excruciatingly neat with every folder in perfect alignment with its companion. Marco's desk was somewhere in between. He had his blotter cleared, but his chair held a box that overflowed with files.

The phone on her secretary's desk began ringing.

Cher debated answering or letting the voice mail pick it up, but the ringing didn't stop. Finally, she leaned over her secretary's desk and grabbed the phone. "Dawson," she said.

Her secretary loved Post-It notes. The yellow sticky papers were everywhere, reminding him of different things to do.

"Cher!" Lily said, sounding surprised. "Why are you answering your own phone? Where's your secretary?"

"I don't know. He's only been working for me two months and already he's figured out my weaknesses."

Lily laughed. "If he brings you more of those heavenly brownies he baked, I expect an immediate delivery."

Cher looked up to see Beatrix Hunter enter, dressed in a sophisticated and elegant dark blue designer suit with a cream silk blouse and a multicolored scarf draped about her shoulders.

"I'll keep that in mind, Lily," Cher said. "So what's on your mind? Do you have something for me?"

Beatrix sat a few feet away from Cher, crossed her legs, and opened her Mark Cross briefcase to pull out a file. While Cher talked to Lily, Beatrix opened the file and started reading.

Lily replied, "I have some info on Helen Ramsey I think you'll find interesting. I emailed it to you. Check it when you have time."

"When you get a chance, could you check for the whereabouts of Sylvia Compton. Last known whereabouts Stillwater, Louisiana."

"Who is she?" Lily asked.

"The murder victim's sister."

"You know, Cher, you have a tendency to over investigate. Why do you want to find her?"

"I think she may have some information about her brother's life. He had a few secrets, and I want to find out what they were."

"We all have secrets."

Boy, did Cher know about secrets. Her own secrets were hers to keep, but Edward Compton by the fact that he was the victim of a murder no longer had control of his. "He had a lot of untraceable money. If Miss Compton knows anything, she might know where the money came from and where it went. That money may also have something to do with his death. Will you do this?"

"Sure. For you, anything."

"Thanks, Lily." Cher hung up the phone and turned to face Beatrix. "Hunter, what are you doing creeping around my office?"

"Just wanting to have a chat with you." Hunter returned the folder to her briefcase, snapped it closed and stood.

Cher opened the door to her office and beckoned the other woman inside. Her secretary had set up a small Christmas tree on top the file cabinet. The tiny silver ornaments reflected Cher's image as she sat at her desk.

Beatrix set a three-gazillion-dollar blue leather Prada or Gucci purse on Cher's desk. Cher wasn't certain which brand-name it was, but having a thirteen-year-old daughter gave her an entree into the world of fashion. Miranda would sell her left kidney for a purse like that one. Beatrix sat and crossed slim legs.

"What do you want?" Cher asked, mildly irritated by the other woman's sophistication and poise. The type of attitude that only came from people who had money.

Hunter tilted her head and smiled at Cher. "I'm in a position to do you a favor."

"A favor?" Cher would rather ask the Grand Salamander of the Klan for a favor than this woman.

Hunter nodded. "I had dinner with a mutual friend of ours."

Cher tapped her fingers on the blotter. "And who would that be?" Not the commissioner again. Beatrix and that man were way too cozy for comfort.

"Lucas Broussard."

"Oh." Cher clenched her fist. She slid her hand off her desk into her lap. This blond bimboette could have any man she wanted. Why Luc? Because you didn't get much better than Luc Broussard. What would her lily-white family say? Cher leaned back in her chair, trying not to be jealous. She took a slow breath. Calming herself, she waited, suspicion knotting her stomach. She was beginning to dislike Beatrix Hunter even more than she'd disliked her before. "And why did you and Mr. Broussard have dinner together?"

"We have a common interest."

"I don't want to know about your love life, Hunter. If you want to date Mr. Broussard, you hardly need anyone's permission." She narrowed her eyes. "How you choose to spend your private, off-duty time is of no interest to me."

"Oh, really! I couldn't tell." Hunter's tone held an almost sarcastic edge.

Cher's spine stiffened. She wasn't going to let Barbie get to her. "Spit it out, or get out."

"How old is your daughter?" Hunter inquired in a too casual tone.

Cher froze. "And why do you ask?"

"Miranda is what, fourteen, thirteen? I met her at the department baseball game last summer. She doesn't look anything like you, she's quite beautiful in a refined way. But she bears a striking resemblance to our mutual friend, with whom I understand you have a torrid history."

Cher swallowed, unable to say anything. What did Hunter know? What didn't she know?

"Dawson," Hunter continued with a slight smile, "I've known you several years now, and I've never known you to be speechless. Not even regarding the quality of the toilet paper the department buys."

Cher fought the urge to grind her teeth. "Are you threatening me, little girl?"

Hunter's eyes widened. "Actually, I've come to help you."

"Help me how?"

Hunter sighed. "Dawson, you're one of the best police officers Phoenix P.D. has ever produced. But even you can't do things that I can."

"Name one."

Hunter smiled. "I can go places you can't."

So Luc had recruited the ice-cold blonde to do his bidding, too. Great now she was stuck with Hunter ... again. "I'm all ears."

Hunter flicked imaginary dust from the hem of her skirt. Her smile had taken on a feral edge. "Lucas is worried. He feels you don't understand the Phoenix social scene. He asked me to help you. But I told him I wouldn't interfere in any investigation in your department without speaking to you first."

"Thanks for the heads-up. How can you help me?" A spurt of rage coursed through Cher. Luc was interfering again. She didn't like anyone pushing their way into her investigations and calling her shots.

"I know the world you're investigating. I already know half their secrets, and they will be more willing to talk to you if I'm by your side. I know everything there is to know about those people, and if we can't get the information, I know where to go and who to talk to."

Cher stared at Hunter. "So you want to be my hoity-toity snitch!"

Hunter shrugged. "For lack of a better explanation…yes."

Cher sat at her desk. "What do you want for all this help?"

Hunter smiled. "I'm not planning on being the department's media officer forever. And with a hefty list of officers ahead of me, my chance of transferring out is narrow. If I help you, with favorable results, I'm hoping you'll consider helping me."

"I'm not bringing you into my unit." Not even if the Commissioner insisted. Hunter didn't have the experience. Her whole career with the department had been spent in media and any practical street experience had been minimal. Like all recruits she'd spent time in a squad car right after graduation from the academy cruising the nicest neighborhood in the city. She just hadn't put in any real time.

Hunter's eyebrows rose. "I just happened to see the memo you twisted out of the commissioner. Even if I'm not going to be one of the five you pick, there will be slots open someplace else. I'll take Sex Crimes, Narcotics or Homicide. I could be an asset to any of those units."

Cher's mind wandered back to when she'd been in Hunter's shoes and remembered the frustration she'd endured as Officer Friendly. Cher closed her eyes, feeling boxed into a corner, and she wanted to scream. "For such a well-bred, upper-class girl you have a larcenous soul, Hunter."

"Thank you." Hunter smiled.

"Okay. You want to be my guide dog, no problem. Just remember who holds the leash."

"I'll remember." Hunter stood and brushed the folds out of her skirt. "I have a couple of things to clear up, but I'll be back tomorrow morning. You and I have an appointment with Misty Van Cleef. She knows everything about everybody. If there is a secret to be known, she knows it." She walked to the door, paused, and turned to face Cher. "You might want to rethink your wardrobe. Something that doesn't scream law enforcement." And then she was gone.

Cher fell back against her chair. She had just been suckered by Officer Friendly and didn't like it. Yet she had to admit, Hunter's proposal had value. Cher knew she couldn't finagle anything out of the rich and powerful. They'd already closed ranks on her once, she wasn't going to give them another chance. If she was going to solve dead Eddie's murder and expose the man who'd taken Eddie's place, she needed to find answers. And those answers were in somebody's mind.

Luc jogged up the driveway to find a van with Atkinson's Messenger Service stenciled on the side parked in front of the garage. A kid, young enough to still have pimples, stepped out of the van at Luc's approach. He held out a clipboard with a receipt on it for Luc to sign. After Luc signed, the kid handed him a thick manila envelope. As Luc opened the door to his house, the van roared to life and was gone before Luc could get his sweat-drenched body inside.

Twenty-four hours was a new personal best for Ben. Luc slid open the envelope as he walked back to his office and sat down in a wing-backed chair situated to one side of a roaring fire. Through the windows, he could see the setting sun. Flames seemed to shoot from it, coloring the sky a mixture of black and orange.

He pulled a manila folder from the envelope and opened it. For a moment he hesitated, feeling as though he were about to betray a trust. But then he thought about his mother and her lifeless body. He needed Cher to understand why his mother had died.

Luc knew that the key to anything was information. He kept records on everyone from the man who cleaned his pool to the chief financial officer of his corporation. Cher was just one more person he needed to know about.

He opened the folder and glanced at the first page. It was a police evaluation form showing her record at the Phoenix P.D. She'd headed up several units in the department before being moved to Cold Case. She'd also received several awards for valor. But he could see that she'd had trouble in the department. She'd taken on unpopular causes that had made her some enemies. He smiled. She'd always been a crusader, and life as a cop hadn't changed her.

He flipped through the pictures. Several Xeroxed newspaper articles showed that she was very active in the community with most of her work involving children, especially young girls. Soccer and softball coach, and even vice president of the grade school PTA. How odd, but as he read on he saw she'd been in the media department for awhile as Officer Friendly. What a ridiculous title for a hard woman like Cher. But as a liaison who spoke to schoolchildren about the police department, he could see that that was probably how she ended up involved at the one school.

He read further. The file was relatively thick. At the back he found personal information. Not much appeared to be known about her early years. Her mother was long dead and her father was unknown. But at age eleven she popped up again with David Dawson as her legal guardian. Later, she changed her name to Dawson. A sheet of paper attached said that David Dawson was a decorated officer who had retired and started his own security business. He was also the president of the local gay and lesbian political action group.

Luc stared at the report on the father. He found a photo attached. David Dawson looked like he was a big man with thick, muscular arms and a strong-boned face. His birth date placed his age at sixty-five, though he didn't look a day over forty. So David Dawson was gay. Luc thought it must have been tough being a cop and being gay. Even today it wasn't easy. He must have had a rough time being a black cop who was gay. Cher had said so little about him and now Luc understood why.

He flipped another page and Cher's elementary and high school records appeared. The records showed discipline problems, and he wasn't surprised. He doubted Cher had ever been an easy person. Getting to know her had been one of the most difficult things he'd ever done in his life, yet once the journey had begun, it had been one of the most satisfying. Though the more he read about her, the more he realized how little he knew her. This file was almost a window into her soul.

He wondered what had happened to her parents. How had she come to live with a cop who seemed totally unrelated to her? Yet as Luc went through the file, he began to see her mature. Her years at Stanford had been exceptional. Even he hadn't known she was a straight A student. She had always played down her accomplishments. Her grade point average was better than his. Much better than his. Way better than his.

She started with the Phoenix P.D. a year after her graduation from Stanford, and for a long moment, he wondered what had happened during that year. When he turned the page he found out. A newspaper article showed a young girl's face. She beamed as she held up a trophy, and Luc realized he was staring at his mother's face only it belonged to a twelve-year-old girl. Cher had her arm around the girl looking proud. The captain stated that Miranda Dawson, daughter of Coach Cher Dawson, made the winning goal to help her team win the regional championships for youth soccer. The trophy was for Most Valued Player.

Luc's hands began to shake. He stared at the girl. A cold shiver started in his arms. Cher was a mother. A proud mother. His mother had told him Cher was a slut. He remembered the devastation he'd felt when his mom had told him she'd found Cher in his bed with another man. For a second he wanted to think the little girl was someone else's daughter, but the aristocratic lines of her face, the lively eyes, and the impish grin was his mother's face fifty years ago. The little girl was his daughter.

He threw down the file and stared at the fire. How could she? She'd had his child and didn't tell him.

Anger flared in him, driving him to his feet. He paced back and forth, clenching and unclenching his hands.

The phone rang. He answered it to find Benjamin on the other end.

"How's the reading going?" Benjamin asked cheerfully.

"What do you know about child custody?"

"Unless your ex-wife is a drunk whore, you're never going to get it." Ben sounded bitter. He'd just been through a nasty divorce. "Why do you want to know, boss?"

"She has my child."

"You lost me."

"Cher Dawson has a child. The child is mine."

"You don't know that." Ben's voice was soothing.

"Yes, I do." Luc glanced at the photo again. "I want a shark. A great white shark." He wanted blood. Cher had denied him his child, he wasn't going to be denied anymore. He didn't care what he had to do.

"Luc," Ben said, "don't do anything foolish. Don't call her. Don't go over there. Do not leave your house. I will be there in twenty minutes." The phone went dead.

Luc disconnected and continued to stare at the photo of the girl named Miranda. What a beautiful name. What a beautiful chid. And she was his.

This girl was everything he and Vanessa had wanted, but had been denied by her cancer and death. He missed Vanessa. He missed her wit and her laugh and the way she reminded him that money wasn't always as important as he insisted it was.

He couldn't wait for Ben. He had to see Cher, to confront her. To see the daughter he'd been denied.

But he couldn't go looking like dirty laundry. He could be in and out of the shower in five minutes, and gone before Ben arrived. Ben would do his best to talk Luc out of anything rash. Luc didn't want to be talked of it. He wanted to nurse his anger. He wanted to confront Cher with what she'd done to him, and he didn't want Ben to stop him.

He dressed quickly and was almost out the door when Ben roared up and parked his Mercedes tight against the garage door, blocking Luc from leaving.

Ben jumped out of the car. "You need to calm down, Luc. You need to step back and let me handle this."

"No," Luc said, "this is not some merger, it's not a takeover bid, this is about flesh and blood. Miranda is my family."

"You have no proof this is your daughter."

"Have you seen her picture?"

"No, why don't you show me."

Luc grabbed Ben and dragged him into the house. "Take a look at this." He thrust the file at Ben. "I'll be right back."

Luc went into his bedroom and opened the closet. In the back was the one thing he had brought with him from San Francisco, his mother's photo album. As a child, he'd loved looking through the album even though his mother had few pictures of herself and most of the pages were filled up with photos of him, but there had been a few, and those few where the ones he wanted Ben to see.

He opened the album to a photograph of his mother at the same age as Miranda Dawson and handed it to him. Ben held the newspaper photo against the photo of Luc's mother. He frowned and glanced at Luc, at his mother, at the girl with Cher. "Well, that certainly is the same face."

"She's my daughter," Luc said in a flat tone. He could ask for DNA testing, but he knew deep in his heart that Miranda was his daughter.

"That doesn't give you cause to go over there and act like a madman. If you want custody of your daughter, you have to play by the rules. You're right, this isn't a corporate merger or a hostile takeover, this is not a situation where you can't make up the rules to suit you. Certain steps need to be taken. Don't go off in the gunslinger mode, you'll shoot yourself in the foot."

"I can't wait. I have to see her tonight."

Ben shook his head. "Listen to me. We have a very powerful leg to stand on due to the fact that she hid your daughter from you. Even though you're one of the wealthiest men in the country, you still need to get a blood test. Then we go talk to a lawyer who specializes in this type of case. If you want sole custody of your daughter, you're going to have to prove that the woman, who you want to find your mother's killer, is an unfit mother."

Luc sat down. "She's PTA. She's a soccer mom, for God's sake."

"Then you better hope she's a soccer mom with a bad habit."

"What do you mean bad habit?"

"Dope, drinking, or dudes. She's going to have to have a skeleton in her closet."

"Cher's foster father is gay."

"Big deal," Ben waved of his hand. "His sexual persuasion means nothing."

Luke glanced through the file again. "You're saying if I want my daughter, I have to destroy Cher."

"Yeah."

Luc couldn't do that. His gut told him Cher was a good mother. Her pride, her determination would never allow her to be bad at anything, and one look at the photo again told him that his daughter was very happy, cherished, and well-cared for. Everything he would have done if he could have.

After a long silence, Luc said, "Okay, Ben, you're right. I can't barge in and make demands. We'll do it your way."

Ben smiled. "I knew you'd see reason. I'll get right to work on this."

Luc walked Ben to the door and watched him pull out of the driveway. Luc forced himself to wait a full fifteen minutes before he went to the garage and got into his Jaguar. Contrary to Cher's comments, he did know how to drive. The garage door slid open, and he backed out and headed for Cher Dawson's house.

Chapter Ten

Cher sat in her car watching Miranda and her soccer teammates as they practiced. She had slid the seat all the way back and propped her brand-new-take-anywhere department-issue laptop computer on her lap. She loved the laptop. She could be anywhere and do all her reports on it, then hook it up to a phone line and send them to her secretary for proper formatting.

The email Lily had sent her on Helen Compton Ramsey was currently on the screen. Cher scrolled through the information, a disturbing feeling growing in her. The first mention of Helen Compton Ramsey was on a marriage certificate for Helen and Grant Ramsey. No birth certificate, no high school diploma. For all intents and purposes, Helen didn't exist, though her name continued to crop up on several business license applications around the country.

A short note from Lily stated that Grant Ramsey was dead, courtesy of an obituary in an upstate New York newspaper, Lily hadn't been able to find a death certificate. The obit announced that he'd died in Hanville on Long Island. No cause of death had been given.

Cher found herself frowning. She hadn't had a quandary in a long while. And now she had a dozen. Helen Ramsey wasn't who she said she was. Edward Compton wasn't who he said he was. Who the hell were they, and did she have enough evidence to pull them both in? Identity theft was probably enough evidence for an arrest warrant, but Cher wanted more. Lily accused her of over-investigation, but Cher always wanted to make certain all the loopholes were closed, and all her questions answered in a satisfactory manner.

Her cell phone rang, and she pulled her purse to her to answer it. "Dawson."

"Lieutenant Dawson," a strange man's voice said, "my name is Colonel McNamara. I'm calling from Fort Huachuca, and my secretary says you've left several urgent messages for me. I have to apologize for calling so late, but I've been in Washington, D.C., the last couple of days and wasn't in a position to return your calls."

"Thank you for calling me back," Cher replied.

"May I ask what this is in regards to?"

Cher gathered her thoughts. "You had a Staff Sergeant Edward Compton working for you who was murdered here in Phoenix four years ago. I'm trying to trace background information on him. His name has come up in another situation."

The colonel didn't reply immediately. "What situation?"

"Sorry, sir, but I'm not allowed to comment on an ongoing investigation. His file is somewhat meager on information. Can you tell me what his job was?"

"Sorry, Lieutenant Dawson, but that's classified information."

"Colonel, he's dead, and everything he knew about the Army died with him."

"You can file for a release of information under the Freedom of Information Act."

"I don't have that kind of time. I'll be retired by then. Can't you even slip me a little hint. Throw me a bone." Cher hated pleading, but the whole case was starting to make her nervous, like she was into something she shouldn't be. Yet she couldn't stop. The need to know what had happened, what was going on, pulled her onward.

"Lieutenant, I'm really not at liberty to say."

Cher took a deep breath. "Let me tell you about the Edward Compton I know. He wears hand-made suits from England and silk shirts that cost more than the car I'm sitting in now. He had a Porsche. I don't know how it works in the military, but I can tell you that if one of my detectives started doing things that aren't exactly legal, Internal Affairs would take a long, hard look at me first because I'm in charge. So I'm thinking the military is the same way. Maybe there was leak of some sort in your office, maybe someone was trading high-level military secrets for cash. If this information were to get out, don't you think someone would come knocking on your door asking what you were doing, or even if you were involved? I've always heard that Leavenworth is not a nice place. So maybe we can help each other."

He chuckled. "You present a very persuasive case. What I can tell you is that Staff Sergeant Compton was in charge of recording classified documents. But, our internal investigations showed that none of our information was tampered with. Sergeant Compton's records showed nothing unusual, financial or otherwise. He lived a very low-profile life here on the base. Drove an old truck and didn't do much of anything to draw attention to himself. Did his job and went home."

"In Phoenix he seems to have had a slightly different life."

"We were made aware of that after his death. But nothing much showed up. If he did participate in illegal activities, he covered his tracks exceptionally well."

Cher chewed on the inside of her cheek. Dead Eddie Compton was a mystery and she was beginning to hate this particular conundrum.

"Thank you, colonel. I appreciate your cooperation."

"I'm sorry I can't be more forthcoming, but I would

appreciate if you would keep me informed of your investigation."

"I'll let you know what happens." Cher disconnected and stared at her computer screen. So dead Eddie was the quiet type. Those were the ones to worry about. She glanced through the file.

Staff sergeant Edward Compton had kept a low profile in Phoenix. Except for his expensive clothes, which unless you knew clothes probably wouldn't send up any red flags. Luc had recognized the tailor because that was what he knew. He was used to paying the best to get the best.

One of the things she'd admired about Luc when they'd been in school was that he wasn't a snob. At times, he'd even been embarrassed by his wealth, and she'd found that endearing about him. That and the sex.

Oh, God, the sex. He'd been incredibly passionate in bed and exquisitely thorough. Even now, fourteen years later, she could still feel his hands caressing her, showing her what her own body could do. Just the memory made her tingle.

She put her phone back in her purse. She had to drag her thoughts away from Luc and return to the report Lily had sent her on Helen Ramsey. According to Lily, Helen had moved around a lot. She'd started a half-dozen businesses in the last fifteen years in almost as many cities. Philadelphia. Manhattan. Dallas. New Orleans and now Phoenix. Each business had been unique, and from what Lily could glean was designed to appeal to a specific clientele. An art gallery in Phoenix. An exclusive woman's boutique in Dallas. An antiques business in New Orleans. Helen had been a very busy woman for someone who hadn't existed until she'd married.

Nothing else jumped out at Cher. Except for Helen's expensive tastes, she hadn't done anything to warrant much more than a cursory investigation. She was another one who kept a low profile.

What lesson could you learn from this, Cher? Not that you've ever kept a low profile in your life. You always have to be the best, the brightest. Look at me. Look at me. The only person she'd ever kept a low profile with was Luc, and look where that had gotten her. She could still remember the litany that went through her head every time she'd looked at him. Don't love him too much. Don't trust him too much. The only thing Luc had known about her besides her last name had been that she'd come from Phoenix.

She knew she'd kept her secrets close to her, not because her foster father was gay, but because deep down inside she was ashamed of who she was before David Dawson had found her, ashamed of who her mother had been. She'd always thought that if she wasn't the best, didn't do everything ten times better than everyone else, then people would whisper she was nothing but low-life trash, no better than her hooker mother.

Miranda pulled open the door and glanced inside. "Tacos."

Cher laughed as she closed down her computer and put it away inside its padded case. "Hungry, are you?"

"Always." Miranda slid into the seat and closed the door, then reached for the seat belt.

Cher reached into her purse and grabbed her stomach acid tablets. Miranda giggled.

Cher started the car and did a U-turn, heading for Miranda's favorite taco place.

Luc parked in front of a huge Victorian house situated back from the road and shaded by several trees, their branches bare of leaves. The front porchlight was on, and he could see that the house was painted in the same bright colors that decorated some of San Francisco's painted ladies. A Christmas wreath hung on the front door.

The neighborhood was old. Few of the turn-of-the-century homes had survived, having been replaced by newer more efficient homes. Until his arrival, Luc hadn't even known Phoenix had such homes. He'd always thought Phoenix was nothing but adobe haciendas, new housing developments, golf courses and cactus. But a little research had given him a new appreciation for the city's rich history.

He stepped out of the car and walked up the front path. A brisk wind curled around him. He stepped up to the front door and punched the doorbell. His earlier anger returned and rose to a fever pitch.

As he waited, he glanced around. He couldn't shake Cher's betrayal. She'd kept his daughter, his blood, away from him. How could she have been so cruel? He'd done nothing to deserve that kind of betrayal. Even if she'd decided she wanted another man. What did she think she was going to do? Drive into the sunset with her ready-made family? She had another think coming.

Through the door, he heard footsteps. The lock clicked open and the door swung wide. A tall man, framed by the light, stood in the doorway. He had gray hair and wrinkles at the corners of his eyes and the edges of his mouth. He was slender and handsome in his jeans and Christmas red sweater. This had to be David Dawson, Cher's gay foster father. He was nothing like Luc had imagined.

"Good evening," the man said in a deep baritone. "Can I help you?"

"My name is Lucas Broussard, and I'm here to talk with Cher."

David Dawson's eyebrows rose. "I see." He did not step away or even indicate that Luc could enter. He simply studied Luc, his mouth turning down slightly, his posture stiffening, a blank look spreading through his eyes.

Hackles rising, Luc stood straight and traded a direct look with man. "You know why I'm here."

Still Dawson didn't move. "Why are you here?"

"I came to see my daughter."

"Cher didn't tell me you were coming."

Luc swallowed impatience. David Dawson was not going to make this easy for him. "Cher doesn't seem to share a lot of information."

A slight smile spread over David Dawson's lips. "She has her reasons."

"I don't care what her reasons are. She denied me my daughter."

"What makes you think Miranda's your daughter?"

"I've saw a picture of her from a newspaper article."

A small glint invaded David's eyes. "Pictures don't always tell the truth. And newspapers almost never tell the truth."

"Miranda is the spitting image of my mother at the same age."

A small chuckle escaped David. "I've been told all black folks look alike. How can you be sure?"

"She's my daughter. I know it."

"Miranda is Cher's daughter."

"And mine." Face to face with David Dawson, Luc's anger drained away, replaced with eagerness to face Cher and meet his daughter.

David started to laugh. "You didn't have a real high

opinion of Cher then, did you?"

Luc wanted to shove the man aside. He needed to get into that house. He needed to see his daughter. "Listen, do you want to have this out right here in front of the neighbors? Or are you going to let me in?"

David seemed to consider his words, but he didn't move. "I don't much mind what the neighbors think of me. I gave up worrying a long time ago."

Luc said, "I don't want Miranda to suffer."

David's shoulders started to shake, then he started to laugh again. "You're a little late with all this fatherly concern."

"I didn't know."

"As far as I'm concerned, you didn't want to know. You never came checking on her."

"What are you talking about?"

Suddenly, David stood aside, frowning. "Call me a cynical ex-cop, but something is rotten in Phoenix. Maybe you do need to come in. Looks like we have some things to straighten out."

Luc glanced past the man. "What about Cher and Miranda?"

"They'll be home in a half hour or so. While you're waiting, you and I are going to have a whiskey moment. Can I offer you a drink?"

"Make it a double." Luc stepped into the house. He'd come prepared to do battle, but this fight wasn't turning out the way he'd envisioned. All these years he'd made Cher the villain and now his position wasn't so righteous anymore.

David led the way into a living room filled with comfortable, traditionally styled furniture and antiques. "I'm going up to get the good stuff. Just give me a minute. Sit down and get comfortable." His tone held a touch of fatherly foreboding.

While David was getting the whiskey, Luc wandered the living room too agitated to sit still. The room was a comfortable mix of styles. Cher had decorated with an eye for color. Things had changed. In their apartment, she'd been very spartan in her approach to decorating. Here there was a friendly elegance with a tasteful blend of muted colors and pleasant furniture arrangements.

Luc finally sat down in front of the fireplace, a huge fire roaring in the grate. The two chairs facing it, had a worn look to them. He could just imagine Cher sitting here with her daughter, or her foster father, sharing the day's activities or discussing the future. On the corner of the hearth sat a basket with needles and yarn. He was amazed to think that Cher had taken up such a homey hobby. A knitted afghan rested across the arm of the wing chair, and he fingered it wondering if she'd knitted it.

He was so surprised at this intimate image of her, that he dropped the yarn. Even with the investigator's report, Luc realized he still did not know her. She'd never let him into her soul.

On the mantel he saw school pictures of Miranda starting from what appeared to be kindergarten to the most current picture. He traced the evolution of her from chubby baby to lanky seventh grader. The last picture showed a beautiful young girl on the verge of womanhood. A hint of mischief resided in her cedar-brown eyes, so like his mother's. Every little nuance of her face showed him her heritage from her nut-brown hair twisted into tiny little braids that formed a halo of ringlets to the classic line of her nose and high cheekbones. She was going to be a knockout when she was grown, and Luc wanted to be in her life so he could see her development.

David returned with two crystal glasses and bottle of Glenfidditch. He set the glasses down on the table that sat between the chair and poured the amber-colored liquid into the glasses and then set the bottle on the table. He sat and Luc had the impression that David often sat in the chair to spend a quiet evening with Cher. In his mind's eye, he saw Miranda stretched out on the floor in front of the fire reading a book, or doing homework, and his heart twisted to realize all he'd missed.

A white cat with a half an ear and one eye strolled into the room. It sniffed at Luc's feet. Luc could see it had a battered look to it as though it had been in one fight too many. Luc had never had pets. His mother had claimed her allergies wouldn't allow him to have one. He watched the animal as the cat peered up at him, and in one fluid motion jumped into his lap.

"If you don't care for animals," Dawson said, "just push Snack back down on the ground."

"Snack?" Luc eyed the cat. The cat stared up at him.

"When Miranda was six, she came running in here one day, grabbed my nine-iron and ran back outside to beat the hell out of a coyote trying to make a snack of this cat. Snack just kind of stuck. And after a couple hundred dollars in vet bills, we just kept her."

A low-throated purr issued from the cat and against his better judgment, Luc found himself stroking the animal who rolled itself into a ball and settled down on his lap. "I've never had a pet." Tension drained away, and he found himself relaxing. He hadn't known that animals had such a therapeutic effect.

David frowned. "I've always been suspicious of people who don't have animals."

"My mother wouldn't allow it."

"She never allowed much, did she?"

Luc thought about that. His childhood had been a little restrictive, but he didn't really want for anything. But on reflection he realized he'd done very little else. He'd never played baseball or gone to football games in high school. He'd worked in his father's office. His father had been his best friend, and Luc still missed him.

One of his most pleasurable memories of his father had been the times he'd covered stories and taken Luc along. He'd taught Luc everything he needed to know about newspapers and writing articles. As a fall back position, his father had said, if his job in the State Department didn't work out. If his dad hadn't died, Luc would probably never have returned to the paper, would never have had the chance to make it bigger and better.

Luc glanced at David Dawson. David sipped his whiskey, a relaxed look on his face. "Mr. Dawson ...."

"Call me David."

"I'm confused here."

"About what?"

"About why Cher kept Miranda such a secret."

David shook his head. "Who the hell knows why Cher does what she does. You should know her. She hasn't changed since she was a teenager."

"But..."

David held up a hand. "Luc, I know you and Cher don't see eye to eye at the present, but Cher keeps her own counsel. If you want answers you need to take this up with her."

"That's no answer."

David shrugged. "The best I can do is give you a clue. Cher's greatest character trait is her loyalty."

"So what's her flaw?"

"Her loyalty."

Irritation flooded through Luc. "I'm not in the mood for this cryptic bullshit."

"Loyalty," David said, "shows itself in the strangest ways. As a cop, that was one of the first lessons I had to learn."

Luc felt like a child being chastised about how life worked. He wasn't the one on trial here. Cher was. She'd stolen his daughter. "She didn't show any loyalty for me." He sounded sulky.

David directed a piercing glance at him. "Maybe you hadn't earned her loyalty yet."

Luc looked away. His gaze rested on a picture of Miranda in her soccer uniform, a soccer ball tucked under her arm, her lips curved into a sweet smile and her eyes filled with amusement. "And how did you earn it?"

David smiled, a distant light in his eyes. "I rescued her."

Luc shook his head. "That I don't believe. The Cher I knew would never need rescuing."

"She didn't try to steal your car when she was eleven."

Luc stared at the man. He had the feeling he was going to get a whole new perspective on who Cher was, or had been. "Cher, who never even cheated on a parking meter, stole your car!"

"She hot-wired my squad car and was ready to take off when I caught her, red-handed so to speak."

Luc couldn't believe Cher had ever been so wild. The Cher he'd known had been so self-contained. "Why would Cher do that?"

"She had to eat. And her momma had taken herself off when Cher was only five. The woman had herself a drug problem. Cher was doing the best she could to survive."

The image of Cher as a juvenile delinquent jarred Luc's memories of her. "But she's a cop."

"She is now. And she's a damn good one. Want to know why? Because she understands the criminal mind. If I hadn't happened along in her life, she'd be dead or doing hard time."

"So that's why you have her loyalty. But that doesn't explain about Miranda."

David sipped the last of his whiskey. "You'll have to talk to Cher. So stop quizzing me. But I can tell you, she did return to San Francisco and was back in twenty-four hours. What happened is for her to tell you."

Faced with David's adamant decision not to tell him about Cher and Miranda, Luc fell silent staring at the flames dancing in the fireplace. He tried to analyze his feelings, but the anger in him kept getting in the way.

David continued. "Cher did what she thought was best. You have to accept that and understand. And if you can't cut her some slack, then you walk out that door right now and never come back."

Luc took a deep breath. "I can't do that."

Luc heard the sound of laughter outside the front door. The door opened and a young girl entered. She glanced back over her shoulder. He heard answering laughter.

Cher followed the girl. She held a small computer bag. Her face was alight with love and laughter. She looked relaxed and beautiful as though she had no cares. Luc's pulse started to pound at the sight of her. This was the woman he'd known before with her eyes dancing with mirth, and her lips curved into a charming smile.

She glanced into the living room and saw him. The laughter drained out of her face, and her eyes went blank.

Chapter Eleven

A bolt of panic shot straight through Cher. Luc was sitting in her living room in her favorite chair with her cat on his lap in what appeared to be a cozy chat with her father. She knew immediately why he was in her home. He knew about Miranda. She glanced at her daughter, her chest tightening until she could barely breathe.

Miranda bounced into the living room and kissed David on the cheek. Luc stared at her like a drowning man waiting for a lifeline. Cher wasn't in the business of being a lifeguard.

"Miranda." Cher said as she curled her fists, "don't you have homework?"

"But, Mom." Miranda shook her head.

"Let her stay." Luc stroked the cat.

"No," Cher hitched a thumb over her shoulder. "Now, Miranda."

Miranda pouted. "But, Mom. Do I have to?" She studied Luc with curious eyes.

Cher gritted her teeth. "Go."

"Whatever." Miranda flounced off, her face a study of rebellion, but Cher wasn't interested in her daughter's feelings at the moment. She was more interested in preserving her daughter's future.

She glanced at the whiskey bottle, then back at Luc, sensing all the unasked questions that bubbled beneath the straight-edged line of his hard mouth.

"Why?" Luc asked, his voice tight and angry.

Her thoughts raced. Because your mother's a bitch. Because I didn't want you to take my daughter. Because I didn't want your mother raising her. Because I love her more than you can imagine. She didn't answer him. She glanced at David. "How much did you tell him?"

Her foster father shrugged. "Not my place." David pushed himself out of the chair. "I think I'll head on upstairs. You two need to talk."

Her heart sank. "I don't want to talk to him. I want him out of my house, out of my city, out of my life." She wanted him on another planet where he wouldn't endanger her relationship with Miranda.

David hugged her gently. "I understand, baby, but Miranda has a stake in this, too." He kissed her and headed up to his second-floor apartment.

Cher glared at Luc. He had invaded her life again, and this time she was more vulnerable than before. Last time her heart was on the line, and now it was her daughter. "Why couldn't you just leave things alone?" she said to Luc, her tone bitter.

Luc put the cat on the floor and stood. "You denied me my daughter, and you want me to leave things alone."

"Miranda is my daughter. Your part in her conception was incidental." Never. Never. Never, would she reveal what happened on her second trip to San Francisco. The scathing humiliation of that second meeting with his mother would never leave her.

"I came for answers."

"I don't have to answer anything. How did you find out about Miranda?"

He had the grace to look embarrassed. "I had a background check done on you."

Cher was appalled and then furious. She did background checks on people because that was her job. She knew he had done the check because he wanted a wedge to force her into continuing the investigation. "I don't want you here. You checked on me because you didn't think I could handle my job. Because I refused to play by your rules. This is so typical. You think your money can buy anything you want, including justice and a peephole into my life." The resentment in her ballooned. "You can't have my daughter. You can't have anything from me except my time at work."

His mouth tightened. "Cher, you have the nerve to get on your moral soapbox after keeping Miranda a secret all these years."

Cher drew back from him. She felt as though he'd slapped her. "I don't have to explain my reasons for what I did." Go away, she demanded silently. "And there is nothing suspect about my conduct." Pity she couldn't say the same about his mother.

He ran his hands over his hair. "Miranda needs a father. I will be a part of her life."

Cher shook her head. "What do you think David Dawson is, chopped chitlins?"

"He's not her father."

"He's not my father either, but he still did a damn good job of raising me right." And more. If not for David she'd be doing ten to fifteen in the pen.

"So you're choosing him over me."

"Life forced me to make a choice. Luc, I never loved a man the way I loved you. Never. I don't think I have it in me to love like that again. But David Dawson saved my life. I owe him everything. He told me I could have the world." All the pain from the past welled up inside her. Luc touched her cheek, running his fingers across her skin. A white-hot bolt of desire shot through her. She shrugged away from him. "If I meant so much to you, why didn't you try to find me?"

His eyes narrowed and his voice was tight with anger. "I wanted to. But my mother told me she'd found you in our bed with another man."

She stiffened. So that's how the bitch explained her abrupt departure. This gave her an out. Maybe she could convince him Miranda wasn't his. "Then what makes you think Miranda is your daughter if you think I'm such a slut?"

"She's mine." His voice was as flat and hard and his eyes.

"If I said she wasn't, would you believe me?"

"Only if it's confirmed by a DNA report."

She tilted her head to study him. "So what you're saying is that you don't trust me."

Luc picked up his glass and drained the last few drops of the whiskey inside. "You didn't give me a chance. You never let me into your life. You kept a big part of yourself a secret."

"If you'd known where I'd come from, what I was, would have you have still loved me?"

"You didn't pick your parents, why would I hold it against you?"

Cher stared at him. "Almost everyone else in my life did. The only thing I was good at were felonies. Most kids spend the first six years in school learning all the basics, I didn't attend school until I was eleven. I didn't know how to read, I couldn't add. The only person who saw potential in me was David. He has my undying loyalty."

"You never gave me the same chance." He paused,

studying her. "David said you returned to San Francisco with the idea of telling me about Miranda. What changed your mind?"

She closed her eyes, all the old memories like sandpaper on her skin. Instinct demanded she keep his mother's behavior a secret. "Things didn't go right. I wasn't thinking like a cop then. If this situation repeated itself today, I would check every angle. But I was twenty-two, pregnant, scared, and trying to hold my life together."

"Are you thinking clearly now? Because you and I need to come to some arrangement about our daughter."

She knew what his solution was. He took Miranda. She got nothing. "You can't take her away from me."

Luc shook his head. "I'm not sure what I'm going to do, but she's my daughter. I can see my mother's face in her face."

Yeah, and that's the pity, Cher thought. What she needed was a retreat until she could figure out exactly what was the best course of action. "Let's take this one step at a time. First off, you want me to solve this murder. You want me to let you back in my life. You want to be a father to a daughter you never knew you had. I can't deal with all these conflicting elements. I need a time-out. You need to go. You and I are going to have dinner tomorrow. We'll discuss the ramifications of your new position as a father then, and in the meantime I will talk to Miranda."

Luc caressed her cheek with his fingers. "I don't want you compartmentalizing all of this."

Cher jerked away, she didn't want his tenderness. She couldn't deal with it or fight against it. "I can't deal with so many jarring emotions."

Luc's jaw hardened. "I want to talk to Miranda, too. I have that right."

"Not until I figure out how to do this." Cher glanced toward the hallway. "Thirteen is a weird age. Miranda has never really asked about your identity. I need to break your appearance in her life as carefully as possible. She could just as easily end up hating you as loving you. So let me do this my way. You've waited this long, another day won't matter."

He was silent for several moments. "One more day."

Cher wanted him gone. He'd created too many new complications in her life. She had to think. She had to talk to Miranda.

She started easing Luc toward the door and out into the night. When she'd finally managed to close the front door, she headed toward her daughter's room.

Miranda's bedroom was a blend of Laura Ashley blue-and-yellow prints, white walls and a wood floor with blue throw rugs. Stuffed animals lined the bookshelves, tucked between well-read books. A collection of paperweights rested on a dainty antique vanity. A wall mural behind the bed showed an acacia tree with a pair of giraffes nibbling the leaves.

Miranda lay in bed, her algebra textbook propped on her stomach. She raised an eyebrow at Cher's entrance. "So, that's him, huh. That's my father."

Cher couldn't tell if Miranda was angry or not. "You were eavesdropping." She sat on the edge of the bed, started to embrace her daughter, but Miranda pulled away slightly. Cher pulled back.

"If I didn't, I'd never find out any information." Though her tone was light, her face was closed and distant.

Cher's chest tightened. Her daughter looked so pretty and so vulnerable. "How do you feel about all this?"

Miranda bit her lip. "I don't know. I feel sort of confused, and even though I want to just scream at you, I can't. If I didn't have a big test in algebra tomorrow, I'd spare the time to be really, really angry with you."

Cher touched her daughter's cheek. "I'm sorry you found out this way. How much did you hear?"

Miranda pointed at the heating grate on the floor. "Pretty much everything beginning with 'go to your room, Miranda,' to 'we'll talk about this later.'" Her voice mimicked Cher's with uncanny accuracy.

Cher kicked off her shoes and crawled into the bed with her daughter. She eased an arm around Miranda's shoulders. "You're not mad at me?"

"I was at first, but then I got to thinking what I would have done if I'd been you. I might have been more truthful, but I know you want to wrap me up in cotton and keep me safe." She stared at the ceiling. "But, if you want to make me feel better, I see front-row tickets to a Destiny's Child concert in my future."

Cher tugged one of Miranda's braids. "Do you think I'm going to try and buy you off?"

"If you want peace and tranquility." She put the textbook on the night stand. "I could be emotionally fragile for years to come."

Cher sighed. "That's it. I'm talking to your grandfather and we're taking the TV out of your room. I'm tired of you watching Jerry Springer."

Miranda grinned. "Take my TV. I have my music."

Cher gave in gracefully. "Well, as long as it's not Eminem." Cher hugged Miranda.

Her daughter squeezed her tightly. "Why didn't you tell me who my father was? I really wanted to know, but every time I asked, you'd get this look in you eyes that sort of made me afraid."

Cher thought of all the years of Miranda's lack of curiosity. "I didn't mean to do that. The memories were more painful than I thought. Besides, you asked so seldom I didn't think you were interested."

"I was. I just didn't know how to ask."

"I didn't know. Remember when you wanted a computer, and every day, I found Post-It notes all over the bathroom mirror and the refrigerator, along with telephone calls from you regarding the benefits of email, the wonders of the Internet. You bugged me twenty-four/seven. I finally gave in to you. If you've inherited nothing else from me, you inherited this relentlessness, this focused determination. You never bugged me the same about who your father was. I thought if you thought it was important, you wouldn't let up no matter what I said. But you never did."

Miranda snuggled her head against Cher's shoulder. "You seemed so sad. Besides, you did tell me that he'd left us. I started thinking he didn't care enough about us to love us, so I didn't ask anymore. But I was hurt."

Cher felt a painful tug in the center of her heart. "You certainly acted as though it wasn't a big issue in your life. After all, most of your friends are on their second, third, and, in a few cases, fourth father. David was your dad. He coached your softball team, he did the father-daughter thing with you. You seemed perfectly satisfied with him. And you loved Robert. You had more stable, adult male attention than all your friends put together. Both Robert and David adored you." Like David, Robert had been Miranda's lifeline. He had picked her up at school and taught her to cook like a French chef. His death had left a large hole in all their lives.

"I miss Robert." Miranda said, sighing. "Pops does, too."

"Me, too. I wish David would fall in love again." She didn't think that would happen.

"Pops is lonely. I know he is. And I think you're

lonely, too."

Cher laughed. Miranda and her famous tactic of changing subjects. Her daughter was way too wise for her years. "Are you saying I need a man? I don't think I want my thirteen-year-old daughter thinking I need a man. You might think you need one, too. And you promised me you wouldn't date until after I was dead and buried."

Miranda rested her head on Cher's shoulder. "I made that promise when I was five years old. You can't hold me to it anymore."

"I have the contract you signed."

Miranda giggled. "Crayon Xs don't count."

"Yes, they do." Cher hugged her daughter tight. She felt so fragile, so young.

"Remember when you said when I was sixteen I could have a car. You'd give me your old one and you'd get a new one. I think I need to aim higher. Luc drives a Jaguar. Do you think I could talk him out of an SUV when I'm sixteen."

Cher grinned. "Don't press your luck."

"How rich is he?"

"Extremely, filthy, mega-rich."

"Ka-ching." Miranda raised a hand like she was playing a slot machine.

Cher burst into laughter. "Finish your studying and then get to sleep."

"Will you sleep in here with me tonight?" She patted the spot next to her on the double bed.

"Sure. Why don't I make some hot chocolate and we'll have a pajama party."

"Cool. He seems nice, Mom." For a second the longing for a father Miranda had hidden deep inside herself showed in her eyes.

"He's going to love you." Cher kissed her daughter on the forehead and went to the kitchen. She sat at the table waiting for the water to boil. She opened the packs of mix and poured them into the cups.

She was afraid of what would happen next. Would Luc insist on his parental rights? Of course he would. He wanted his daughter, she'd seen it in his eyes. And now that the secret was out, there was no putting Miranda back in the genie's bottle.

The water boiled. Cher poured hot water into the mugs and began stirring in jerky, circular movements. Maybe Luc knowing about Miranda was a good thing. And with the wicked bitch of the west being dead, she wouldn't have to sweat that woman's undue evil influence upon her innocent daughter. The need to tell Luc everything about his mother had been on the tip of her tongue, but she'd kept silent.

She wasn't going to be the harbinger of evil. Luc didn't know what his mother had done, and Cher would never tell him, no matter how much she wanted to.

Luc sat in his car releasing his anger. For a long time, he stared at Cher's home. He watched the lights go out in the living room. He sensed the comfortable hominess that existed inside. Cher had created a family for herself, and he was the outsider with no family left to turn to. He remembered in school when his mother had acted as though Cher were the outsider despite Luc's insistence that he loved her and wanted to marry her. But that had changed when his mother had made her cool announcement that Cher had been with another man and had left. Because Cher had hidden her secrets so well, had never let him into her heart, he had not questioned his mother. She had seemed to have all the answers to keep him from running after Cher. She had soothed his feelings with comments about Cher's inappropriateness. Cher would never be one of them. One of their kind. He needed to let her go. And when he'd married Vanessa, his mother had been ecstatic, confiding in him that Vanessa was right kind of wife for him.

He couldn't contain the jealousy in him. When he and Cher had been together, she had never talked about getting married and having babies. She had always lived in the present, and there was an irony in that she now had everything he'd ever wanted, and she'd built it all for herself without him.

He went back over his conversation with Cher. He realized she had never truly answered his question about why she'd left. His past experiences with her reminded him that she never did anything without reason. She was hiding something. Not just Miranda, but something else. Something that had to be devastating. She was so tough, so self-contained. And so full of secrets.

He started the car and headed toward the house he'd bought to establish his residency in Arizona. He wasn't anxious to return to the sterile place, made more desolate by the fact that Cher and Miranda would be so far from him.

The phone in his car rang. He answered and found Ben at the other end.

"I told you to stay away from Cher." Ben's voice was hard and angry.

"I couldn't," Luc replied. "I had to see Miranda. I had to meet her."

"The last thing you needed to do was confront Cher with guns blazing." Ben was silent for a second. "If you want to annihilate her in court to get custody of the girl, you have to look like a victim."

Was that what Luc wanted? Did he want to destroy Cher just to assert his parental rights over Miranda. "There has a to be another way."

"After what she did in taking your daughter away!"

"Dragging Cher through a nasty court battle can't be good for Miranda. I don't want her hating me before she knows who I am." If Miranda hated him, he would never forgive himself. He had to figure out a way to keep everything as amicable as possible...for his daughter's sake.

"Excuse me!" Ben sounded exasperated. "Is this the same man who caused a hostile takeover of one of the largest independent book publishers in California? And now you want to play patty-cake with the woman who betrayed you? What the hell is wrong with you?"

Luc sighed. "Ben, this is a child, not a business. Business means anything goes, and we all understand those rules. I know your divorce was nasty, but this isn't the same situation. Cher hid Miranda away from me for a reason. And I know her well enough to understand that in her head it was a good reason. I am not going to make this a blood war until I find out what happened to make her do this."

Benjamin breathed hard. "Luc, I know you, and you'll never be satisfied until total surrender. Just say the word, and I'll have the custody papers filed and the hearing scheduled immediately."

"No, that's not how I want to do this."

"Then what?" Ben was a bull dog when he needed to be. But that was not what Luc needed at the moment. He wanted a friend. Someone to listen to him as he thought his way through this convoluted maze.

Luc cautioned, "Ben, let's just wait and see what develops. I'm having dinner with Cher tomorrow night."

"That sounds kind of cozy. I get it now. You don't want to go after custody of the kid because you still want the woman."

Luc braked in the middle of the street. A car behind honked and swerved around him. Luc couldn't respond to Ben because he didn't trust himself to keep his emotions under control.

He stepped on the gas and turned into the housing development. "Ben, I'll call you later. I need some time to sort things out."

He disconnected as he turned into his driveway. The garage door rolled up and he pulled into the garage. The overhead light showed the empty walls. He didn't want to go inside to the rest of his empty rooms and what had suddenly turned into an empty life.

Chapter Twelve

Cher sat back in her desk chair and stared at the pack of cigarettes on the corner. With arms crossed, she debated whether to smoke or not to smoke. Her fingers itched to break open that pack and light up. She wanted that cigarette so bad she was considering breaking her promise to her daughter. Yet at the same time, she didn't want her suit to smell like smoke. She'd worn the dark plum dress and matching jacket to please Beatrix Hunter and hopefully look less like a cop.

Outside in the squad room, Wyatt Earp Whitaker was having a good-natured argument with Marco Jackson. Through the open door, she saw Marco sitting on the edge of his desk laughing.

Even Jacob Grayhorse's dour expression had been replaced with a smile, and Cher wondered what amused them. The door to the squad room opened and a well-dressed man walked in. He looked around. Jacob approached him, listened as the man spoke, and then gestured at Cher's office. She'd seen that face before. She searched her memory and came up with a name. Bad Eddie Compton come to call. Her week getting better and better.

Edward Compton had finally come to the land of the enemy. She didn't know if she was glad to see him or not. But she had to admit this kinda made him seem guilty and he was doing some quick repair work. If it were her, she would have stayed in San Francisco until the cops dragged her kicking and screaming out of her house.

Cher studied him as he walked across the squad room. He was a tall, slender man with skin the color of burnished walnut. His eyes were dark and alert. He exuded good breeding, and Cher wondered who the hell he really was. She searched for the familial resemblance to Helen Ramsey, but found nothing to indicate they were related. A small, niggling suspicion started in the back of her head. If this man and Helen Ramsey were brother and sister, Cher would eat her desk.

He stood just outside her door and looked at her, making eye contact. He looked arrogant, like he couldn't be bothered with this investigation, and probably hoping she wouldn't be bothered with murder either.

"May I come in?" he asked in a cultured tone that reeked of money and voice lessons. Just beneath the surface lurked something that told Cher his poise and his demeanor came from practice, rather than birth.

"Please, Mr. Compton." Cher stood and gestured at a chair.

He moved gracefully into the room and closed the door. "So you're Lieutenant Cher Dawson. I was expecting someone a little more steely-eyed and hard. Not this vision of nubian perfection."

Cher could only stare at him. She was going to be sick. She tried to summon a smile, but her lips felt stiff. "Thanks."

He looked her up and down, an appreciative glimmer in his eyes. "But I must say, the reality is quite delightful and not at all what I expected."

Cher felt maybe she should dig a finger in her ear just to shock him. "Have a seat. May I offer you coffee, soda, a bottle of water? The water is from Japan. My father has a client who sends us this fancy Japanese brand. You might like it."

He thought a moment. "Some water would be nice."

She opened her compact refrigerator and carefully took out a small bottle, holding it by the neck and handed it to him. He wrapped his fingers around it and cracked the seal on the spout. He took a long sip, holding the bottle with delicately poised fingers.

He set the bottle on the corner of the desk and smiled a well-practiced smile, and Cher tried to see what in this glossy facade of a man had attracted Luc's mother. He sat gracefully and crossed one knee over the other, swinging his well-clad foot slightly. "Lieutenant, let's cut to the chase. I understand that my late wife's son is not satisfied with the information regarding his mother's tragic passing. Please help me understand how you, a member of the Phoenix Police Department, can be investigating a San Francisco death for which an involvement on my part was completely and totally exonerated?"

"What makes you think I'm investigating the death of Victoria Broussard?"

His eyebrows arched. "Then what are you investigating?" His tone was polite, but there was a hard undertone.

This man was smooth and Cher was impressed by his stage presence. "It would be improper for me to speak of any investigation that I might or might not be doing."

He gave a slight smile. "My sister informs me that you have been asking questions."

"If you know I spoke with your sister, then I'm sure she explained the subject matter." She could tell he was fishing. Some alarm had gone off in his head, and he wanted to know whether or not to worry. Cher wanted to tell him to worry. She wanted to ruffle his calm air of composure. "Eddie, you came to see me. Obviously, you feel we have something to discuss. If you need to unburden yourself, please do so. I'm willing to listen."

A shadow of annoyance crossed his face and was swiftly gone, replaced with a calm, innocent gaze. "I have nothing on my conscience."

My granny's fanny. "Then why pay me a visit?"

He gave her a measuring look. "Lieutenant, perhaps I am only here to ask a stunningly beautiful woman to lunch." Again, a winsome smile curved his lips. A smile that would probably melt the panties off a lot of women.

Cher leaned over her desk, resting her arms on the blotter. "Eddie, I am so impressed that you came all the way from San Francisco in your hand-made Italian loafers just to ask a working girl like me out to lunch. I really know, deep in my heart, I should be flattered, but somehow I can't find it in myself to dredge up the sincerity." This was a man who had relied on his charm for too many years. Cher was immune to him. She could see that he didn't quite believe she wasn't going to roll over and expose her soft underbelly just because he'd graced her with a winning smile. "But since you're here, I do have some questions." Being a cop meant being suspicious. She delighted in the suspicious part.

He raised a hand. "Ask away."

"Where were you born?"

He didn't quite frown. "What does this have to do with anything?"

"When were you born?"

"Why these trivial questions?"

"Maybe I'm a trivial kind of girl."

A look of alarm spread across his aristocratic face. "I don't see any connection. My life is an open book."

With blank pages, Cher thought. "Indulge me."

He rattled off all the pertinent information that Cher already knew belonged to dead Eddie. How nice! He'd managed to memorize the facts faultlessly.

"You're looking at me strangely," he said when he'd finished his well-rehearsed rendition.

"I'm trying to picture you as a child in Louisiana. Tell me more."

"There's nothing to tell. I was born, went to school, grew up, and left."

"Tell me about Stillwater."

"Little town, nothing of note, good people, and no future." He looked smug and in control. He finished the bottled water and tossed it in the trash. "Nothing as glamorous as Phoenix."

"If you think Phoenix is glamorous, Stillwater must be a major backwater town."

"Extremely provincial." He tilted his head.

"That's a big word for a country boy like you."

"Detective, you truly can take the country out of the boy, if you put your mind to it."

"I'll keep that in mind."

He stood. "I hope I've satisfied your curiosity. And if there is any way I can persuade you to dine with me, allow me to give you my card." He reached into his jacket and pulled out a crisp white business card.

"I'm not calling you in San Francisco."

He removed a pen from an inner pocket and scribbled on the card and handed it to her. "I'm staying with my sister. This is her phone number. If you'll excuse me, I have an another appointment."

"Thank you for squeezing me in."

"My pleasure, Lieutenant Dawson."

Cher watched him leave her office. She had to admit he had a pretty nice ass, even if the rest of him was a little too showy, like an unsound thoroughbred. He was not a man built for going the distance. No Triple Crown winner in him. He'd be winded at the half-mile post.

When he was out the door she opened the center drawer of her desk and drew out one of her many sets of chopsticks from too many lunches at the Chinese place on the corner. She unwrapped the chopsticks and carefully reached into the trash can and with one stick inserted into Eddie's water bottle, she removed it and set it on her desk. She found an evidence bag in a drawer and gently slid it over the bottle, tipped the bottle into the bag and closed the top. She labeled a tag and attached it to the bag. Eddie had very nicely left his fingerprints on the glass and some DNA in the spit on the mouth of the bottle and she intended to have it typed. She wasn't certain what she was hoping for, but she knew she'd need it. Always be prepared, David had told her.

"Whitaker," she called out the door, "what are you working on?" She got up and walked to the open door.

"Working on my transfer papers, what else?" he yelled back.

"Still!" She leaned on the door jamb. "You must not really want it if you're taking this long to fill in all those boxes."

He grimaced. "Give me time. I want to do this right, so you can't turn me down."

She grinned. "Take all the time you need. Just remember I have first dibs on your time. Get in my office." She turned around and walked to her desk.

Whitaker slouched into her office and leaned against the door while Cher rustled through the file on the dead Eddie Compton. She wrote down a phone number and handed the paper to him. "Call this man, Kingsley Walker. He's the sheriff in Stillwater, Louisiana. I want to find out information on Eddie Compton and who he ran with."

"Why don't you talk to him? Don't you think a big, bad lieutenant has more juice than a lowly sergeant?"

"You speak his language."

"You mean red neck?"

Cher shook her head. "Just remember, you said that. Not me." She pointed at his desk, and he left, mumbling something she couldn't quite hear.

A few minutes later, Beatrix Hunter sashayed into the squad room. Her blond hair swung back and forth in tune with the hem of her very chic, very designer label outfit. Cher wasn't sure who the designer was, but she pretty much figured that it came right off the runway and probably cost more than what Cher made in a month.

Cher suddenly felt dowdy in her plum-colored jacket dress.

"Ready to go?" Beatrix smoothed the cuff of her well-cut jacket and fluffed the edges of the Ann Klein silk scarf artfully arranged about her neck.

Beatrix always sounded perky and upbeat like that perfect girl in high school that everyone hated. Cher wanted to growl at her. Beatrix had the ability to make every woman feel second-rate. Cher included. "Yep."

"You look like a Christian about to face the lions."

"I feel like one."

Beatrix waved her hand. "You'll be fine. You look so lovely today that Misty Van Cleef will never question your pedigree."

"You make me sound like a grayhound."

Beatrix simply smiled. "Not exactly the breed I would use to describe you."

"What breed would that be?"

"Oh no!"

She checked her appearance in the mirror. "You're right, on second thought, don't answer that." She grabbed her purse. "Let's get going. I want to get this interview over with."

Misty Van Cleef lived in a trendy black-and-white

house. White floors, black furniture. White walls, black drapes. The only spot of color was on one wall where a huge abstract painting in fuschia and electric blue hung over the black marble fireplace.

Cher sat on a black, butter-soft leather chair that was so comfortable she thought she'd fall asleep.

Hunter and Misty Van Cleef stood in front of the huge painting extolling its virtues. Cher thought it was ugly and dumb.

"He's an up-and-coming painter." Misty was a graceful woman with light brown hair tinted with platinum highlights. Her reed-thin body was encased in black silk slacks and a white silk blouse. She wore a black and white Chanel scarf about her slender throat and huge diamonds in her ears. She was the epitome of taste and elegance and probably hadn't had a decent meal since puberty.

Cher stifled a yawn. Hunter was good at the small chatty stuff that Misty seemed to enjoy.

Finally, the two sat across from Cher. Misty arranged herself sideways on the sofa and daintily sipped a glass of white wine.

"So tell me," Misty said with a gracious smile aimed at Cher, "what do you want to know about Helen Ramsey?" Her voice was cultured. She'd probably graduated from Vassar.

Hunter crossed her legs. "Lieutenant Dawson is in the midst of an extremely delicate investigation, and you are the only person in the city we can rely on for discretion and accuracy."

Misty preened. She touched her hair and gently ran thin fingers through it. "Your mother said your police job was just a rebellious childhood phase. But you seem to have found your niche, Beatrix. Your parents must be proud."

Hunter chuckled. "They're a bit uncertain about what to make of my career decisions."

Misty patted Hunter's wrist. "Only because marriage doesn't seem to be on the horizon for you."

Hunter edged away. "It's difficult enough meeting nice gentlemen with breeding. Much less the one you want to spend the rest of your life with."

Misty's laughter was a tinkling musical note. Cher gritted her teeth. She silently commanded Hunter to get on with it so they could get out of this stifling house.

"Misty," Hunter said, "tell me how you met Helen Ramsey."

Misty took another sip of her wine. "She operates a gallery, and we met when I was in my primitive phase." She waved her hand at the room. "I wanted everything in pre-Colombian and African. Helen had quite a delightful collection of third world art."

"How often do you redecorate?" Cher asked. How nice to know her ancestry was considered third world chic.

"Every couple of years." Misty glanced around the

room, pride in her blue eyes. "I get bored with the same look."

Cher felt a spurt of annoyance. A kid could get beaten to death, a hooker die from a drug overdose, but God forbid that Misty Van Cleef should ever be bored. "And the last time was?" Misty was a woman with way too much time on her hands.

"Last month, but my pre-Colombia phase was three years ago." Misty touched a finger to her cheek. "Helen was so very knowledgeable. She helped me with my redecorating, and we became friends, of a sort."

"Tell me about her brother."

Misty giggled again. "What a delightful man. Very charming in an old world sort of way. Very European. Helen told me they are from a very old Creole family in New Orleans. Good breeding always shows." Misty turned to Cher. "Where are you from, Lieutenant Dawson?"

"I'm a local girl." Cher made a note to herself to check on where Stillwater was in relation to New Orleans.

"Tell me," Hunter said, "how you knew Victoria Broussard."

Misty shook her head. "I met Victoria when she came to Phoenix several years ago. We attended several Republican fund raisers together and discovered we had a lot in common."

"Would you call yourself friends," Cher asked, "or

merely acquaintances?"

"Since I did make a point of introducing Victoria to Edward, I would say we were more than acquaintances, but less than confidants. She was one of us."

"In what way was she one of you?" Cher asked puzzled.

"Well-bred and cultured. One could tell Victoria was born to this life." Misty sounded very smug.

As opposed to Cher who had not even been born in a hospital. "How about Edward and Helen, did they fit in?"

Misty nodded. "Edward is very charming. And Helen is absolutely enchanting."

"So they fit into what you expected them to be."

Misty paused a moment, her eyebrows raised. "Of course, my dear. They may not have been from Phoenix, but they had all the qualifications for admission into our world."

Cher wanted to gag. How could this woman be so blind? Edward Compton was evil. Cher dealt with evil every day. She could smell it, taste it, hear it coming a mile away. Edward Compton was no more of Misty's self-indulgent, self-centered, overfed and over-privileged world than Cher was.

Cher glanced at Hunter whose eyes were glazed over and Cher realized she was bored out of her skull. Maybe Hunter wasn't so bad after all. She'd made an effort to escape from the world she'd been born into and attempted to find something meaningful. Cher hated having to revise her opinion of Hunter. Hunter fidgeted. "How did Helen Ramsey and her brother end up in Phoenix?"

Misty smiled. "Helen is such a versatile person. She's been everywhere and owned several businesses. She had a boutique in New York, a restaurant in Philadelphia, an antiques dealership in New Orleans, and she is a computer genius. If not for Helen, I don't know what I would have done. She introduced me to the wonderful world of Internet shopping. She helped my husband purchase polo ponies online and..." Misty fluffed her Chanel scarf, "just between us girls, half price on the Internet. I may be wealthy, but I do appreciate a good bargain."

Cher made another note to self, recheck Helen's businesses and see what she could find. Years ago when Cher had worked fraud, she'd investigated a case with a guy who did what Cher called a hitch and ditch. He married the women, took their money, and then hit the road. She wondered if Eddie was running the same scam. That would account for Helen's movements around the country. She'd start a business, reel the wealthy, lonely women in and Eddie would swoop down and save them from their loneliness. He had that con-artist smell about him. He was too slick, too perfect, too everything to be real. The hairs on the back of Cher's neck stood up. The case was coming together. She could feel the link between the two Eddies and Helen developing. All she had to do now was find out where that link began. She already knew where it ended. The problem was that she had too many incompletes. She needed to start finding how everything fit in the puzzle.

Now if she could just get her personal life on track.

On the way back to her office, Cher called Lily on her cell phone to ask her to run a second check on Helen Ramsey and find out what she'd discovered about Sylvia Compton. The unknown sister and pretend sister nagged at her. She also asked Lily to see if Helen had a business partner in any of her enterprises and who that person was.

Lily had nothing on Sylvia Compton except a birth certificate and a record of her high school graduation. According to Sylvia, she could be one of those people who fell through the cracks. Or she could be dead, though Lily had not found a death certificate. Cher thanked her and asked her to keep trying to find Sylvia, though Cher wasn't certain there'd be anything to find. Sylvia was as elusive as her dead brother.

The squad room was a hive of activity. Marco was on the phone. Jacob squinted at a paper while making notes in a battered notebook and Allen was hunched over his computer.

Cher entered her office and found Whitaker sitting in her chair. "Are you comfortable?"

He swiveled it back and forth. "You have a nice chair. It's all broken-in in all the right spots. When I think of all my hard work and diligence to you and this unit, you should give me this chair as a reward."

"How about, as a reward, I don't transfer you to parking meter patrol?"

"Ouch!" His face scrunched up. "You really know how to hurt a guy."

Cher pointed her finger at him and then jerked her thumb over her shoulder. "Out."

"Out of your chair? Out of your office? Out of your squad? Out of your life?" His lean face looked hopeful.

"Out with the information." She sat down and wriggled. "Thanks for keeping my chair warm."

He flipped open a blue spiral notebook and studied it for several seconds. He glanced at Cher. "According to my notes, Sheriff Red Neck is out of town. Won't be back until late tomorrow."

"Wasn't there anyone else you could talk to."

Whitaker shrugged. "You didn't tell me to talk to anyone else. You stated quite plainly to speak to Sheriff Red Neck."

"Get out." Cher swallowed irritation.

"Out of your chair? Out of your squad? Out of your life?" He looked hopeful as he stood.

Cher started laughing. "Whitaker, I'm just keeping

you around for the laughs. You're like a vaudeville act: good, bad, and indifferent all rolled into one."

Whitaker half saluted and left while Cher sat back and stared at the open file in front of her. She damned Luc for coming back into her life and for presenting her with such a puzzle while adding so many complications.

Gerard's was small and intimate with tiny tables graced by a single lit candle in white holders, snow-white tablecloths and a friendly food smell that promised to sate even the most finicky appetite. Christmas lights lined the walls, and a brightly decorated tree had been set up in the center of the room. Ben had recommended Gerard's, and Luc understood why.

As Luc waited for Cher, he studied the tables of men and women. Gerard's was not a family themed place, but a premier French restaurant for couples intent on seduction. Now that he was sitting, he wasn't certain this place was the correct one for a candid conversation with Cher.

A waiter hovered just at the edge of Luc's vision ready to be of service without seeming intrusive. Luc had ordered the bottle of wine cooling in a silver bucket next to the table. Luc's glass was half empty.

He glanced at his watch for the third time. Cher was late, and Luc tried to remain patient. He'd never known

Cher to be late. If anything, she was a time freak, arriving an hour before an event to avoid being late. He remembered a Christmas party, their first real date, and she had insisted he pick her up two hours beforehand. The party had been in San Francisco and she wanted to factor in time to be lost even though Luc had known exactly where he was going. Halfway to the party he'd realized that the extra hour with Cher had been a boon. He'd deliberately gotten lost just to keep her with him.

When Cher finally entered the restaurant, following the hostess, he gulped. She walked slowly between the tables with the self-confident air of a woman who understood what she wanted and when she wanted it. Men's heads turned, and Luc felt a prickle of jealousy. He didn't want other men looking at her, admiring her. He wanted her to himself.

She wore a skimpy black dress that fit her body like an Italian leather glove. A slit up the side showed her long, slender legs and Luc's mouth went dry. He couldn't take his eyes from her shapely calves. He remembered the feel of those legs wrapped around him even after all these years. He remembered the depth of her passion and wondered what had happened to it.

This sexy, enticing woman was the mother of his child. He forgot all his anger at her deception as she approached him.

Despite fourteen years, she was still incredibly beautiful. She'd slicked her hair back and secured it with sparkly gold combs. Her dark eyes glowed. Her full lips were painted red and beckoned to be kissed. Luc's stomach tightened, and he knew he still desired this woman. He wanted her in his life and in his bed.

Luc stood at her approach. "Cher, did you know you're unusually late?"

The hostess pulled out Cher's chair, and she slid into it with a graceful movement. "I'm unusually busy." Her voice was tart.

Luc sat down, drinking in the sight of her. The candlelight cast a soft glow over her features. "You're unusually beautiful."

She inclined her head in a gracious gesture. "Thank you. I have to admit, Miranda chose the dress and insisted on doing my hair. She has your taste in clothes. I'm perfectly happy if my colors match."

That was one of the things that had attracted Luc to her. She had no artifice, no airs. What a man saw was what he got.

"Miranda is to be commended. What other traits do I share with her?"

Cher sipped her water, replacing the glass carefully. She studied him before replying, as though trying to see what was on his mind. "We can break it down into three categories."

"And those are?" Luc inquired, hungering for anything about Miranda that Cher could offer.

She tilted her head at him. "The good, the bad, and

the ugly."

For a second he was taken aback. "I'll bite. Give me the bad first, but I don't want to know about the ugly." He wanted to think his daughter was perfect, but reality reminded him that she was just a child with all the flaws and imperfections of childhood. If she grew up and turned into half the woman Cher was, he would be happy.

"She has your arrogance, but a good sense of humor to temper it."

That was harsh, but he could take it. "And the good part is?"

Cher smiled. "She has your ability to control her anger. She thinks before she speaks, and she's very diplomatic. I can't believe she's my daughter at times. I say what I think. She's very careful about every word that comes out of her mouth."

Bluntness had been another thing about Cher that had attracted him to her. She not only said what she thought, but she practiced her own brand of honor and truth. The strength of her moral standards had thoroughly intrigued him. Her father had done a good job raising her.

But, he had a thousand questions he wanted to ask her. Why did she sleep with another man? What about him had sent her running away? Why did she hide Miranda from him? He couldn't think where to start. All he could think about was the way her dress molded to her breasts and the way the candlelight flickered off her skin, adding a burnished look. He wanted to touch her. All the years, and all the time between, all the anger and recriminations melted away, and he was caught in the memory of how she had been before.

"Our daughter sounds very mature." He couldn't help the touch of pride that crept into his voice. He had spent most of the night and half the day thinking about Miranda and wondering who she was. His impatience to finally meet and learn to know her had almost snapped. A dozen times he thought he might order the car and go to Cher's house, but he knew that any attempt to contact Miranda could be disastrous. He wanted to handle Cher as carefully as possible. If anything, she'd grown more prickly with the passage of time.

Cher chuckled. "Please don't tell her that. At times, she does act like a thirteen-year-old going on forty, but the reality is, she's still thirteen. She loves shopping at the mall, buying clothes she doesn't need, talking on the phone for hours at a time, and all those other teenage girl things designed to annoy parents."

"She sounds perfectly normal." Now that he knew Miranda existed, he so desperately wanted to be a part of her life, to experience all those annoying things that parents had to contend with. And to be a part of Cher's life again. If she would let him. "Why did you hide her away from me?"

Cher's face changed. Before there had been laughter

and a lightness in her eyes, and suddenly her lips thinned and her eyes went blank and still.

Luc looked her directly in the eye. "David said you returned to San Francisco to tell me about Miranda. Why didn't you?" He had spent the day trying to think of all the reasons why Cher had kept his daughter a secret, but nothing came to him.

She looked down at the table. "I chickened out." Her voice was tight and tense.

"No, not you. Nothing frightens you." Never had she let fear rule her.

She raised her head. "There are a lot of things that frighten me."

The waiter politely asked if she would like some wine, and Cher nodded. Their conversation waited while the waiter filled her glass and refilled Luc's. Then he slipped away to another table while Cher took a sip of the wine.

"Do I frighten you?" Luc asked.

She wet her lips. "I have come face-to-face with the worst life has to offer. You don't frighten me. But what you are, where you came from scared the shit out of me."

He sensed there was more to that statement than she was willing to reveal. He could certainly understand her feelings. At times, his mother had frightened him, too. "Part of me was hoping you'd bring Miranda."

"I thought about it for a minute, but she's on the firing range with David, and I didn't want to disturb her time with him. They go every Thursday night. It's a major bonding time for them."

"You are allowing my daughter to use a gun!" Luc hated guns, even more since his mother's murder.

Cher sat back in her chair, her face calm. "You need to calm yourself down. This is not the place to debate how I'm raising Miranda."

"But I want an explanation on why you let her use a gun." He was over-stepping his bounds but the gun issue worried him.

Cher looked amazed. "You can't just step back into my life and start telling me how to raise my daughter. I really don't owe you an explanation, but I will give you one." She took a deep breath, and Luc could see she was gathering the threads of her argument. "She lives with two cops. There are firearms in the house. She had better know the rules. If something happens when she's at the house alone I don't want her to be afraid to protect herself or think that guns are toys for her amusement."

"Do you see evil around every corner?"

"You grew up in privilege and were protected from the evils of society. I have seen the evil. I live in a world where there are two kinds of people—predators and prey. I'll be damned if my daughter is going to be prey. If it were possible, I'd get her a permit to carry. It's a big, nasty world out there for women. Newsflash: it's not getting any better."

"How can you let a thirteen-year-old use a gun?"

Cher's lips thinned. "She grew up with guns. It's a part of my life. I don't believe every person walking the earth has the privilege to own a gun, but it's part of what I do, and Miranda has to learn how to respect the power."

Once again he was reminded that despite her beauty, she was lethal in a way that made his skin tingle. "I'm not sure I like what you do for a living."

She jerked as though he'd hit her. Her eyes narrowed and she bared her teeth. "I'm a grown-up. I really don't need your permission." She jabbed her finger at him. "And if I wasn't a cop, you wouldn't be in Phoenix asking for my help."

He didn't want to be reminded about why he was in Phoenix. What he wanted to do was talk about Miranda and them. He was a little shocked with himself to realize his mother's death was no longer a priority. She had been replaced with his burgeoning desire for Cher and the knowledge that he had a daughter.

Not that he didn't want justice for his mother, but his daughter's future was more important. She was the future. Nothing he did now would change the fact that his mother was dead.

"What plans does Miranda have for the future?" How does a man make up for thirteen lost years of a child's life? What questions should he ask?

Cher smiled, a light in her eyes that was almost tender. "I think she's going to be a writer. Considering the amount of paper she consumes, her writing seems important to her."

"Fiction or nonfiction?" He couldn't have asked for anything better. Mentally, he rubbed his hands together. He thought of all the things he could do to help her in her choice.

"Probably fiction. She has a tremendously active imagination."

Even better. "My publishing company has a fiction line that includes young adult books. What does she like—romance, mystery, science fiction?"

Cher shook her head. "No. No nepotism." Her voice was fierce.

"Why not? Your father was a police officer. Don't you think that aided you in your career?"

She leaned her elbows on the table, her face taking on a intensity that startled him. "Let me tell you about David Dawson and my career. I didn't want his help, and he didn't offer it. Matter of fact, I think he talked to his buddies to make it harder for me. I started out as that simperingly sweet Officer Friendly who went to schools to talk to kids to show them how trustworthy cops could be. Five minutes into that gig, I was ready to eat my gun, I was so bored. Then when I finally was allowed to transfer out, I ended up on the ugliest beat in Phoenix where the things I saw gave me nightmares for mouths. From there I went to bunco for a whole six months, and homicide, then did another year in Internal Affairs and finally the Cold Case Unit. When I told him I wanted to be a cop, my father did everything he could to discourage me. But when I endured, he finally decided I had made the right decision. I earned my stripes, and I'm not going to let you hand over Miranda's like some sort of prize doll with no personality of her own. She's going to work for her future the same way I did."

But Luc wanted to help his daughter. She shouldn't have to work so hard to get what she wanted. "I could give her so much. Why won't you let me help?" He could pave the way in so many different directions. He'd already called Stanford to see how he could get Miranda in.

"Don't do Miranda any favors. She's enough like you I can almost guarantee she won't appreciate them."

"I have always appreciated everything that was done for me. And I worked hard, too."

"And you wouldn't be where you are today if your parents hadn't been who they were." Her voice was almost bitter.

Luc realized he was on the losing end. And he always knew how to cut his losses. "I don't want to argue, Cher."

"All we seem to do is argue. You asked me out to dinner, and I'm hungry. Can we order now and put that hovering waiter out of his misery? He's been trying to get our attention for fifteen minutes." She flipped open her menu and glanced through it.

A rumble of hunger rolled through him as well, and

he knew if he wanted to keep Cher mellow, he needed to feed her. Food had always worked wonders in the past. Hopefully, the good food here would advance his plans for the future.

Luc wasn't about to abandon his subject.

Chapter Thirteen

Cher was almost too stressed to eat the grilled sea bass the waiter put in front of her. Luc was being way too pleasant for a man who intended to take her daughter away from her. He'd brought her to the most expensive restaurant in Phoenix, plied her with incredible wine and fed her food fit for the gods. She hated when he was nice to her. His charm put her off guard, like the months after they'd first met and he had wooed her with soft words and passion.

She hadn't learned her lesson. She kept having to remind herself that he had an ulterior motive and he wasn't being nice because he liked her.

Luc put down his fork. He folded his hands together. "I've decided to make Phoenix my permanent base of operation."

She wasn't hearing this. Cher pressed her tongue to the roof of her mouth to stop the angry words from streaming out from her lips. Be calm, she demanded of herself. "Nobody owns a media empire in Phoenix."

"There's a first time for everything. I'm only two hours from San Francisco."

Cher held her breath for a long beat and then expelled it. "You're not taking Miranda away from me."

"Miranda's not a bone I can steal, but I do have rights. Ones I fully intend to recognize as her father. She is my heir. I would prefer the two of us come to an agreement that didn't involve lawyers and a legal battle."

Cher couldn't think of an answer to his statement. Her palms began to sweat and her stomach knotted. The last thing she wanted was to let him back into her life no matter how he made her blood race and her body tingle. Every nerve ending was raw with her need to touch him. "You're a young man. You can remarry and have more children."

"I could say the same for you."

Cher shook her head. "I'm thirty-five. I have maybe five good years left on me. You, you'll fire live rounds until the day you die. I have to be careful about who I date. I have an impressionable young daughter."

"Does being a cop color everything in your perception?"

"There are freaks and perverts out there who look for women like me who have a young daughter. And even if

I bring home some nice guy, who's going to say he's going to stay for the long haul. You date a guy. He likes your kids and your kids like him. Then one day, he's out the door. Your kids are devastated and you're left with performing damage control, or worse, the heavy."

"You never used to be so negative."

Cher closed her eyes. What did he know about her? She opened her eyes and gazed at him. "I live in the real world. And my world isn't nice. And under the surface, your world isn't very pretty either. The only thing you have going for you is money to distance yourself from the crap and cushion the blow."

"That's not fair."

"The world isn't fair." Cher sipped her white wine. "You waltzed back into my life fully intent on forcing me to do your bidding. And now that you know you have a daughter, you're going to use your money to wreck my life. And you're telling me life is fair. It's only fair for you because you can buy fairness. I have to suffer."

"I'm suffering, too."

"I know that. You lost your mother, but you can't replace her with my daughter."

"You keep referring to her as 'your' daughter. She's mine, too. I intend to be her father in every way and not just a sperm donor."

"At the time she was conceived, you weren't 'just' a sperm donor."

"Then why are you treating me like one now?"

She stood and tossed her napkin on the table. "This isn't going to work."

"What do you mean?"

"You get a lawyer and I'll get a lawyer and we'll let them duke it out." She grabbed her jacket and turned.

Luc stared for a second as she walked toward the door, skirting the tables. He reached into his pocket, pulled out his wallet, tossed enough money on the table to cover the meal, and raced after her.

"Cher." He pulled open the door and followed her out to the parking lot. "You can't leave."

"I can do anything I want."

He grabbed her by the shoulders and spun her around. She glared at him. He pulled her toward him and kissed her.

Her body was rigid against him. Her clean, fresh scent invaded his nose, tickling his senses. Cher never wore perfume, but her fragrance always reminded him of a field of Jamaican wildflowers.

Her fingers curled around his arms. She wasn't fighting him. Her mouth opened slowly. Tentatively his tongue explored her bottom lip. She began responding. Her body went soft against his and her fingers started massaging his arms.

A shudder of need raced through him. His blood was on fire. He hadn't experienced this kind of rush since he spent that last day with her.

Cher pushed him. "Get away me." She dragged the

back of her hand across her full lips. "Let's get one thing straight. I know the attraction is still there, but I don't have time to indulge. I have your case to solve, and we have a nasty custody battle to fight. The sex thing is off the table. Got it?"

A glimmer of hope ran through him. Maybe he could still have her. And Miranda. "You're still attracted to me?"

She leaned back on the car and crossed her arms. "I don't want to be."

"Why not?"

Her lips thinned. She stared up at the dark sky. "Because it's inconvenient."

He knew from past experience when she couldn't look him directly in the eyes, she was torn. Could he use that to bind her to him? "Inconvenient?"

"Yes."

This explanation he had to hear. "Why is that?"

"Because I'm trying to solve your case. It's natural that you look to me for comfort."

"I don't really have a stake in solving Eddie Compton's murder."

"Really?" She rolled her eyes. "Now I might believe that if you hadn't thrown around your considerable bank roll, or you hadn't been dogging my every step like I'm some wet-behind-the-ears rookie on her first big case."

He could admit to that. He had manipulated her. "I've bulldozed you." He wasn't sorry. She'd do the same if given the chance.

"Normally that's my job." She gave him a weary smile. "I don't like being on the other end of the shovel."

"You never did."

"I know for a fact that if Eddie Compton had been murdered by a plain Joe Blow from Tucson, you wouldn't give a damn. But he's connected to you personally, and you're bound and determined to see justice done for your mother. I resent being used. Any detective with street savvy could have handled this case, but I get to do the honors. I'm a very busy woman."

She had never pulled her punches, and listening to her made him realize how badly he wanted her. "Am I wrong in wanting that?"

"Hell no. Your methods are bad, but one killer off the street is always a good thing."

"What does that have to do with us?"

She tensed. "Everything."

"Explain."

She tilted her head and eyed him for a moment before answering. "I feel like I'm taking advantage of a victim's trust. That would be an ethical violation."

"I don't care." And he didn't. He glanced up and down her body. He couldn't wait to get her into the hotel room and undressed. If she didn't make a move soon, she'd be having sex in the car.

She blew out a long breath. "To be honest, I'm about

five seconds from not caring myself."

Luc couldn't help himself. He smiled. "Interesting."

Her voice was sharp. "Wipe that smirk off your face."

He touched his chest hoping to appear somewhat humble, although he was far from feeling humility. "Forgive me, I'm not making a joke of this."

Her full lips quirked. Her shoulders straightened.

Experience told him she was ready to surrender, she just needed to find a way to keep her dignity. He could respect that. "Cher, I'm not making fun of you." She was right, he was a manipulator. One with no shame. That's why he had a thriving business. He was a man who knew how to reel in the fish and make the fish consider it an honor and then thank him.

"All right," she said, "one time. Then it's over. We go back to being enemies, back to our separate lives."

"I wasn't aware we were enemies."

She ran her hands through her hair. "Times awastin'. We can stand here and fight, or we can heed the call of nature. Make a choice."

"We can't go to my house. I barely have a bed." He barely had a home. He thought of the empty rooms and knew he had to do something fast. If Cher was willing to share, he would need a place for Miranda to sleep. He wondered if she would like a pool, or a horse. He had room for both.

"I'm not taking you home." She tapped the roof of

the car. "And I pride myself on never doing sex in the car."

"The hotel." He gestured at the building behind him. When he had chosen the restaurant, he'd had no idea where this intimate little dinner would lead. With the prospect of touching her, of running his hands up and down her body, the idea of going to his house seemed distant. He wanted her now.

She glanced over her shoulder at the building. "You always were a big planner."

That's why he got what he wanted. He nodded in acknowledgment as he slid his arm around her and led her toward the hotel lobby.

The door to the hotel suite closed. Cher was trapped. She'd committed herself to having one last fling with the one man she had never stopped loving.

All during the check-in process, she had the feeling the hotel staff knew exactly what they were going to do. The knowing looks on their faces bothered her all the way up in the elevator and through the door.

"Are you nervous?" Luc turned on a lamp illuminating the blue-and-green living room with two sofas, two wing-backed chairs and a dining table with side chairs. A hall, with a Pullman kitchen set-up along one wall, led to the bedroom. Even with only sex on his mind, Luc went first-class.

After all these years, he still knew her moods as if a little neon sign flashed on her forehead announcing them. "I am." She hated admitting she was nervous. Her stomach knotted, and she tried to appear casual as though she went to hotels once a week for sex and was used to the drill.

He tossed her a curious look. "Why?"

“Because...” Her voice trailed away. She couldn’t tell him why she was nervous. She removed her jacket and threw it across the arm of an overstuffed wing-backed chair. "Will you do me one big favor?"

"You’re answering my question with a question.”

She nodded. She had no more answers, and she didn’t quite trust her voice. She wanted only to fall on him, to rip off his clothes and be as close to him as she could.

“What favor?" he asked.

She took a deep breath. "Stop being the caring, sensitive lover. You really make me feel guilty."

He laughed. "I don’t think you’re feeling guilty. I think you’re angry at yourself. You don’t like feeling out of control."

She put her hands on her hips. He was right. Unlike most women, anger was easy for her. He reached up and touched her cheek, the trapped feeling returned.

Her eyes darted around the room. She couldn't look at him. Although she craved his touch, she knew it exposed her weakness. The spicy cologne he used surrounded her. It hadn't changed. She didn't remember the name, but she remembered he had it made for himself at a shop in San Francisco. After all these years she tried to forget the details. Good to know she was successful at fooling herself.

"Are you mad at me?" She had to ask.

"It's a waste of time. What happened between us is over. I choose to look to the future."

She been mad since the day he stormed back in her life.

Why wasn't he? "Why?"

"I think my anger is for Edward Compton. I know in your head you had a good reason for hiding her from me. One day you're going to tell me. I'm willing to wait." He ran his thumb along her bottom lip. The touch was so gentle, it seemed more like a caress.

Cher closed her eyes, wishing his touch didn't feel so good. "Is it important?"

"At this moment, no."

"Getting me into bed is important right now?"

"I'm a man. I compartmentalize."

"Hmmmm."

"You know, sometimes you talk way too much." He leaned over and kissed her.

His lips felt warm and tender. Her blood began to thunder in her veins. His other hand cupped her cheek. His tongue slipped into her mouth, caressing hers. All the old feeling blindsided her. She was lost. Utterly lost.

Luc broke away from her. He smiled. "You are more beautiful now. Your face finally grew into your soul."

"I don't care if that's a line, you have me."

"Come to bed." He held out his hand to her.

Cher paused for a second, still a bit unsure. This was a major step, once taken, she couldn't go back. Was she willing to risk the heartbreak that would come? Or did she have the guts to play this out. She waited for the panic to come, for the voice in her brain that kept her on the straight and narrow to speak up, but it didn't. She grasped his fingers. Their entire past melted away, and nothing mattered but that moment. And making love to Luc.

He held her fingers lightly as he walked her over to the huge brass bed. She followed him, surprised that she wasn't at all afraid where this would lead. All she knew was that this was right. As she walked, she reached behind her and grabbed the zipper and began pulling it down. The soft whisper of silk whispered down her back.

When they reached the bed he turned around. He let go of her hand. "Making love to you was as close as I ever hoped to getting to heaven."

Had his mother lied? Had his marriage really been the love match of the century. Old girlfriend. Good family. Everything a man could want.

A hint of sadness appeared in his eyes. "Vanessa was a good woman. She was my friend, but she never made me crazy. Not the way you did." She made him crazy? She'd never known that. Funny that this should surprise her. He always had such a cool exterior. The only time he gave anything away was in bed. Never anytime else. "Is that what I do? Make you crazy?"

"Every minute of every day."

"Were you happy with her?"

"I don't want to talk about the past. What matters now is you and me." He reached over and slipped the strap of her dress off her shoulder. "Beautiful."

Cher closed her eyes, almost fearing the passion that blazed in his eyes. She had gone so long, denying her hunger for him, she was suddenly afraid at the depth of the intensity for him.

"Look at me," he commanded softly.

Cher opened her eyes. A sigh broke from her lips. She never sighed. That was for girls in the throes of their first real crush. Not grown women who had lived a dozen lives. She reached up and snaked her arm around his head, pulling his mouth to hers. The softness of his lips captured her. Her insides melted. Finally she was able to submit to him. Luc tasted of wine and chocolate. Intoxicating. She ran her hands over the firm muscles of his chest. Under the fine cotton she could feel the hills and valleys of his muscles. She heard the faintest groan from him and deepened the kiss. It was almost as if their tongues warred with each other. The fire in her blood escalated until she thought she would be consumed by the flames. Being with him was so right, she hoped that when everything was said and done, she wouldn't have any regrets.

He moved closer. His arms went around her.

Cher relaxed completely. All her defenses fell away, and she was at peace with her decision to take him to her bed. Her hand went to the belt at his waist.

Luc pulled back. "You're sure."

"I'm sure. Get naked."

"Bossy, bossy."

"You have a problem?"

"I'd prefer to undress you."

Smiling, she decided she could go for that if he was game also. "Only if I get to undress you."

"Please do."

Slowly, she unknotted his blue silk tie. When it was free, she tossed it over her shoulder. Slipping the jacket off his broad shoulders, she smiled. To think she almost forgot the excitement she had always felt when she took off his clothes. She began to unbutton his shirt, the cotton warm from his skin. She pushed the shirt off his shoulders and down his arms. Cher caught her breath. The years had been so kind to him. She knew he had blossomed into manhood, but the rippling biceps and rock-hard chest and stomach were an unexpected delight. Luc had the most divine honey-colored skin. He was smooth and perfect, like the statues she had seen in a museum. Her very own marble god come to life.

"You're staring."

She couldn't stop herself. He was better than before. Better than she wanted. "The years have been kind to you."

"And you, too."

"No. This is not the body you remember. Things have shifted. Expanded. Drooped."

"I still think you're perfect."

"Just close your eyes."

"I'm going to turn on all the lights."

He placed his palms flat on each side of her neck. Slowly his hands began to descend.

Cher thought she was going to explode. She sighed again.

His thumbs hooked under the straps of her black bra. He pulled the straps down until they dangled about her upper arms.

She thought seriously about getting the heck out of there. Luc let go of the straps and reached around her and unhooked her bra. The satiny material slipped over her skin. She closed her eyes and held her breath. She didn't want to see if he didn't find her thirty-five-year-old body attractive. He said nothing. The seconds crept by. Cher fought the urge to bring her arms up and hide her breasts.

His voice came out in a breathy sigh. "Magnificent."

"Thank you." She exhaled softly gaining her equilibrium. Cher reached down and took his hand. She guided it to her breast. His warm fingers caressed her skin with gentleness. She began to shiver from the sensation. She noticed that his hand shook as he covered her breast.

Knowing he was as nervous as she gave her a sense of heady delight. When they were young, there had never been anything tentative about him.

"Why are you so apprehensive?" he asked.

"I don't make a habit of seducing the men in my life."

"I'm glad."

Secretly she was too. That made making love to him so special. Putting her hand up to his dark nipples, she felt his strength under his skin. Her hands trailed down his chest to his washboard stomach. Under her hands his muscles contracted. She heard him groan. His skin seemed to get hotter. Or maybe that was just her palms. She wasn't sure. She stopped when she made contact with the waistband of his pants. Biting the inside of her bottom lip, she knew she had to continue, but she was still a bit hesitant. Her hands dipped lower over the fine wool of his pants. He sucked in a quick breath as she grazed his eager erection. Luc was so ready for her, but it wasn't enough. She wanted to feel more of him. She needed to see him. Have him inside her moaning her name. She wanted him more now than she ever did when they were together years ago.

Her throat went dry as she pulled down the zipper of

his pants. Metal rasped. Material ruffled. Her heart raced in her chest. Carefully, she slipped her fingers inside his pants to find silk boxers. She smiled. Some things never changed. He'd been a boxer man back then, too.

"Cher," he groaned.

She touched the heated flesh of his penis. Warm silk, hot hard flesh scorched her fingers. "Tell me what you want."

He grabbed her hand and pressed it harder against him, his eyes intense and filled with longing. "Everything you have."

"It's yours." And she meant it.

He grabbed her upper arms and pushed her down on the bed. "Good." The bedspread felt rough on her skin. She watched him rip off his shoes then his pants. He reached in the back pocket and took out his wallet. His hands shook as he withdrew the condom from his wallet.

She didn't know if she should be happy or not. A condom meant no more babies. She was okay with that. Quickly she slipped out of her pantyhose and slip. She sat up and touched the tip of his manhood. He was thick with need for her. She let her hand travel down his heavy length. The skin was smooth and powerful. He grew harder and hotter in her hand. She wanted to thank God for being so good to him. So kind to her.

"Don't," he said.

His demand baffled her. "Why?"

"Trust me."

She raised her hands in a gesture of supplication, then scooted back on the mattress. Her gaze went to his eyes. She still had power over him, and he still had the same power over her.

Cher wanted him as she never needed another man before. In that instant she realized why. She still loved him. More than likely she never stopped loving him. With Luc every time had been special, something she never experienced before or since. As each second passed, her love for him expanded. So did her trust. He would never hurt her. He couldn't. She lay down at peace with her choice to let this man make love to her.

Luc joined her on the center of the bed. He leaned over and took her in his arms. He smiled just before he lowered his head to kiss her.

Cher wanted the kiss to go on forever. She could touch his bare skin from now until her last breath and never get enough of the feel of him. "Hurry. I want you inside of me now."

"We have time."

"I told you before. Don't go all sensitive lover on me, okay. Not now."

"You want me to just do it?"

Did he realize she had been on overdrive since the second he walked back into her life. "Yes."

He kissed her hard on the lips, then raised his head. "No."

She laughed against his lips. "I can make you."

"Really? Give it the old Stanford try."

"If you insist." Using her body weight, Cher flipped him on his back. In one fluid movement she straddled him. "Now you have the right to make love to me. You have the obligation to make me come. You also have the right to come yourself. If you don't understand these rights, you have the right to have a refresher course until you understand your rights and obligation."

He looked up at her smiling. "Is this how you subdue all your suspects?"

"Why? Would you go out and commit a crime?"

"Only if you're the arresting officer." She didn't answer. Instead she bent over and kissed him. She grabbed his wrists and pulled them over his head. She lowered her body until they were chest to chest. She kissed his lips, his neck. She nipped his earlobes. He wriggled frantically underneath her. A heady sense of power raged through her. If only she had her handcuffs with her.

After she explored all of the smooth skin above his neck, she lowered her lips to his chest. Carefully she took one of his hard nipples in her mouth. She laved his nipple until it peaked. All the while she felt him squirm beneath her. She gripped her thighs harder on his waist. She could feel his erection in the small of her back.

Cher swished her hips. The heat and friction grew inside her. Liquid fire pooled in her belly. She was so ready for him now. Circling his nipple with her tongue, she decided she had tortured him enough. She was ready. She wanted him inside her. Now!

She let go of his wrists. "Don't move."

He nodded and smiled.

Then she snatched the condom off the night stand. She put the edge of the plastic packet between her teeth, grasped one corner with her hand, and ripped it open.

Luc snaked his free hand around her waist and pulled her to him. "Did you really think I was going to let you have all the fun?"

Eye to eye with him, she grinned. "You weren't having a good time?"

"Don't get mouthy, or I'll..."

She batted her eyelashes at him. Luc was the only man she every felt safe flirting with.

He took the condom pack from her. "Let go of me so I can get in this thing." He removed the condom from the package and slipped it on.

"Need any help?"

He licked the skin on the side of her neck. "No."

A shudder of delight plunged down her spine. Cher wanted to skip all the preliminaries and get to the main event. It had been a long time since she was this turned on. Since the last time she was with him. She felt his hands on her back. She shifted her weight and raised herself up on her knees. She looked into his eyes. They burned so bright with sensual fire, she thought she might ignite. "Love me. Now. Please," she begged.

"Yes." He grip her waist and lifted her briefly, then lowered her over his erection.

His heat and power filled her. She wanted to force him to go faster, but his grip on her waist was too strong. In that instant she realized that he was the one in control of their lovemaking. She didn't feel weak, instead stronger. With him she had always been able to give herself over to passion and not feel like a weakling. He accepted her as she was.

Their bodies and lips melted together as if they were one person. His tongue entered her mouth as he began to thrust up into her. All thoughts drained from Cher as her body moved in sync with Luc's. Under the onslaught of pure pleasure, Cher let the rhythm of their bodies drive her faster. Her back arched as she felt herself near climax. Her body tightened. All her senses were on alert. She could smell the scent of sex heavy in the room. His slick skin slid over her. The sound of his breathing mingled with hers. An expression of lust and wonder was stamped on his face. She put her mouth on the pulse beating in his neck and tasted the salt of his skin. Cher could feel herself coming apart. Her world was going to shatter in a million pieces, and she didn't care at all. All she wanted was to be one with this man.

Luc groaned. "Cher." He said her name over and over in a chant of reverence.

With each thrust she moved closer to falling off the

earth. She gripped his arms, wanting to find some balance, but he drove into her with relentless passion. As though he wanted to mark her as his. She was willing to let him.

Over and over he branded her with his intensity. His thrust became quicker, more powerful. The blood rushed out of her head. Her climax started slowly, washing over her body in waves. Her stomach tightened. Her mind when blank.

Inside she felt an explosion of pleasure that seemed to last forever. Her entire frame shuddered, and she fractured into a million pieces. Luc's body stiffened next to her. He called her name. For a brief second the world stopped, and she collapsed in his arms. Complete.

Chapter Fourteen

Cher stood in the center of the room, with a sheet wrapped around her, clutching her clothes.

Luc held up Cher's panties. "Aren't you forgetting something?"

She snatched them from him and went into the bathroom. When she returned, she was dressed.

Luc watched Cher slip her feet into her high heels. "Why can't you stay the night?"

"Because staying out all night doesn't look right." Cher picked up her purse and turned to face him.

"We're grown-ups."

"With an impressionable young girl as part of the package. If she sees me coming home at six in the morning, she might get the feeling she can do the same."

"Don't you allow her to be young?"

"Hell, no. Rule number one of a teenager, you give up one millionth of an inch and she will take you on the marathon run of your life."

"You're not spending the night with a stranger. I am her father."

Cher shook her head. "And I'm her mother. I can't afford a reputation."

He began to laugh. "How pompous you've grown over the years."

Cher smirked. "Trying to be like you."

"Me!" He sat up and swung his legs over the edge of the mattress. He could feel another argument coming on.

She put her hands on her hips. "All right. Let's call an end to this. I'm tired. It's after midnight. I'm packing a gun and the safety is off."

"Your threat of violence isn't impressing me."

"Come on over for breakfast. Then you can take Miranda to school."

"You've told her about me?"

"Not exactly. The heating grates in the house are open to every room. Miranda could work for the CIA. She knows everything."

"Should I bring something?"

"You mean something like doughnuts or eggs benedict? Friday is waffle day, just bring yourself. School starts at 8:30 so you need to be there by 7:30." She slipped on her jacket. "Don't be late."

"That's all?"

"I'm giving you some time with Miranda. Eventually you'll have to meet her face-to-face. I'm taking tactical advantage by allowing you on my home ground."

"Thank you, Cher." He wouldn't mess it up.

"Don't thank me yet. Twenty minutes with a teenager and you might think about running away."

He walked over to her. She backed away slightly, but he caressed her cheek. "Time with Miranda means a lot to me." Her skin was velvet and silk, and he was transported to the precious moment when she had clung to him and begged for more.

"This doesn't mean I'm rolling over."

"I expect no less from you." He kissed her, and for a moment he wavered between dragging her back to bed or letting her leave.

Cher gently disentangled herself. "I'll see you in the morning."

He could do nothing but let her go. He walked her to the door of the suite.

"Good night, Luc." She kissed his cheek and was gone before he could think of anything to stop her.

Cher sat in her car for several minutes reflecting on what she'd just done. She'd compromised her case, her life, her relationship with her daughter.

How could she have been so weak as to allow herself to be enticed back into his bed? For fourteen years she'd tried to keep her feelings for Luc hidden deep in her mind and now all the memories of what they'd once shared returned like long-buried demons.

She started the car and tried to push her feelings back into the bottle. Maybe one time. She thought if she gave in to her desires, got everything out of her system, she could go back to her insulated little world.

All during the drive home, she couldn't stop thinking about what letting Luc back into her life meant. Her career was turbulent enough as it was, and Miranda could be as volatile as any teenage daughter even though she was a terrific kid. She could handle that, but Luc meant new problems. If she allowed herself back into a relationship with Luc, she didn't think she could put all the pieces back together when it died. She hung on to her emotional stability by a thread. He was rocking her world yet again. And this time, she wasn't young and resilient.

When she let herself into the dark house, she found David asleep on his favorite recliner, his reading glasses slipping down his nose and his book open across his lap. Snack had curled up against his stomach and purred contentedly when Cher patted his sleek head.

In the kitchen, Miranda was nodding over a cup of hot chocolate.

Miranda perked up when Cher entered. "It's about time, young lady," Miranda scolded. "Doesn't the word curfew appear in your vocabulary?"

"This talk is sounding a little too familiar." Cher turned the gas on under the teapot to heat the water. She pulled a mug out of a cabinet and added hot chocolate to it.

Miranda yawned. "That was the world's longest dinner. It's almost one. What did you do all this time?"

Cher tried not to blush. She wasn't about to tell Miranda anything. "We had a lot of talking to do."

"Right." Miranda had a look in her eyes that was a little too knowing for a thirteen-year-old.

Cher felt defensive. She didn't have to explain her actions, no matter what those actions were. "You better get to bed."

"Wait a second. I want to hear all about your date."

Cher frowned. "You're sounding like me. Who turned over the title of mom to you?"

"This is my life here you and my dad are deciding."

"We've decided to let you live."

"Gee, thanks. Is that all you talked about?" Miranda cupped her chin in the palm of her hand and stared intently at Cher.

"We talked about a lot of things." The water boiled and Cher poured it into her cup. She sat down at the table to study her daughter. Miranda had a feral look on her face that told Cher she wasn't going to go to bed without something. "Luc is coming for breakfast and is going to take you to school. So if you want to look bright and chipper, you better get your beauty sleep."

Miranda shoved away from the table. She kissed Cher on the cheek, deposited her cup in the sink, and went to bed.

Cher sat for a long time in the kitchen staring at the clock. In six hours, Luc would appear at the front door. She needed her beauty sleep, too.

Luc pulled into the driveway and sat in the car staring at the front door. He wore the wrong tie, and for a man with more than fifty ties, he should have known to go more casual. He looked like he was ready for a corporate takeover.

His palms sweated and his heart pounded like a sledgehammer against his ribs. He thought he was going to have a heart attack.

A knock sounded on the window and he turned to find his daughter peering at him. He opened the window and she grinned at him. "You can come in now," Miranda announced. "I'm perfectly safe. I've had my rabies shots."

Luc swallowed. "Thanks for the health announcement." Close up, she was beautiful with her dark hair pulled back from her face and her eyes glowing.

She opened the door and stood waiting for him. "Come on." Her voice held a hint of impatience.

"I'm a little nervous."

"So am I. But the show must go on." She turned and headed up the walkway.

He stepped out of the car and watched her climb the steps. Even in her black jeans and red turtleneck sweater, she had a poise and elegance that reminded him of his mother. He followed her into the house, stopping to sniff the salty smell of cooking bacon and the yeasty aroma of waffles. His mouth watered. He couldn't remember the last time he'd had waffles for breakfast. His mother had believed in cottage cheese and fruit.

Miranda closed the front door and led the way down the long hall to the kitchen. Cher stood at the stove dressed for work in a dark blue pantsuit with a huge white apron covering her from neck to knee.

She turned and waved a fork at him. "Sit down."

The table was set for three.

"Coffee?" Miranda held a carafe.

He nodded. He couldn't speak, his throat was so tight. This was such a homey scene.

"Black," Cher said, "one sugar."

"You remember." Luc was amazed.

"I also remember Sir Mortimer Wheeler's box. Don't get excited."

"Box?" Miranda asked. "What are you talking

about?"

Cher took a sip of her coffee. "It's a method of archeological excavation. You remember. The Grid System. Dividing the site into squares, etc."

Luc was lost. He vaguely remembered something.

Cher shook her head. "Never mind. I just remembered I also wrote that paper for you. Easiest three hundred bucks I ever made."

Miranda stared at him, her mouth open, her eyes wide. "You cheated in school! You let my mom do your work for you? That's illegal."

Luc could feel a heated flush creep up his cheeks.

Cher saved him with a wave of her cooking fork. "Miranda, I wear the badge in this family. I will determine the illegality of any action regarding the adults in this room."

Miranda glared at her mother. "But you told me..."

Cher cut her off. "It was an extenuating circumstance, sweetheart. It was either write his paper, or I wouldn't have had the money to fix my car. I would have had to walk the dark, crime-ridden streets of Palo Alto, risking life and limb. I might not be here today to tell you this story."

Miranda frowned. "If you weren't here, I wouldn't be here."

"Exactly," Cher said.

Luc burst out laughing. He wanted to kiss Cher. She looked delectable standing over the stove, her hair mussed and her eyes bright with laughter. Her eyes met his and her smile faded slightly as though divining his thoughts. A slight blush crept up her cheeks. She turned abruptly back to the stove.

Miranda told Luc where to sit, and he pulled out the chair. She sat across from him. He felt uncertain and anxious.

"Here I am"—Miranda said with a grin, — "busting my rear end to get a straight A average, and I find out my own father and mother cheated in school." She gave a little cry. "I'm going to need therapy."

Luc stared at her. "Are you serious?"

"About the therapy or the straight As?"

Cher started laughing. "Luc, she's pulling your leg about the therapy. If I remember correctly, I did tell her that I cheated once, and I felt horribly guilty. I made a mistake and would never do it again."

"That's a hint, right?" Luc said.

Cher nodded. "Very much so."

Luc gave Miranda a solemn look. "I'm sorry I cheated. I feel horribly guilty and will never do it again."

A look of total disbelief crossed Miranda's aristocratic features. "I'll believe that when pigs fly. I did a lot of checking about you on the Internet yesterday and no man gets to your position in wealth and power by being Mr. Nice Guy all the time."

Luc took the cup of coffee from Miranda. "In big business, we all know the rules. Survival of the fittest is number one. I've never been investigated by the Securities Exchange Commission, nor have I ever defrauded an investor."

Miranda poured orange juice. "That doesn't prove anything except that you've never been caught."

"That's enough, Miranda," Cher said. She placed a plate of bacon in the center of the table. Then she opened the oven and drew out a plate piled with waffles and set it on a hot pad. "Breakfast is served."

Breakfast was fun. Luc ate heartily, but when it was time to take Miranda to school, he found himself tongue-tied again.

Miranda slid into the car seat next to him. "Do you know you own a Fortune 500 company?"

Luc started the car and pulled away from the curb. "I'm aware of that." Luc wondered where she was going with this conversation. Only an hour in her company, he already knew that she had her own roundabout way of getting to a subject.

"Did you know that Forbes magazine considers you to be one of the most powerful media tycoons in the world. You're right up there with the Murdoch family and Ted Turner."

"I know that, too." He braked at a stop sign. "So what you're saying is that you're impressed with my money?"

She fingered the lapel of his jacket. "And your sense of style."

"That sounds a little shallow."

"I'm thirteen." She shrugged. "I don't have to be deep until college."

"Have you decided where you're going to college yet?"

"I don't even know what I'm going to do this weekend. Why would I be thinking about college?"

"Because it's never too soon." Boy, he sounded pretentious. In fact, he sounded like his father when they'd first had this conversation when Luc was in high school. "What do you like to do?"

"I like to write. Ride horses. Take karate lessons. Shoot guns. Regular stuff."

"I don't think shooting guns is regular."

"When you live with cops, you have to know the rules. I took firearms safety when I was eight years old. Mom made me. Mom doesn't think everyone in the world should own a gun, but we have enough firepower in our house to start a small war, so I need to know what I'm doing."

Luc still didn't like guns, but he had to concede to Cher's wisdom. "What subjects do you like in school?"

"English and history. I love history. I thought about being a history teacher, too. Then I could talk about it and write about it. But I also love science. I really love science. All those little cells and what they do in the body. Maybe I'll go to medical school. Or into research. Or be a Pulitzer Prize-winning writer. I have options."

And big dreams, Luc thought. He wanted to know more about this odd child he'd fathered. "Your mom gave me permission to pick you up after school and spend the afternoon with you. What would you like to do?"

"You're worth $870 million. I want to go shopping. Me and my friends." She slanted a glance at him. "And we have to buy some stuff for my mom. She's been wearing the same clothes for years because she socks every penny away for my college education. Now we can spend that."

"You know how much I'm worth?"

"Yeah, but I'm not sure if that's liquid or paper assets. The article wasn't clear on that."

Luc reeled. This wasn't a thirteen-year-old girl, but an underage financial wizard in disguise. "I don't know myself. I'd have to talk to my accountant. I do have a bank account with about thirty-five thousand in it."

"That's good. But you know, in three years, I'm going to be sixteen. I do want to have a brand-new SUV. Also, you know that island you own in the Caribbean, I want to have a sixteenth birthday party there with all my friends flown in and a band. I don't know which one yet, but I'll let you know."

"I want. I want. I want." Luc was amazed. Fatherhood and greed all in one day. "Is that all you know? I'd like to be more than just a financial source to you."

Miranda laughed. "You can't blame a girl for trying.

I got caught up in the moment."

They were approaching the school. Luc parked a half block away. A couple of girls waved at Miranda. "How come you never asked about me?" He was sort of hurt that Miranda had exhibited so little curiosity about who her own father was.

Miranda shrugged. "I was curious. But my friend Julie has had four stepfathers in the last seven years. My friend Andrea's mother has a new boyfriend every three weeks living in her house. One of them tried to touch Andrea, if you know what I mean, but my mom took care of that. So I decided that my mom was protecting me because something about you wasn't right. Mom is really big into protection."

"Now that you know the truth. What do you think?"

Miranda shrugged again. "My mom was protecting me. You asked about why I'm asking you for all these things. I don't know how long you're going to be around, or even be interested in me."

Luc reached out and touched her arm. "I'm interested. I won't disappear tomorrow because I'm thinking about your college education even if you aren't."

Miranda faced him, a solemn look on her face. "I appreciate all that. But I'm going to win the Westinghouse scholarship in science. That will save you some money."

"I can afford any school you want to attend."

"I know that. And you know what, I think I can get

the grades to get into any school I want. And every school has scholarships. So I'm planning my fall-back position." A young girl knocked on the window. Miranda waved. Then she turned to Luc and said, "I have to go. I don't want to be late for first bell." She reached over and kissed him on the cheek and then opened the door and was gone before he could think of an appropriate response.

He watched her take long, graceful strides up the steps to the school surrounded by a half-dozen girls. Just before she entered the gates, she turned and waved at him. She pointed and several girls stared at him. Then they all disappeared through the gates giggling.

Luc pulled out of the parking spot, giving it up to a woman who had been waiting to drop off a carload of boys. He turned a corner and drove, his mind not on where he was going. After a couple more turns, he found himself on a street shaded by a canopy of oak branches. Stately Victorian houses lined the street.

He stared at the houses. Except for Cher's area, he didn't know another street with Victorian homes existed. One was for sale. He parked in front of the Victorian and studied it. The outside was in need of some paint and fixing, but the location was only a couple of blocks from the school and not far from Cher's house. He hated the stucco ranch house he'd bought in such a hurry. The house had no history, no personality. For an interim home, it was fine, but he found himself unable to be comfortable in it. Having lived in San Francisco all his life, he liked homes with character that had stories to tell.

The For Sale sign had a box attached to it. Luc got out of the SUV and opened the box and took out a piece of paper describing the house's features and at the bottom gave a contact point. As he slid back into the driver's seat, he reached for his cell phone. He knew what he was going to do.

He wasn't going to disrupt Miranda's life. But if Cher was going to allow him to be a part of it, he wanted to make the transition easy. He'd buy this house, refurbish it and make it into a home for him and Miranda when she visited. Cher, too, if she wanted.

As he buckled his seat belt, he realized that he had turned into his father. When his father had married, he'd moved his business to San Francisco because that was where Luc's mother wanted to live. And here was Luc making the same decision. He already knew he would move his corporate headquarters and any employees who wanted to come to Phoenix. He would remake his life to accommodate his daughter, and Cher if she wanted to be a part of it.

After last night, he knew he wanted Cher back in his life, and he would do anything he could to get her. He realized that he'd never stopped loving her, never stopped missing her. He couldn't let go again.

The phone was ringing as Cher entered her office. She answered it.

Whitaker said, "I talked to that sheriff in Louisiana. Seems that Edward Compton was quite a baby hell-raiser back in his juvenile days. In fact, that's why he was in the Army. Join or go to jail. Uncle Sam wants you."

"Is that all you found out?"

Whitaker continued. "Seems he had his own little posse consisting of his sister, Sylvia. Everything big brother did, baby sister had to do better. The sheriff tried to catch Miss Sylvia at all sorts of doings, figuring she was the real ring-leader, but couldn't prove anything."

Cher twisted the phone cable around her finger. "What did they do? Tip cows. Steal tractors? Make moonshine?"

Whitaker laughed. "Some illegal gambling, fighting, driving under the influence and drag racing. Nothing big."

"Typical small-town teenage stuff."

"That's what the sheriff said. I asked her..."

"Her?"

"The sheriff. Kingsley Walker is a she."

"I want you to call her back and see if she has pictures of these kids and may even their friends." An idea formed in Cher's head, more strongly than before. She wasn't quite certain what she was fishing for, but she could feel as though the solutions were just out of reach.

"Will do."

"You didn't have a problem that the sheriff was a woman?"

"Heck no. She said I should come down and go fishing on my next vacation. Picture this: me on the bayous drinking beers and sucking crawfish. Isn't that a pretty picture?"

Cher wanted to throw up. But resisted for the sake of keeping her office clean. "Thanks, Whitaker."

"Anything else I can do to help you solve this case, boss?"

"Not in this lifetime."

"I'm taking personal time this morning. I'll see you after lunch." He disconnected before Cher could ask him what he was doing. That was Whitaker, full of surprises. Cher hung up the phone and attacked the pile of files on her desk.

By noon, she had attended two meetings and ground her teeth over her budget. She felt frazzled and unappreciated when Luc appeared at the door. He had a light in his eyes that she hadn't seen since that last day when they'd been together in the shower.

"I was just going to call you." Cher pointed at her chair and he sat down. "In my effort to be more cooperative, I wanted to schedule a meeting and bring you up to date on what's going on."

"Good, good, I want to hear everything but it's noon, let's take a ride. I have something I want to show you."

"Let me talk first since I'm in such a generous mood."

"I like you best when you're generous." He leered at her. "Had I known that making love to you would put you in such a great mood, I'd have gotten you in the sack a lot earlier."

"Yeah," she said with a wry grin, "you realigned my planets."

He seemed on edge. He fidgeted until Cher wanted to grab him by his power necktie and pull. Then she realized he wasn't wearing a necktie. He wasn't even wearing a suit. He wore casual pants and a pullover sweater and looked relaxed, more relaxed than he'd been since he'd reappeared in her life. As though a little lovemaking had realigned his planets, too.

He crossed his arms over his broad chest. "What's on your mind?"

"When you were doing your background investigation on Edward Compton, did you do anything on Helen?"

"You've asked me that before." He looked at her, an expectant light in his eyes. "So what is your big news?"

"Did you find out anything about Helen's husband?"

He shook his head. "She said he died in a swimming accident off Key West in 1987."

"In Florida? That eliminates a pool accident. Wait a second." She plowed through the pile of papers in the file she started on Edward Compton. What had Lily's email said? She found the email and handed it to Luc. "This says he died in New York. Are you sure she said Key West?"

"Yes." Luc frowned as he read.

Cher grabbed the phone and dialed Lily's number. When Lily answered, Cher asked. "Have you found out anything more on Helen Ramsey and her businesses?"

"I'm waiting on one last report, but from what I'm seeing, there's nothing there. No business partners, no licences in any other name, but hers."

"I need a favor, then."

"Anything," Lily said.

"You have a homicide detective down in Miami, don't you? See if you can shake loose anything on a drowning in 1987. A black male. Name: Grant Ramsey."

"But," Lily said, "I told you he died in New York."

"Check anyway. And find a photo of him, if you can."

"What about Helen?"

"I know what Helen looks like."

Lily laughed. "I mean the background check."

"Send me what you have. Maybe's there something there, but I'm beginning to doubt it."

"I'll do what I can." Lily hung up.

Cher placed the receiver on the cradle. "We're close."

"To what?"

"The end. Finito. Finis. Solved. One for the win

column."

He leaned forward. "How do you know?"

"I just know." She jiggled her eyebrows. "Trust me. I've been a cop for a long time."

He jumped to his feet. "Now, we're going to have lunch, and I have to show you my news."

"This sounds intriguing." She opened the bottom drawer of her desk and pulled out her purse.

"Don't you love it." Luc spread his arms. "This is a home."

The house needed a new roof and one corner of the porch sagged, but the bones were good and even Cher could see that once a little money had been spent on it, the house would be gorgeous. It reminded her of the day David had shown her their house. He'd been so proud of his find, despite the work they would eventually put into it. Luc had the same expression on his face, the same sense of pride in his voice.

Cher walked through the massive rooms torn between delight that Luc was going to show such an interest in Miranda and deep fear that she would lose her daughter to this man who could buy her anything.

"Do you think Miranda will like it?" Luc asked as he walked up the stairs to the second floor. "She'll have her own bathroom." He flung open a door and showed her the front bedroom.

He grabbed her hand and pulled her inside. A bay window overlooked a tall cottonwood tree. Beyond, the street was a winding ribbon of concrete. In the distance, Cher could almost see the red tile roof of Miranda's school.

One of the things Cher had always loved about Phoenix was its architectural diversity.

She turned and looked at Luc. He watched her waiting for her answer. "The house is lovely, Luc. Miranda will love it."

"What about you? Do you love it?"

"Who wouldn't love this house?" She turned around again and could see how much Miranda would enjoy all this.

"Good. Glad you like it. I'm going to build a pool..."

She held up a hand. "Don't buy my daughter."

His mouth dropped open. "I'm not trying to buy her."

"You can give her everything." Her lips quivered. "I can't compete with you and what you can do for her. Don't punish me by flaunting your money because I didn't tell you about Miranda." She'd voiced her most primal fear. She'd put her soul on the table and exposed her greatest fear to him.

He wrapped his arms around her shoulders and pulled her against him. He kissed her hair, her forehead, her cheek, and finally her lips. Heat grew inside her, and she swayed against him. When his lips left, she almost pulled him back to keep the kiss going forever.

"I'll never take Miranda away from you." He rested his forehead against hers. "You gave me a beautiful daughter, and I will be forever in your debt."

She wasn't certain she believed him. She wanted to, but he was a man who understood what wealth could buy. He threw his money around without even thinking about its effect. He might not do it on purpose, but Miranda was a very impressionable thirteen. Cher wasn't going to allow him to spoil Miranda for no other reason than the fact that he could.

She leaned against him, her heart pounding so loud she thought it would pound its way out of her chest. Despite her misgivings, her love for him grew and became so powerful she didn't know why he couldn't feel it.

If only his mother still didn't stand between them. The woman might be dead, but her actions lived on.

Cher's cell phone rang, breaking the moment. She pulled back and opened her purse. "Dawson," she said.

"It's Lily. I faxed a photo of Grant Ramsey to your office. I talked to Detective Grayhorse. He seemed to think you were out on a long, long lunch with Mr. Broussard. I'm not interrupting anything important, am I? Like naked stuff." Lily's maniacal chuckle filled Cher's ear.

"Lily, when you laugh like that, you make me think of a troll."

"Funny," Lily said. "I'll laugh about that later when I have time. By the way, tell Mr. Broussard, newspaper mogul, that I found the photo on the society page of one of his newspapers and I talked to my guy in Florida about the drowning you asked me about. He says no drowning in Florida for Grant Ramsey, but he did find a twenty-year-old gun permit for a Smith and Wesson .38 registered to Grant Ramsey."

"A .38 Smith and Wesson." Something went off in Cher's head. She covered the mouthpiece and said to Luc, "your mother was shot with a .38, wasn't she?"

He nodded.

"So was dead Eddie. I need to see the ballistics report on the gun that was used on your mother." She uncovered the mouthpiece. "Lily, I'll catch up with you later. I owe you big."

She disconnected and said to Luc, "The kissing can wait, we need to get back to the office." She whirled away and raced down the stairs. While Luc locked the front door, she opened the car door, leaned against it and dialed the office.

"Grayhorse," she said when he answered, "I want you to call the lab and have them send up a ballistics guy. On my desk are two reports, one labeled Edward Compton and one Victoria Broussard. Have him compare the two ballistics reports inside each of them for me."

As Luc raced down the street, she could feel the whole case coming together.

Cher's office was a beehive of activity. Luc watched in amazement as her detectives seemed to bounce all over the place.

The detective with Indian features walked up to Cher and grinned at her.

"Do they match?" Cher's voice held an edge of impatience.

"Like peanut butter and jelly," the detective answered.

"Where's the photo that came over the fax machine."

"On your desk."

Cher took the two reports and walked swiftly into her office. Luc had never seen the look of total concentration on her face before. As though he no longer existed.

She picked up a paper from her desk, looked at it and then walked swiftly back to Luc holding the paper up. "Where do we know this guy from?"

Luc took the fax. The man he knew as Edward Compton stared back at him. The caption said, Grant Ramsey weds local socialite, Doris Hyatt, in wedding of the century. The grainy, smiling face of an attractive woman stared back at Luc. She held on to Grant's, aka Edward's hand. In the background Helen Compton Ramsey held a half-raised flute of champagne.

She pointed to the fax. "Looks like bad Eddie is going to be jail-bird Grant in the not-too-distant future." Cher turned to Whitaker. "Whitaker, get Judge Fredricks on the line. He never goes to lunch. Give him the scoop, I want a warrant for everything Grant Ramsey, aka Edward Compton, and Helen Compton Ramsey own. Storage facilities, boats, houses, cars, garages anything registered to them in the state of Arizona."

Luc stared at the photo unable to take his eyes away from it. Edward, no Grant, was a bigamist. Luc glanced at Cher. She was smiling. "You're enjoying yourself, aren't you?"

"Yeah," she replied, "I love it when things come together. I get an ego rush arresting a suspect who thinks he's smarter than I am."

"Do you have enough evidence?"

"I have the ballistics reports, I have the photograph with Helen in the background. I'd like to find the gun. I'd love a confession. But I can take what I have so far to the bank and see what turns up from the search."

Luc could feel her repressed excitement. Her eyes shone. Her body was tensed, her back straight and her feet slightly apart. She curled and uncurled her fingers. Her service weapon clung to her hip. She was like a warrior queen, a tiger circling for the kill. He was awed by her, and humbled.

This was a woman who didn't need him. As much as he had liked Vanessa and enjoyed her company, she had needed him with a deep-seated sense of dependence. Cher had walked out of his life, continued without him to become the person he'd first glimpsed and fallen in love with fifteen years ago.

She was a woman in charge of her life, herself, and her future. Luc wanted to be a part of her future. This Cher was the one he hungered for, not the Cher who had goaded him into attending classes and helped him write his papers so he could graduate. But this Cher, this fully developed woman who'd given him a daughter and made herself into who she was now.

He felt as though he'd been punched in the stomach. One of the detectives bumped into him, and he moved out of the way of traffic. The whole squad room was galvanized as Cher coordinated the afternoon with her detectives.

"Jackson, get me the county attorney's office on the phone," Cher said, "I want one of his people here when we interrogate Mr. Ramsey-Compton, or Compton-Ramsey, or whoever the hell he is."

Luc caught Cher's arm. "I want to go with you when you pick up Edward Compton, I mean Grant Ramsey."

Cher shook him off and laughed. "The days of deputizing a civilian are long over, Luc. Just find a corner and sit. I'm not leaving you out."

Two hours later, Cher and Grayhorse brought Edward Compton into the squad room. The handcuffs on his wrists jingled as he stalked across the room and was ordered to sit.

Edward, aka Grant, looked as though he'd been awakened from a nap. His eyes were unfocused, and his hair wasn't sharply combed. He wore wrinkled gray slacks and a black sweater. His dark skin had a gray pallor to it. He slumped into the chair, his eyes drifting around the squad room and rested briefly on Luc before passing on. Generally, he looked defeated, and Luc wondered what about him had attracted his mother.

A woman, dressed in a black suit and carrying a black briefcase, had joined the group. Everything about her screamed lawyer. She and Cher conferred in a corner and then Cher nodded at her detectives who hauled Edward to his feet and took him out.

"Come on." Cher grabbed Luc by the arm and pulled him out after Edward. "This should be interesting."

The interrogation room had a one-way mirror. Cher leaned against a wall of the room while her detective, Wyatt Earp Whitaker, sat at the small square table with Edward. Luc stood on the other side of the mirror observing with the woman who he'd been introduced to, but whose name he didn't remember. She was a County Attorney, and she smiled as Cher and Whitaker asked Edward one question after another.

"You can't try me a second time for Victoria's murder." Edward had a touch of bravado in his voice.

"Who said anything about Mrs. Broussard?" Cher said.

"You think I don't know? Victoria told me all about you, Cher Dawson."

Cher's lips thinned. "That's Lieutenant Dawson to you. I don't care about what she told you about me. Eddie, this is how I see it. You are not the mastermind of this plot. You look good, but you don't have a lot rattling around between your ears. So that basically makes you an accessory."

"To what?" Edward demanded.

"Let's start with the real Edward Compton, and then we can add bigamy, fraud and a list of charges as long as your arm once the County Attorney's office has sorted it all out. Edward, or should I call you Grant, give me what I need. Ms. Harrison and I will guarantee you won't get a lethal injection verdict."

"I didn't do anything." His voice was sulky and petulant.

"Yes, you did. Don't make me work harder. I get cranky when I have to work so hard." Cher gestured at him. "Look at you. You're sweaty and twitchy. You're lips are quivering. The next thing I know your eyes are going to roll around in your head. You're guilty. Tell me what I want to know and save me some time."

"What do you want to know?"

"Let's start with the gun."

"What gun?"

"The .38 Smith and Wesson registered in your name, Grant Ramsey."

Luc didn't believe Edward could get any sweatier, but the color drained out of his face and he stared at Cher his mouth open and his eyes filled with naked fear.

Cher gave her predatory smile. "The one that killed the real Edward Compton. Grant, let me lay this down with you. I was lying to you earlier. You can be retried for Victoria's murder. It's called a federal violation of her civil rights. Now consider that this is going to be mixed in with identity theft, with you having stolen Edward Compton's identity, I can turn this all over to the FBI, and you will be serving your time in Joliet, or some equally ugly, dangerous, where no-one-serves-lattes prison and you can't get a court for squash. If you want to serve your time with mafiosos, terrorists, and kidnappers, then don't tell me anything. If you were just a hapless little accomplice in the overall scheme of things, then tell us now."

"Sylvia did it. It was all her idea.

"Sylvia?" Cher tilted her head. "Are you telling me that Helen Ramsey is really Sylvia Compton?"

He nodded. "She hated the name Sylvia and changed it to Helen."

Cher had been thinking that Helen was another alias, and here Helen really was Edward Compton's sister. The dead Edward. She resisted the urge to rub her temples. A headache floated just along the edge of her thought. "Where is Sylvia— I mean Helen?"

"I don't know. Getting her nails done for all I know. She left this morning and didn't say anything. She killed Victoria and she killed Eddie."

"Why did you kill Victoria?" Cher asked.

Grant Ramsey shrugged. "Victoria came home earlier than expected and found Helen and me in bed together. After all, she still thought Helen was my sister."

"And Helen is your wife, isn't she?"

He nodded. "She killed her real brother because Eddie wanted out. He had himself a cute little chick on the side he wanted to marry, but she was churchgoing goody-goody."

"Tell me what Eddie did for you."

Grant shook his head. "He was the computer geek. Because he was in the military, he had access to all kinds of records." And that was all he said.

Someone brushed past Luc. He turned and saw Jacob Grayhorse open the door to the interrogation room. "Lieutenant," he said, "you have an urgent phone call. The lady won't give up."

Cher nodded. "I'll be right there." She handed a pad of legal paper to Grant. "Write it all down. Confession is really good for the soul." She left and Luc watched as Grant picked up a short, stubby pencil and started writing.

As she passed Luc, she touched his shoulder. Her

eyes gleamed in the shadowed room. "It's coming together." And she passed him and walked into the squad room.

Luc watched Grant Ramsey as he bent over the paper and pressed the pencil to it and started writing. Luc was confused and not certain he was truly understanding what had happened. The best he could figure out was that Helen had killed her own brother, her husband had assumed her brother's identity who then married his mother and whom Helen had killed because his mother had found Helen and her husband in bed together. He fought the urge to rush out of the room and go find the bitch.

Several minutes later, Cher returned and from the way she walked and the smile on her face, Luc could tell something had changed.

"Grant," her voice was deceptively gentle. She opened a folded sheet of paper, "or should I say Grant Huntington aka Leroy Hunt aka Robert Noble aka Timothy Roderick aka Claude Butler aka ... need I go on? You have quite a list of identities here. Each one with a broken-hearted bride left behind who claims you swindled them out of a hell of a lot of money. That's what Eddie did, didn't he? He had the ability to set up all the identities. He had access to all those government computers and could arrange things, couldn't he?"

Again, Grant nodded. "He taught everything he knew to Helen. She was better than her brother. I don't know how she managed to get into government files, but she did."

That was why Luc's original investigation of Grant, after taking Edward's identity, didn't show anything out of the ordinary. Helen had hacked into the government's databases and changed the information. And because death certificates weren't cross referenced with birth certificates, no one would have known the original Eddie was dead until the file had been unearthed at Cold Case and entered into its database.

Grant broke down, tears sliding down his face. "It was all her idea. Honest, it was," he said, sobbing.

Cher patted Grant on the shoulders. "There. There. It's okay. We all make mistakes."

Luc almost laughed at the bored expression on Cher's face. He could tell she'd heard it all before.

Once the floodgates were open, Grant couldn't stop talking. He gave it all up, from Helen's initial need for money to the fact that he'd fallen hard for Victoria Broussard. Allowing Helen to kill her had been the hardest decision he'd ever been faced with in his life.

Luc couldn't help a moment of cynicism. Yeah, right! Luc thought. Hard decision to make. Kill someone, or not. How hard had that been? Just because his mother had caught Edward—make that Grant—in bed with his real-life, honest-to-God wife.

Cher left the interrogation room. She had a smile on her face that went from ear to ear. "There are just days when I love my job."

"And is this one of them?"

"Oh, yeah!" She touched his shoulder and crooked her finger. "Come with me."

Luc followed her to her office. "I'm hoping you're taking me to your office to seduce me."

"Something even better than that."

"What's better than a Cher Dawson seduction?"

Cher opened the door to her office and stepped inside. "Are you okay? He's not going down for your mom's murder, but he is going to be doing some state time. And from the look at his track records, Louisiana, New York, Georgia, and Pennsylvania are all going to want their shot at him, too. I've a ton of phone calls to make."

"I want to celebrate. Come to dinner with me tonight."

She glanced at her watch. "I can do that. I'll bring Miranda."

"As a buffer?"

"Luc, I don't know what the parameters are of the 'thing' we have. I don't want to give you any false hope, nor give Miranda any false hope until we iron out some details. For the record, we've been busy."

"So, does this mean you think we're having a relationship, or we're not having a relationship?"

A struggle of emotions crossed her face. "We're having a 'thing.' I don't know what to call it. I've never felt anything like this before."

"We could get married. For Miranda's sake."

She whirled on him. "Have you been sniffing the ink off your money?"

"What's so difficult about getting married? We almost did it once. We're older, wiser, and the heat is still there. Probably more so than when we were younger. I think Miranda wants us to get married."

"No," Cher said, "she's playing it cool. That's her way. She has a lot of you in her. Besides, what kind of half-assed, out-of-the-woods proposal was that?"

"What do you want? Romance? You hated that when you were younger. If I ever bought you a flower, you thought I was cheating on you."

"I never said that."

"You never would say it. That would be giving away some of yourself, that part of you that you always kept out of reach from me. But it was always there in your eyes. I saw you with Grant. You used to question me the same way you questioned him. Fierce, intense, no quarter given, take no prisoners."

"Then what attracted you to me? If you felt I was so inflexible and unyielding."

"Because you were the only woman who never needed me. My wife needed me to shield her from life. My mother needed me to keep her lifestyle. Every woman I ever dated needed me for something: status, money, sex. But not you. You were with me because you wanted to be."

Cher held up a hand. "You stop that right now."

He frowned. "What?"

"Are you telling me that you were attracted to me because I didn't need you? I needed you every day. You gave me your faith. David has faith in me. You took me at face value and didn't want me to be something I wasn't. I didn't have to be a sorority girl, or a raving beauty. I could just be me."

"You never told me this."

She tilted her head at him, her eyes dark with a new look. "I just thought you knew."

"I didn't know."

A knock sounded on her office door. "Damn." She stalked to the door and flung it open. "What?"

Whitaker stepped back from the onslaught. Then he pushed past her and turned off the intercom. "You know as juicy as this conversation is, we're guys, and we get all embarrassed at this emotional shit. Jackson just pulled out a box of tissue. Him and Grayhorse are sobbing in the corner. You have totally ruined your rep. Who knew you were a girl under all that hard-nosed shit?"

Cher covered her face. Luc found laughter bubbling up in him. She was embarrassed.

Cher pointed at the door. "Luc, you need to leave. I'm going to die of embarrassment. I'll pick you up later. Around seven or so. That will give me plenty of time to wrap this up."

Luc left the office and found five or six male cops sitting on desks as though they were waiting for him. At his entrance into the squad room, they all started clapping.

One of them slapped him on the back. "All choked up, man."

Another grinned. "Right on, man. Mars and Venus. Mars and Venus."

Cher frowned at the sight of all the men. "All right, if one word of what was said in that office is ever repeated, the body count will escalate. I don't know who half of you are, but I suggest you get back to work. Whitaker, get Beatrix Hunter on the phone, we're going to need media to take charge of the information on this case. And wipe that smirk off your face." She disappeared back into her office, slamming the door.

Chapter Fifteen

Luc had to escape. He'd never, in his whole life, exposed so much of himself and or learned so much about Cher. He needed to get ready for dinner. She wanted a proposal, she was going to get one. The best one he could come up with. He glanced at his watch. He had exactly one hour and fifty minutes to get ready to knock her socks off. Since she insisted on bringing Miranda, he'd call his daughter and let her in on what was going to happen. He had the feeling that despite Cher's objections earlier, Miranda very much wanted them to get married and make a family.

All the way home Luc was euphoric. Something had changed and even though he couldn't put a finger on it, he knew. What he knew, he wasn't certain, but he had feeling that his future with Miranda would contain Cher as well. He could hardly wait. He had to call a jeweler. Cher wasn't sentimental, and he knew his mother's jewels were too flashy for her. Something with sapphires, square cut. He remembered a sapphire ring she'd never taken off because David had given it to her. It was her birth stone. He knew an engagement ring and a wedding ring would mean more to her if it contained sapphires.

Using his cell phone, he called Benjamin and asked him to check the phone book for the nearest jeweler. And as Benjamin search the phone book, Luc appraised him of the situation with Edward Compton aka Grant Ramsey and his wife Helen formerly Sylvia Compton.

Ben took the convoluted explanation in stride. "I found a jeweler at the Biltmore Fashion Square, which is on your way home. If you can't find what you want, there a Sak's Fifth Avenue in the mall, too."

"Thanks, Ben."

Ben asked, "Do you want me to go to the station and make sure all the Ts are crossed and Is dotted as far as Edward Compton is concerned?"

"No," Luc responded. "Cher has taken care of every detail. They have an APB on Helen and should have her in custody shortly."

They rang off. Luc drove to the mall. He hadn't been there before, but he liked the look of it. He parked his car and entered, stopping at two jewelers before finding a store with the right kind of sapphires.

The jewelry store had a collection of several dozen

sapphire rings and the third one they presented to him, Luc knew Cher would love. The sapphire was a deep clear blue, square cut, four carats set in platinum. Exactly the type of cut Cher adored, though he figured she'd rather have a new gun. He bought the ring anyway and before leaving the mall he stopped at Sak's and found a silk scarf with a vibrant rose pattern. If Cher didn't like the real thing, maybe this scarf would be to her liking. He had the clerk thread the scarf through the ring and then wrap it.

Cher was a hard woman to shop for. He wanted to make his proposal memorable, but as he stood in the center of the store, he couldn't think of anything else that would create the romantic ambiance he wanted. But a glance at his watch reminded him he needed to get home, he was almost out of time.

As he was leaving the mall the bright lights of a travel agency caught his eye. A huge poster advertising flights to Paris stopped him. Paris. What could be more perfect than a weekend in Paris? Just him and Cher. He walked into the agency, booked two tickets and a weekend at the Ritz Carlton. Miranda might feel out of sorts at not being included, but he decided he would make it up to her some other time.

He pulled into his driveway feeling extremely satisfied with his purchases. The garage door rolled up and he parked his car.

He entered the kitchen from the garage and walked

right into the muzzle of a gun held by Helen Compton Ramsey. For a long moment, he couldn't move. "How did you get in here?"

"You are so like your mother. You need an army of servants to take care of things for you. Have you ever thought about locking a door in your whole life?"

"I locked the front door."

She sighed. "But you didn't lock the back one." She waved the gun toward the hall that led to the front part of the house. "Let's go."

"Go where?"

"We have things to do. You are getting me out of here."

The muzzle of the gun looked very large and extremely deadly. Luc froze. He imagined Miranda finding his lifeless body on the kitchen floor and knew he couldn't let that happen. "What do you want?"

Helen studied him. "What the hell do you think? I want money, five million deposited in my account in the Caymans, and safe passage to St. Kitt's on your corporate jet."

"I'm not going to help you. You're going to kill me."

She smiled at him. "If you don't get on the phone and start making the arrangements, you're right. I'm going to kill you and then I'm going to kill your daughter, and then I'm going to kill your bitch."

Luc swallowed his fear. He glanced at the clock on the stove. Cher would be arriving in less than an hour with Miranda. He had to do something. "This is going to take some time."

"Then shut up and start calling." She pointed the muzzle straight at his forehead.

Luc gulped. He nodded and headed toward his study. He picked up the phone and dialed Cher.

"Dawson, make this quick," she said.

"This is Luc Broussard, just listen," he said quickly before she could continue. "I want you to fuel the plane," he enunciated the words clearly, "and be ready to take off." He glanced at Helen. "You did say St. Kitts, didn't you Helen?"

The muzzle of the gun was pointed directly at his forehead. "You heard me the first time."

Luc said into the phone. "File a flight plan for St. Kitts."

There was a second's silence. "I understand," Cher said. "The cavalry is on the way." The phone went dead.

Luc hung up. "The pilot will need a half hour to fuel the jet and file a flight plan. I'm assuming you're using one of your several passports?"

"Grant couldn't keep his mouth shut. Jesus-God, he's an idiot." The gun lowered briefly then resumed its position.

Luc couldn't take his eyes off the gun. "I have to call my broker to get the cash."

"Make it quick. I have an account at the Grand Cayman's National Bank under the name of Mary

Smith."

Luc dialed Benjamin and when the answering machine came on, Luc calmly left a message asking Ben to call back as soon as possible. "Sorry," he said to Helen, "my banker appears to be at dinner."

"Then I guess we'll wait."

"Whatever shall we talk about?"

Helen sat down in a wing-back chair and gestured to the opposite chair. "Don't get snooty with me. You're an idiot, too. All men are spineless twits, can't keep a secret. All Grant had to do was keep his mouth shut. Your mother knew how to keep her mouth shut. I had to dig long and deep to find out about her."

Luc leaned forward. "What secrets could my mother have?"

Helen laughed. "You fool. Since we have time, let me enlighten you. Did you know your mother was a prostitute?"

Luc sat back, shocked. He could only shake his head.

Helen giggled. "Not your average run-of-the-mill street hooker, but a high-class top-of-the-line call girl. She had a specialty."

"How do you know?" His mother a prostitute! He shook so violently he could hardly stand. How could she have sold her body for money? All these years she talked and acted as though she came from the bluest of the blood family. She'd lied to him. And because she'd lied, he wondered what other secrets his mother had told.

"One thing about a good con, you make it your business to know. That's why she didn't want Cher around. Cher knew the streets. She would have known that your mother's act was nothing more than a good con. Her own mother was a working girl. Your precious Cher came from the same, sordid cesspool. What do you think about your precious mother now?"

"I don't believe you."

Helen smiled. "You can believe whatever you want, but I have proof. I have your mother's arrest record. One of her clients wanted a freebie and when he turned nasty, she got busted, and the whole sordid story is on record in Manhattan North. Your mother was a piece of work. She was not about to let her baby boy marry into something she tried desperately to leave behind."

"I'm not following you."

"Of course. Your mama didn't tell you, did she? When I saw Dawson in her office, I knew your mother hadn't said a thing about what she'd done, and Cher didn't tell you either. Let me say, your mother was a viper in the grass. You wanted to marry Cher and live happily ever after, but your mother didn't want you bringing the ghetto home, son. So she put a stop to it."

Against his better will he asked, "How?"

"Victoria was a smart one. She dug up all that info on David Dawson. Gay. Black. And wanting to be the police chief. What a laugh! Your mama showed Cher what she had, and Cher made her decision. David was a naughty, naughty boy. But Cher chose him over you. Hard to believe, isn't it?"

Luc could only stare at her. So much was explained.

"But," Helen continued, "that's not the good part. When Cher came crawling back to whine about being pregnant, your mama wrote her a check and told her to get rid of it. Told her, you were already married to that sniveling, sickly piece of work, Vanessa. She must have been exciting as cold chitlins in the morning."

"No." Luc shook his head. "I don't believe you."

"That's too bad. You're not going to be able to ask her. Tell you what, you find yourself a little piece of paper and we're going to write down my safety deposit box number and we'll just leave that little note for Cher. I'll even give you a chance to say good-bye to your one true love. It will be interesting reading for Cher while I'm sunning myself on a beach in St. Kitts."

"You know, Helen," Cher said as she walked into the room, her gun drawn. "There isn't going to be a St. Kitt's in your future."

Cher had her gun raised at shoulder level and Helen said calmly, "I'll kill him."

"I have absolutely no problem shooting you in the back."

Luc gulped. "Wait a sec, my life is on the line here."

Helen shrugged. "Do I care?"

Cher replied. "I do. Put your weapon on the floor,

Helen. No one needs to get hurt here."

"No." Helen's voice was petulant.

Sirens suddenly pierced the air.

"Helen," Cher said, "you are hearing the sounds of Phoenix's SWAT team. One of the finest in the nation, I might add. These are the kind of guys that can shoot a hole in a dime at three hundred feet. What do you think your chances are with them?"

Helen shook her head. "I'm not going to jail."

Cher slid farther into the room. "Helen, you're a wealthy woman. You know wealth buys justice. The right lawyer and you'll probably beat this rap. All you have to do is tell them 'When I was six years old, my uncle Bubba raped me and traded me around to all his friends.'"

Helen smiled. "No one ever took advantage of me."

"It's your defense, not the truth."

Helen smiled. "So you're telling me all I have to do is tell a jury that my hubby slapped me around and threatened to kill me if I didn't go along with his plans."

"I'm not telling you anything, but if that's your story, you can't tell it to the jury if you're dead. And trust me, I shoot marksmen level, I'm not missing at this distance. And neither will the boys outside. I'd rather let them do it so that they have to fill out all the paperwork. Though probably there won't be a lot. You are holding a gun on one of the wealthiest men in this country. Give it up, Helen. This man is a personal friend of the governor.

Your death would be considered justifiable homicide."

Helen's gun wavered. She glanced back and forth between Cher and Luc. Red strobe lights flashed across the walls.

Cher continued, "If you shoot him, I won't be able to help you, at all."

Helen stood and faced Cher, her gun still on Luc. "Do you really think I can beat this rap?"

Cher shrugged. "If you're dead, you'll never find out, will you?"

Helen hesitated a long moment. Her gun wavered unsteadily. Sweat popped out on her forehead.

"Tick. Tick," Cher said. "The SWAT boys are in position. I'm waiting for your decision."

Helen shook her head. "I can't think."

"Then let me help you." Cher walked up to Helen and simply took the gun right out of her hand.

Luc almost had a heart attack. His life and schooling had prepared him for the shark tactics of business, not the desperation of crime.

Cher pulled a radio out of her pocket. "Okay, boys, everything's under the control. The front door is open."

Seconds later, the hall was filled with burly men in black who clattered through the house holding the most lethal-looking rifles Luc had ever seen. One of them took Helen into custody while Cher handed over Helen's gun to another one. "Log this in as evidence and see that it gets to ballistics. I think this Smith and Wesson has quite a history." Cher walked over to Luc and touched his shoulder. "Are you okay?"

"Tense moment." Luc swallowed. "But I'm fine."

"That was smart of you to call me."

"I didn't know what to do, but I did know I wasn't going to let her leave the country." Luc grabbed onto the back of the chair. His legs felt like rubber, and the room swirled slightly. Would Cher think less of him if he sat down and continued to pretend he was all right?

Cher walked to the sideboard and poured him a generous glass of bourbon. She handed it to him and pointed at the chair. "Take this. I want you to sit and relax. This nice officer is going to ask you what happened. I have some things to take care of, and I'll be back as quickly as I can."

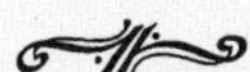

That was close. Cher tried not to think as she watched the last of the police cars leave, returning the street to normal. The curious neighbors had been dispersed, and Cher was alone for a moment.

She forced herself to breathe. She had almost lost Luc a second time. Her palms still sweated at the fact that Helen had intended to murder him.

"Why didn't you tell me what my mother did to you?" Luc asked.

Her legs wouldn't support her. She sank into a patio chair and looked a him. "Who wants to know what their parents are really like?"

"I would have chosen you. I wanted you. I loved you. I would have fought for you."

"There was nothing to fight over. I owed David more than I owed you."

"You loved David more than you loved me?"

"No." She took a deep breath. All her fears resurfaced. "I loved you more than anything. You were everything to me. But, David saved me. He gave me a future. The Cher Dawson you knew would never have existed without him. he loved being a cop, and I couldn't let your mother destroy him."

"Why couldn't you trust me?"

"You didn't have the power to protect David. I did."

He grabbed her by the shoulders and drew her to her feet. "I didn't marry Vanessa until a year after you left me."

"Your mother was good." Cher's voice was weary. Now that the excitement was over and Luc was safe, she wanted nothing more than to go home and crawl into bed.

"I love you." Luc kissed her.

"But can you forgive me?"

"The past is over. We have to move on. My mother is dead and what she did was unforgivable."

"I don't want you to hate her. She thought she was

doing what was best for you."

"I'm a grown man. I can handle disappointments. I'm not surprised about my mother's action. If it came down to it, I would have done everything I could to protect my father, too. I just wish you'd trusted me enough to give me a choice." He snaked his arms around her.

"Forgive me?" She lifted her face.

"Finally," he kissed her.

"Finally what?" she asked when the kissed ended.

"Finally, you realized you don't always have to be the tough guy with me. I'm going to love you anyway I can get you."

She smiled. "Wow!"

"I want you to know that it was Paris and a weekend at the Ritz Carlton. I had my proposal all planned. But I am not going to wait. Hell, I'm not even going to ask. You're marrying me." He dug into his pocket and pulled out the box. "Here. Open it."

She backed away and accepted the box. Her fingers trembled as she carefully unwrapped it. Inside the box the sapphire ring winked against the folds of the scarf. "My kid loves you, my cat loves you. I'm good."

"Say it."

She hesitated, making him wait, just because she could. She could see the hunger on his face. She grabbed his tie and pulled his face to hers. "I love you." She kissed him.

(Summer Anthology)	*T. T. Henderson*	
	Jacquelin Thomas	

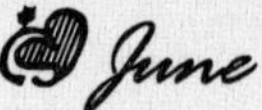

Subtle Secrets	*Wanda Y. Thomas*	*$8.95*
Indigo After Dark, Vol. III	*Montana Blue/Coco Morena*	*$10.95*
Impulse	*Montana Blue*	
Pant	*Coco Morena*	

OTHER GENESIS TITLES

A Dangerous Love	J.M. Jefferies	$8.95
Again My Love	Kayla Perrin	$10.95
A Lighter Shade of Brown	Vicki Andrews	$8.95
All I Ask	Barbara Keaton	$8.95
A Love to Cherish (Hardcover)	Beverly Clark	$15.95
A Love to Cherish (Paperback)	Beverly Clark	$8.95
And Then Came You	Dorothy Love	$8.95
Best of Friends	Natalie Dunbar	$8.95
Bound by Love	Beverly Clark	$8.95
Breeze	Robin Hampton	$10.95
Cajun Heat	Charlene Berry	$8.95
Careless Whispers	Rochelle Alers	$8.95
Caught in a Trap	Andree Michele	$8.95
Chances	Pamela Leigh Starr	$8.95
Cypress Whisperings	Phyllis Hamilton	$8.95
Dark Embrace	Crystal Wilson-Harris	$8.95
Dark Storm Rising	Chinelu Moore	$10.95
Everlastin' Love	Gay G. Gunn	$10.95
Forever Love	Wanda Y. Thomas	$8.95
Gentle Yearning	Rochelle Alers	$10.95
Glory of Love	Sinclair LeBeau	$10.95
Indiscretions	Donna Hill	$8.95
Interlude	Donna Hill	$8.95
Kiss or Keep	Debra Phillips	$8.95
Love Always	Mildred E. Riley	$10.95
Love Unveiled	Gloria Green	$10.95
Love's Deception	Charlene Berry	$10.95
Mae's Promise	Melody Walcott	$8.95
Midnight Clear	Leslie Esdaile	$10.95
(Anthology)	Gwynne Forster	
	Carmen Green	
	Monica Jackson	
Midnight Magic	Gwynne Forster	$8.95
Midnight Peril	Vicki Andrews	$10.95
Naked Soul (Hardcover)	Gwynee Forster	$15.95
Naked Soul (Paperback)	Gwynne Forster	$8.95
No Regrets (Hardcover)	Mildred E. Riley	$15.95
No Regrets (Paperback)	Mildred E. Riley	$8.95
Nowhere to Run	Gay G. Gunn	$10.95

Passion	T.T. Henderson	$10.95
Path of Fire	T.T. Henderson	$8.95
Picture Perfect	Reon Carter	$8.95
Pride & Joi (Hardcover)	Gay G. Gunn	$15.95
Pride & Joi (Paperback)	Gay G. Gunn	$8.95
Quiet Storm	Donna Hill	$10.95
Reckless Surrender	Rochelle Alers	$8.95
Rooms of the Heart	Donna Hill	$8.95
Shades of Desire	Monica White	$8.95
Sin	Crystal Rhodes	$8.95
So Amazing	Sinclair LeBeau	$8.95
Somebody's Someone	Sinclair LeBeau	$8.95
Soul to Soul	Donna Hill	$8.95
The Price of Love	Beverly Clark	$8.95
The Missing Link	Charlyne Dickerson	$8.95
Truly Inseparable (Hardcover)	Wanda Y. Thomas	$15.95
Truly Inseparable (Paperback)	Wanda Y. Thomas	$8.95
Unconditional Love	Alicia Wiggins	$8.95
Whispers in the Night	Dorothy Love	$8.95
Whispers in the Sand	LaFlorya Gauthier	$10.95
Yesterday is Gone	Beverly Clark	$10.95

All books are sold in paperback, unless otherwise noted.

You may order on line at www.genesis-press.com, by phone at 1-888-463-4461, or mail the order form in the back of this book.

ORDER FORM

Mail to: Genesis Press, Inc.
315 3rd Avenue North
Columbus, MS 39701

Name ______________________________

Address ______________________________

City/State ____________________ Zip __________

Telephone ______________________________

Ship to (if different from above)

Name ______________________________

Address ______________________________

City/State ____________________ Zip __________

Telephone ______________________________

Qty.	Author	Title	Price	Total

Use this order form, or call 1-888-INDIGO-1

Total for books __________

Shipping and handling:
$4 first two book, $1 each additional book __________

Total S & H __________

Total amount enclosed __________

Mississippi residents add 7% sales tax